The
Media Murders

a J.T. Ryan Thriller

A Novel
By

Lee Gimenez

RRP

River Ridge Press

The Media Murders
by
Lee Gimenez

This is a work of fiction. The names, characters, places, incidents, and dialogues are products of the author's imagination and are not to be construed as real. Any resemblance to actual persons, living or dead, is entirely coincidental.

Printed in the United States of America.

Published by
River Ridge Press
P.O. Box 501173
Atlanta, Georgia 31150

First edition.

Cover photos: Copyright by Andrea Izzotti and Ostill; used under license from Shutterstock, Inc.

Cover design: Judith Gimenez

ISBN-13: 978-0692747407

ISBN-10: 0692747400

Other Novels by Lee Gimenez

Skyflash

Killing West

The Washington Ultimatum

Blacksnow Zero

The Sigma Conspiracy

The Nanotech Murders

Death on Zanath

Virtual Thoughtstream

Azul 7

Terralus 4

The Tomorrow Solution

Lee Gimenez

The
Media Murders

a J.T. Ryan Thriller

Chapter 1

The man felt no remorse for the three people he would murder tonight.

But he'd been in this line of work a long time. Empathy for his vics never entered the equation.

He raised his night-vision binoculars and gazed at the small jet parked on the airport tarmac. The pilot and crew were already aboard, doing final prep before takeoff. The sole passenger, David Matthews, would be arriving soon.

The hired assassin was in a dimly lit alley between two hanger buildings. And although the airport was large, this area was used by private aircraft and was far less busy. Still, the night sky was crowded with commercial jetliners as they circled the airport, preparing for final approach before landing.

Lowering his binoculars, the man took in a breath, inhaled the jet fuel aroma that pervaded the air. He was wearing a blue flight mechanics jumpsuit; clipped to his lapel was a forged security badge which allowed him free access to the area. He was a wiry man with non-descript features, which helped him blend in a crowd, a useful attribute in his profession. His pockets held a Glock 9mm with a suppressor attached, a switchblade, and a garrote, items he always carried and hopefully would not need tonight. But he was a methodical planner and knew his business was unpredictable.

Hearing the growl of a truck engine, he tensed and took a step back deeper into the shadows as he waited for the fuel truck to drive past. He glanced at his watch, growing impatient, wanting the job done. *Time is money*, he thought. *I've got other work to do.*

The assassin raised his binoculars again, and as if on cue, he watched an airport van drive toward the small business jet and stop beside it. A tall man carrying an overnight bag got out of the van. David Matthews. Matthews climbed up the air-stairs and into the plane. The co-pilot pulled up the stairs and the cabin door closed.

Although the assassin was wearing ear plugs, the high-pitched whine of the jet's twin engines was clearly audible as they spooled from idle to the roar of full standby.

A minute later the small plane rolled forward on the tarmac and merged onto one of the taxiways. He watched as it began following a larger business jet to the main runway. The larger jet sped down the runway and lifted off. Matthews's plane was next, soaring into the night sky a minute later.

Reaching into his pocket, the man took out a rectangular device. After waiting several more seconds, he pressed the detonator button on the device.

Watching the sky intently, he frowned when nothing happened. The spark generator he'd inserted in the fuel tank should have ignited immediately.

Then it happened in a split-second. The dark sky lit up as the small jet exploded into a fireball. He heard the roar of the explosion as the fragments of fiery metal cascaded down.

The man turned and calmly walked away, knowing O.O.V. was now back on track.

Chapter 2

Atlanta, Georgia

Erin Welch was in her FBI office when her desk phone rang. Turning away from the computer, she picked up the receiver.

"Welch here," she said.

"It's Mark Parker," she heard.

"Mark. It's good to hear from you. It's been awhile."

"Sorry about that. I've ... been busy."

"Tell me about it," Erin said, staring at the stacks of case files on her desk. "I'm sure you're like me – always drowning in work." Erin recalled Mark Parker's background. He was a reporter at WMN, one of the largest TV news companies in the world. Parker was also very good at his job, earning three Emmy Awards for his investigative reporting.

"So, Mark, is this a social call or business?"

"Neither. It's something ...." He didn't finish the sentence.

"Okay. You want to do it over the phone?"

"No, Erin. That won't work. We need to meet."

"Sure. My afternoon's pretty clear – I don't have any appointments. Come over to my office."

"That's not good either."

"If it's really important," Erin replied, "I could come over to WMN – you're only a couple of miles away." Parker and Erin had known each other since college days; both had graduated from the University of Georgia and had stayed friends. During her years at the FBI, the two had conferred on cases to their mutual benefit.

"I'd rather not meet here, either," the reporter said cryptically. "Remember where we used to hang out when we got our first jobs in Atlanta?"

"Sure, Mark, I remember – neither of us made much money back then."

"Meet you there in an hour."

Erin heard a click and realized the man had hung up. *Strange conversation. Is he in trouble?* she thought, as she gazed out the floor-to-ceiling windows, which gave her a panoramic view of the downtown skyline. Erin was the Assistant Director in Charge (ADIC) of the FBI's Field Office in Atlanta; one of the perks of overseeing the operation was her corner office on the building's 14th floor. *The downside of it,* she mused as she stared at the stacks of files on her desk, *is that the buck stops with me. I've got 25 agents who report to me, but if they screw up, it's my ass that's on the line as well as theirs.*

Erin glanced at her watch. She'd spend the next half hour finishing emails, then head out to meet Parker.

***

Erin Welch pulled her Jaguar sedan into the restaurant's parking lot and turned off the engine. It was three p.m. and the lot was almost empty. Which made sense, since it was well past the lunch hour.

Climbing out of the car, she scanned the exterior of the IHOP. She hadn't been here in years, but the place looked the same. Going inside, she found Mark Parker already there, sitting at a booth in the back of the restaurant. The place was almost deserted, except for a few people at the counter.

He rose when he spotted her and after shaking hands she sat opposite him at the booth. The waitress came, took their coffee orders and moved away.

She appraised him thoroughly, noticed the graying hair at his temples and the dark circles under his eyes. Although he was only in his mid-thirties, he appeared much older and haggard.

"So, Mark, I was surprised by your call. It's been over a year since we talked. I remember I was working on a drug case then and you gave me a good lead."

He seemed distracted and his eyes darted around the room and toward the restaurant's front door. "You weren't followed, were you?"

She thought that was an odd question. "No, I wasn't."

"You're sure?"

"I'm an FBI agent, Mark. I'd know."

He appeared relieved. "Okay. Good."

"Are you in trouble, Mark?"

"No."

The waitress returned, set their coffee cups on the table and moved away.

The dark roast brew smelled delicious and she took a sip as she appraised him again. He had a wary look in his eyes that implied the opposite of what he'd just said.

She leaned forward in her seat. "We've known each other a long time. You're a good reporter and a good friend. If you're in trouble, maybe I can help."

Parker nodded, slid his coffee cup aside, and in a low voice said, "Did you hear about the private jet that crashed a couple of days ago?"

"I saw something about it on the news. The plane took off from Atlanta airport and went down soon after. From what I remember the three people on board all died, but fortunately the jet went down in an unpopulated area and no one else was hurt."

"That's right, Erin."

"What does that have to do with you?"

5

"I know one of the people who died. In fact, I'd met with him recently."

"Who was it?"

"His name was David Matthews."

She took another sip of coffee. "His name sounds familiar."

"It should be. He is, or was, an investigative reporter for the *New York Times*."

"I remember now. He won a Pulitzer a few years back."

"That's right, Erin."

"You said you met with him recently? What about?"

His eyes darted nervously around the restaurant again, then he fixed his gaze back on her. "We were collaborating on a story together."

"I thought reporters liked to work alone, get the scoop, and break the story themselves."

"This is different. It's too big a story – too many people are involved. Important people."

Perplexed, she said, "Too big a story? You work for World Media Network, one of the largest news companies in the U.S."

Parker shook his head slowly. "Things have changed in the news business."

"Changed how?"

"Reporters have restrictions on what we can report."

She smiled, amused at his comment. "Censorship? You've got to be kidding. You report the facts. It's what you do for a living."

The haggard look etched deeper on his face. "I wish that were still true."

"Look, Mark, I can see you're under a lot of stress. I want to help. Let's start at the beginning. What was the purpose of your meeting with Matthews?"

"I can't say. At least not yet. It's confidential."

She nodded. "Okay. He was in a plane crash. I'm sure you're upset because you knew him. I can understand that."

"It's more than that, Erin."

"What do you mean?"

He lowered his voice to a whisper. "I don't think the crash was accidental."

Erin leaned back in the seat. "I read the news report. The NTSB is investigating, but all indications point to a mechanical malfunction that caused the plane to go down."

"That's why I called you, Erin. You need to investigate this."

"The Bureau doesn't get involved unless there's criminal activity."

Parker shook his head. "I don't trust the NTSB."

She had known Parker for a long time, knew he was a solid reporter. But what he was saying wasn't making much sense. "I want to help. But you're acting a little paranoid right now. You say you don't trust the National Transportation Safety Board, the federal agency in charge of investigating U.S. plane crashes. And you don't trust WMN, the news company you used to rave about. Tell me, why didn't you want to meet at your office today?"

His eyes grew wary again. "They're listening."

"Who's listening?"

"I'd rather not say." Parker glanced at his watch. "I've got to go."

Suddenly, he reached out and gripped her hand hard. "Please, Erin. Look into the plane crash." His eyes bore into hers and she saw fear there.

"Okay, Mark, I'll look into it."

Relief flooded his face. Without another word, the man got out of the booth and quickly left the restaurant.

Erin, baffled by the strange conversation, sat there for another few minutes, trying to sort out what Parker had told her. Picking up her cup, she drank the coffee, which was now cold.

Chapter 3

J.T. Ryan saw the muzzle flash and instinctively dropped to the ground, the round missing him by inches. His adrenaline pumping, Ryan rolled to his left over the asphalt pavement and took cover behind a low wall.

Ryan was itching to fire back, but he needed the man he was chasing alive. The criminal, a thug by the name of Carpenter, was a mid-level guy in a counterfeiting ring, and the FBI needed him to lead them to the bigger fish.

He heard footfalls on pavement and he glanced around the wall – he spotted Carpenter running down the alley away from him.

They were in an old, mostly deserted warehouse district south of Atlanta. The area had once been a thriving textile manufacturing zone, but most of that had moved to China. Now the mostly empty buildings were used for illegal activity, like the counterfeiting operation.

Sprinting up, Ryan gave chase at full speed, his lungs burning from the effort, and he closed the distance.

Suddenly Carpenter halted, turned back and fired off another two rounds. Ryan ducked as the bullets slammed into a nearby wall. He had been a private investigator a long time and knew his luck wouldn't hold. He had to take Carpenter down now.

Pointing his revolver, Ryan fired once, aiming for the man's leg. Carpenter howled and clutched his thigh, his pistol clattering to the pavement.

Pocketing his gun, the PI rushed forward, slammed into the man, knocking him to the ground. Carpenter was big and brawny, and though he was bleeding, he managed to stagger upright.

Ryan, who was also tall, and more muscular, hit him with a fierce uppercut, and followed it with a solid punch to the gut. Groaning, the thug went down to one knee, then sagged to the ground. Pulling out plastic flex-cuffs, the PI bound the man's hands behind his back. Then he rolled the now unconscious guy on his back.

Carpenter was bleeding from the lower part of his thigh. Taking out two more flex-cuffs, Ryan tied them together and looped the plastic around the man's leg, cinching it tightly into a crude tourniquet.

Standing, he pulled out his cell phone and keyed in a number. "It's Ryan," he said.

"J.T.," Erin Welch replied when she picked up. "Did you find him?"

"Yeah. I got Carpenter."

"Is he alive?'

Ryan chuckled. "Of course he's alive."

"I know how you work, J.T."

The PI laughed again. "I guess you do." He stared down at the unconscious man. "Listen, send an ambulance – unfortunately I had to wound him to put him down."

"Figures," she replied sternly. "He better not die, or I'll renegotiate your fee. We need him alive, remember?"

"Don't worry, it was just a flesh wound."

"Yeah, I bet. Okay, give me your location. I'll send the EMTs and a couple of my agents."

He told her where he was and said, "You'll notify local PD?"

"Of course, J.T. Don't I always?"

"And it's a good thing, too," he replied. "For some reason, I'm not too popular with police departments."

Ryan heard a sigh from the other end. Then she said, "You do good work. I just wish I didn't always have to clean up your messes."

Then she hung up.

With a smile, he put his phone away.

***

Ryan was driving his Tahoe SUV north on Interstate 75, maneuvering around the slower moving vehicles. Although it was eight p.m., traffic was still heavy. It was something the Atlanta tourism bureau never talked about – the city's streets and highways were always a mess, no matter what time of day. Ryan loved the area, but hated the traffic.

Just then a pickup truck cut in front of him and he slammed his brakes and hit the horn. Glancing at his watch, he realized he was already late for his planned dinner with Lauren.

Hours later he pulled into Lauren's driveway and turned off his SUV. Lauren Chase, his longtime girlfriend, lived in a modest brick home in Roswell, a northern suburb of the city. Climbing out, he strode up the steps and rang the doorbell.

Lauren opened the door, a frown on her pretty face. A petite woman in her mid-thirties, she had sculpted good looks, long auburn hair, and hazel eyes. The freckles on her face highlighted the reddish tone of her hair.

"John Taylor Ryan," she said in a stern voice. "Do you know what time it is?"

Ryan stepped inside. "I'm sorry, hon. I was working on a case and traffic was a mess."

The frown didn't leave her face, but she at least went up on her tiptoes and gave him a quick kiss on the lips. "Dinner's cold. I'll go a reheat it." She went toward the kitchen.

That's when he noticed two things, clues why she seemed so upset. First, she was wearing a dressy outfit, a new stylish dress he'd never seen before. And second, candles were lit on the dining room table. He followed her into the kitchen.

"What's the special occasion?" he asked.

Lauren faced him, her eyes brimming with tears. "Damn you, J.T. I can't believe you forgot." She crossed her arms over her chest.

He stared blankly at her, racking his brain.

She shook her head slowly. "It's the anniversary of when we first met."

Not good, he thought. *Not good at all.* In years prior he'd taken her out to dinner at an expensive restaurant and bought her flowers. But he'd gotten so involved in his recent case he'd completely forgotten.

Ryan approached her and gave her a big hug. He was tall and ruggedly handsome, and his strong arms engulfed her petite body. He gazed into her green eyes. "I'm really sorry, hon."

She wiped away a tear. "Are you?"

After a long moment the stern look left her face. "All right, J.T. You know I can't stay mad at you for long. Now let me finish reheating dinner so we can eat."

"Can I help?"

"Yes. You can get out of my kitchen," she said with smirk. "You're dangerous in here."

Ryan smiled, glad she was in a better mood. "Hey, I can cook. Before we met, I did okay."

"You can make a ham sandwich, and *maybe*, just maybe, fry an egg," she said with a chuckle. "Now, out!"

He poured her a glass of chardonnay, grabbed a beer from the fridge for himself, and went into the dining room. Lauren came into the room a few minutes later, placed the platters of food on the table and sat across from him.

He lifted up his bottle of Coors and she clinked it with her wine glass.

"I love you, Lauren Chase."

"I love you, too." She wagged a finger at him and smiled. "But you better not forget next year."

"Don't worry, I won't."

"So, what were you working on today, J.T.?"

"Finishing up on an FBI case."

Lauren scrunched her pert nose. "Working with Erin Welch again, I assume ...."

"I thought you liked her now."

"I do. I just don't like the Bureau sending you on dangerous assignments."

He took a sip of beer. "I'm a PI. I'm paid to do dangerous work. Just like I did when I was in Special Forces in the Army. It's what I do."

"I know. I just wish you ...."

His work as a private investigator was a bone of contention. What had prevented them from getting married years ago. Lauren wanted to have children, but was afraid he'd be killed and she'd be left a widow, raising kids on her own.

Ryan loved her more than anything and he reached over and covered her hand with his. "You know I can't give that up. You really think I'd be happy selling insurance? Or being a school teacher?"

She shook her head, a sad look in her eyes. "No, you wouldn't. I know that."

He looked down at the heaping plate of food – it looked and smelled delicious. The pasta's savory aroma filled the room. "Lasagna? I hate lasagna."

"J.T.! It's your favorite dish! I cooked it special for tonight."

"Got you," he said with a chuckle.

Lauren laughed. "Okay, buster. You did. Now quit kidding around and eat your food before it gets cold again."

He hadn't had much to eat all day and he was famished. Picking up his fork, he plowed into the meal.

They ate and drank and had a relaxing, enjoyable dinner. Lauren was a professor at Georgia Tech and she filled him in on her day. He described his day, and as usual left out the grittier parts of his job.

It was past midnight by the time they finished dinner.

She yawned, finished her glass of wine, and rested it on the dining room table. "I've got an early day tomorrow. Will you help me clean up, J.T.?"

Gazing at her, he gave her a sly smile. "Let's leave it. We've got more important things to do right now."

"I've got a conference tomorrow. I've got to get some sleep."

"Oh no, you don't, Lauren. It's our anniversary, remember?"

She smiled demurely, knowing his meaning. Although she was a tigress in bed, you'd never know it by her shy demeanor. Her face flushed red, accentuating her freckles. "Yes, I remember. And I want what you want, but ...."

"Do I need to spank you, Ms. Chase?"

Lauren's face flushed a deeper shade of crimson. "Promise?"

Ryan laughed, rose, took her hand and led her into the bedroom.

She smiled shyly again as he stood in front of her. The sight of her, even fully clothed, aroused him. He breathed in her scent, a lavender perfume.

Without a word, he slowly caressed her face with one hand, tracing her cheek, chin, and neck. "I love you very much, Lauren."

"I love you too."

He bent down and kissed her on the lips. She kissed him back, hungrily, and he wrapped his arms around her and held her for a long time. She tasted salty and delicious. When they separated he could tell by the sparkle in her eyes that she was just as aroused as he was.

She began to take off her dress and he said, "Let me do that."

The teal blue dress she was wearing buttoned down the front and he slowly and methodically unbuttoned it while holding her gaze. He slid the garment off her shoulders and it fell to the floor. Even though they'd been together for years, the sight of her still took his breath away.

Lauren made a move to unsnap her shear lace bra.

But he pushed her hand away and he began tracing his fingers over the garment slowly, teasingly, massaging her breasts over the silky material. Then he caressed her nipples, now erect.

Goosebumps rose on her skin and she gasped. "Take it off, J.T. I want you now."

Ryan placed a finger on her lips. "Not yet."

He needed her urgently, but he wanted tonight to be something special, something she'd remember for a long time.

Leaving her bra on, he slid his hand over her flat stomach, paused, then slid it lower over her panties, edging his fingers until he was over it. He felt her wetness through the silky material and began to stroke her lightly, delicately, until she closed her eyes and let out a low moan.

"Please, J.T.," she whispered hoarsely. "Make love to me now ...."

Ryan didn't reply. His fingers continued to gently caress the wet silky fabric.

With her eyes still closed, her labored breathing changed to short, sharp gasps.

Suddenly Lauren's eyes snapped open and she had a wild, ravenous look in them. The shyness of earlier was all gone.

She pushed his hands away. "Two can play this game," she growled.

Then she quickly unzipped his pants and reached inside. Ryan groaned in pleasure.

They held each other's gaze a moment, then he kissed her hard and she kissed him back, her tongue exploring his mouth.

Knowing he wouldn't be able to hold off much longer, he broke off the kiss and tore off her clothing, while Lauren, her eyes wild and her breathing ragged, began pulling off his shirt and pants.

Hungry for each other, they never made it to the bed that first time, instead making love on the bedroom's carpeted floor.

They got very little sleep that night.

Chapter 4

J.T. Ryan walked into the FBI building in downtown Atlanta, and after checking in at the reception desk, he got a visitor's badge and went through the security checkpoint. He took the elevator to Erin Welch's floor and minutes later strode into her corner office.

"How's my favorite Assistant Director in Charge?" Ryan said with a chuckle, as he sat in one of the chairs fronting her desk.

She pointed to the tall stack of files on the desk. "Cut the crap, J.T. It's been a long day already."

He laughed and glanced out the office's floor-to-ceiling windows. It was a cool, rainy day, and ominous clouds hung over the skyline like a dirty blanket.

Erin opened a desk drawer, took out an envelope and slid it across her desk. "That's your check for the counterfeiting case."

Ryan picked it up and put it inside his jacket. "Thanks. How's the case going?"

"Very well. The guy you arrested, Carpenter, is singing like a jaybird. We've already located two of his accomplices." She paused a moment. "You did a good job."

"Is that *praise* I'm hearing?"

She gave him one of her steely FBI stares. "Faint praise. You already have a big ego. If I said you did a great job you'll raise your rates."

Ryan laughed. "I'm worth every penny."

She pursed her lips, then must have realized he was making a joke. An amused look crossed her face. "You're not as smart, or as funny, as you think you are."

"Lauren tells me the same thing," he replied.

"How is she, by the way?"

"She's doing well."

Erin tucked her long hair behind her ears. "That sweet girl is a saint for putting up with your BS all the time."

Ryan nodded, and leaned back in the chair as he studied the woman. As usual she was stylishly dressed in a charcoal gray Christian Dior jacket and matching skirt, an elegant white blouse, and a pearl necklace. She was in her late thirties, tall and attractive, with the good looks of a model. But she appeared different today and now he realized why.

"You changed your hair color," he said.

"Good detective work, J.T."

"You've been a blonde since we met. Why the change to brunette?"

Erin tapped her Mont Blanc pen on the desk before answering. Then she waved a hand in the air toward the bullpen, the rows of desks that crowded the large, open room outside her office. Almost all the desks were occupied by male agents. "The answer I gave those guys is that I got tired of being a blonde. But the real reason: I don't like the 'dumb blonde' jokes some of my guys told behind my back."

He was surprised by her answer. "You're one of the smartest people I know. And the best Bureau agent I've worked with."

She frowned, obviously thinking he was making another joke. But she realized he was being serious and said, "Thanks, J.T. The problem is, the FBI hasn't changed that much. Sure, we have more women agents now, but I'm the only female ADIC. It's still a boy's club in the upper ranks."

"I understand."

She leaned forward in her chair. "I just started working on something new. I need your help with it."

"A big case?"

Erin shook her head. "I don't think so. In fact, it's not an official FBI investigation. I'm just looking into it for a friend of mine. It's regarding a plane crash that happened in Atlanta a few days ago."

"That's usually handled by the NTSB, right?"

"Correct. Like I said, this isn't a Bureau investigation. I just want you to poke around, see what you find out."

Erin pulled a file from a drawer and handed it to him. "There's not much here, J.T. Just the news reports, and notes of my conversation with the NTSB agent who's in charge of the investigation. Also notes of my meeting with Mark Parker, the WMN reporter who's a friend of mine."

Ryan opened the file and scanned it. "Okay, I'll check it out."

Erin gave him a steely gaze. "And this time, J.T., don't shoot anybody."

Ryan chuckled as he rose.

Then, with a mock salute, he turned and left the office.

Chapter 5

The WMN building was an imposing, contemporary steel-and-glass, twenty-story structure located in the heart of downtown Atlanta. The news company had grown quickly, and was now much bigger than its cross-town rival, CNN.

Over the years J.T. Ryan had been there several times, working on cases. But even so, he was impressed with the glass and chrome open atrium that soared to the 10th floor. To the left of the reception desk was the eight-foot tall logo of the news company, WMN in marble letters superimposed over a backlit map of the world. Below the company's initials was the full name, World Media Network.

Approaching the reception desk, Ryan handed the attendant his card and asked to see Mark Parker, then took a seat in the lobby to wait.

Ten minutes later a young Asian woman came out of the elevator and walked toward Ryan.

"I'm Mei Lin," she said, "Mr. Parker's assistant." She was attractive, with large black eyes and short black hair that framed her doll-like face. She appeared to be very young, no more than a teenager, but Ryan knew many Asian women often looked younger than their actual age. The petite girl was no more than five feet tall and he towered over her.

The PI flashed his ID at the woman. "I'm J.T. Ryan. I'm working with the FBI on a case and I needed to speak with Mr. Parker."

A worried look crossed her face. "I'm sorry, Mr. Ryan, but he's not here."

"When do you expect him?"

She glanced nervously at her watch. "He should have been here early this morning. I left a message at his apartment and on his cell, but I haven't heard back."

"I see. Is he usually late?"

"Actually, no. He's a very prompt man. In fact, we had an important meeting this morning. I was shocked he missed it."

Ryan nodded. "Maybe he was working on a story."

The young woman shook her head. "Along with being his assistant, I'm a reporter also; we work on stories together. I'd know if he was looking into something new. You work for the FBI. Is Mark in trouble?"

"It's an ongoing investigation," Ryan replied. "I can't comment on it." He took out a business card and handed it to her. "My number's on there. Please give me a call when he shows up."

"Of course."

Turning, the young woman strode toward the elevators as Ryan left the building.

Back in his Tahoe SUV moments later, Ryan exited the parking lot and made his way south toward Atlanta's Hartsfield airport. Reaching the airport area, he wound his way through the heavy vehicle traffic until he came to a large, lightly wooded field about two miles east of the airport.

A section of the field had been roped off with yellow tape. The ground within the roped off area was littered with metal and plastic fragments of every shape and size, the remnants of the private jet that had crashed. Men in blue polo shirts and tan pants were on the field, picking up and bagging scraps of evidence.

Nearby were three sedans and a Ford cargo van, all with NTSB markings on them. Ryan also saw an Atlanta PD uniformed officer standing by the vehicles. Getting out of his SUV, Ryan walked over to him.

"I'm looking for Agent Tim Caruthers," Ryan said, as he showed the cop his ID.

The uniform pointed to a tall, rangy man in the field. "That's him over there."

Striding over, the PI held out his creds.

"Agent Caruthers? I'm J.T. Ryan. I'm working with the FBI."

Caruthers glanced at the ID and gave the PI a disdainful look. "You have no standing here, Ryan. I'm running the NTSB investigation. I already talked to that uppity FBI woman, what's her name."

"Erin Welch, and she's an Assistant Director in Charge."

"Whatever," the agent said, rolling his eyes. "If, and that's a big if, we need the Bureau's involvement, we'll call."

Ryan grit his teeth. The man was beginning to piss him off. But then, he'd never been a big fan of government types thinking they were better than ordinary citizens. The PI took a deep breath and calmly said, "I'm just trying to help. Maybe you could just fill me in on your preliminary findings."

The NTSB agent glared at him and put his hands on his hips. "This is an accidental crash, no doubt about it. An unfortunate mechanical problem that cost the life of three people. There's absolutely no need for the FBI to be involved."

Ryan pointed to the men collecting the fragments of the plane. "Looks to me like you're still processing evidence. I'm not sure how you can be so certain it's accidental."

Caruthers's face turned crimson and he jabbed his index finger on Ryan's chest. "I don't care what you think, asshole. Now, get the fuck out of here before I kick your ass!"

Ryan immediately saw red. He swatted the man's finger away, then with both hands gripped him by the throat and began squeezing. The agent's eyes went wide as he fought back and tried to pull away, but he couldn't break the PI's vice-like grip.

The APD cop noticed the fight and ran over. But instead of breaking it up right away, he watched a few moments, an amused look on his face. No doubt, Ryan thought, the cop had put up with the NTSB agent's arrogant attitude for days and was enjoying himself. Eventually he said, "Okay, you two, break it up."

Ryan let go and Caruthers fell to one knee, coughing and wheezing as he massaged his throat.

The PI nodded to the uniform and walked away toward his vehicle.

***

As soon as Ryan walked into his office in midtown Atlanta, he felt his cell phone buzz. He pulled out the phone and took the call.

"It's Erin," he heard the FBI woman say in an aggravated tone.

"I was about to call you."

"Ryan, I just got off the phone with the regional director for the NTSB. I can't believe you almost strangled Agent Caruthers."

"You told me not to shoot anybody, remember?"

"Ryan!" she screeched.

"Okay. Bad joke. But listen, Caruthers deserved it. He called you 'uppity'."

"He did?"

"Yes, Erin, he did. And anyway, he started it. He poked me in the chest first." Ryan chuckled. "I should file assault charges."

There was a long sigh from the other end. "Why can't you play nice with others?"

He laughed, then said, "There's another reason the guy pissed me off – he told me the investigation showed the plane crash was an accident. From what I saw, they're still processing evidence. No way he could know for a fact it was accidental. He's either incompetent or covering something up."

"All right, J.T. Let's put that aside for now. We've got a bigger problem to deal with."

"What's that?"

"The WMN reporter, Mark Parker."

"I went to see him at his office, Erin. But he wasn't there."

"There's a reason for that," Erin replied. "Parker's dead."

Chapter 6

Erin Welch pointed to the top of the condo tower, fifteen floors up. "He jumped from up there."

Ryan gazed up at the building.

Erin and Ryan were standing in the large grassy area in the rear of the structure. The space was immaculately landscaped with lush shrubbery and elaborate stone paver walkways. The building was located in Buckhead, an affluent community filled with many other high-end condo towers.

Police wooden barricades had been erected around the scene, keeping out the gawkers who were milling around. A couple of uniformed cops were also there, bored looks on their faces.

"Where's Parker's body now?" Ryan asked.

"County morgue," Erin replied.

"You think it was a suicide?"

Erin pursed her lips. "Buckhead PD thinks so." She took out a clear plastic baggy from her jacket; in the bag was a single sheet of paper. She handed him the bag.

Ryan scanned the note scrawled on the paper. It read, *I can't take it anymore. Mark.*

"Is that his handwriting?"

"It looks similar," she said. "I'll have an expert examine it to be certain."

Ryan pointed to the grassy area where the body had been found. "What was the T.O.D.?"

"The coroner puts the time of death around four a.m. this morning. A resident of the building was coming back from jogging at around eight and found the body among the shrubbery."

"They're doing a tox screen?"

Erin nodded. "We should have the results back by tomorrow."

"You met with him, Erin. You said he looked scared, possibly paranoid. Maybe he was having mental problems and it got too much for him and he decided to end it."

The FBI agent looked doubtful. "Could be. But I've known Mark for years. He was never a quitter. It was that drive that made him such a good reporter."

"The timing of this whole thing bothers me."

"In what way, J.T.?"

"First, there's a plane crash involving a prominent reporter. Then there's a suicide of a second reporter who was working on a related case. All in the span of one week. Coincidence? I don't believe in coincidences."

She nodded. "Neither do I."

"So where are we?"

"This started," Erin said, her voice hard, "with me doing a favor for a friend. But we're way beyond that now. I'm making this an official FBI investigation."

"I guess that means you'll be assigning your agents to handle it. Guess my work is done."

She stared at him for a long moment, then an amused look crossed her face. "I don't know, J.T. Your skills may come in handy. As a contractor ... you can do things my guys won't touch."

He smiled. "What you really mean is: I'm not afraid to get my hands dirty and I'm willing to break the rules to get the job done."

She said nothing and smiled back.

"Does this mean I keep working the case, Erin?"

"I may regret it later," she said, "but, yes, it does."

Chapter 7

Mark Parker's condo was an upscale two-bedroom apartment furnished with expensive chrome, glass, and teak furniture. Abstract art hung on the walls and the hardwood floors gleamed from a recent polishing. The place was what J.T. Ryan expected, considering the WMN newsman was a well-known and highly-paid television reporter. The man was not married and had been the sole occupant in the condo.

Ryan was in the apartment now, methodically searching each of the rooms, looking for any clues regarding the man's death. He found nothing suspicious in the living room, dining room, kitchen, master bedroom, or bathrooms. The PI found only one bottle of wine in the place, indicating Parker was not a boozer. And he didn't find any antidepressants or any other prescription medicine, meaning the reporter was probably not having any mental issues. In fact, the newsman's only vice seemed to be smoking. The strong smell of cigarettes hung in the air, and full ashtrays were in every room.

Ryan had saved the second bedroom, which had been turned into a home office, for last.

He walked in and scanned the space. A teak desk and matching teak bookcases dominated the room. A four-drawer filing cabinet was in a corner.

Approaching the desk, he noticed something right away. Next to a stack of books on the desk was a framed photograph of a young woman. Picking up the picture, he saw it was of Mei Lin, Parker's assistant. She was wearing shorts and a halter top and was smiling into the camera.

Setting the photo down, he began searching the desk drawers, but found nothing out of the ordinary. Next he tackled the filing cabinets and saw gaps in them, as if some files had been removed. He noticed something else – there was no laptop, or a desktop PC in the room. There was also no printer. Looking behind the desk, he did find cables and a charger for a computer. From local PD he'd learned that when they searched the victim and the condo, they found no cell phone, computer tablet, or a laptop, which was highly unusual. The forensics techs had also dusted for prints, but found none. The place had been wiped clean.

It was obvious to Ryan that Parker's death was no suicide. Most likely the man had been overpowered, knocked out, and pushed off the roof of the building. And the killer, or killers, were pros.

Chapter 8

J.T. Ryan pressed the apartment's buzzer and waited. A moment later Mei Lin opened the door.

"Mr. Ryan," she said, "come in. Ms. Welch from the FBI called earlier and told me you'd be coming over this evening."

Ryan stepped inside and she closed the door behind them. Lin motioned toward the small, sparsely furnished living room. "We can sit in there."

Unlike Parker's condo, this apartment was plain and cramped. The woman must have kept a cat, because a feline scent permeated the place.

They sat across from each other on lumpy couches that had seen better days. He studied the pretty, Asian woman, who was wearing jeans and a faded Atlanta Falcons t-shirt. Her eyes were red-rimmed as if she'd been crying.

"Would you like some coffee, Mr. Ryan?"

When he declined, she tucked her legs beneath her.

"I'm sorry for your loss," Ryan said sympathetically.

Lin nodded. "He was a great reporter. We're all going to miss him at WMN."

"You were close to him, correct?"

"That's right. As well as being a reporter myself, I was his assistant for two years. He was like a mentor to me."

"But he was more than that," Ryan stated.

"What do you mean?"

"I saw your photo in his apartment. I'm assuming you were romantically involved."

She was about to deny it, then simply shrugged. "I guess it doesn't matter now. Staffers aren't supposed to be ... you know ... but now that he's ...." Her eyes brimmed with fresh tears and she brushed them away.

Ryan waited a minute for her to regain her composure.

"Ms. Lin, from what I've gathered so far, I don't believe he committed suicide."

"You don't? What else could it be?"

"I think he was murdered."

Her eyes went wide. "Murder? Are you sure?"

"Not 100 per cent, no. That's one of the reasons I needed to talk with you. Was he despondent? Did he ever talk about suicide?"

"Absolutely not! In fact, on a personal level, we were happy. We talked about the future. We even talked about getting married one day ...."

Ryan leaned forward in his seat. "Okay. As you know, he met with Erin Welch before his death. According to her, Parker was acting strangely – he was afraid of something. Something connected to a story he was working. He also met with a *New York Times* reporter, a man by the name of Matthews. Matthews died recently when the small jet he was in crashed."

Lin nodded, her face showing alarm. "I don't know the details of why Mark met with him. It was a story he was working on his own. A big story. Like I told you before, Mark and I always worked on things together. But on this, he kept me out of it."

"Why do you think he excluded you, Ms. Lin?"

"Mark said it would be safer for me that way. He felt the story was too dangerous and he wanted to protect me."

"Did he tell you what it involved?"

She rubbed her temple as if she had a headache. "Not in so many words. But I'm pretty sure it had to do with censorship."

"What do you mean, Ms. Lin?"

"Call me Mei – everyone does." She paused a moment. "Since you're not in the business, you're probably not aware of what's going on."

"You're right."

She un-tucked her legs and placed her feet flat on the floor. Then she leaned forward and lowered her voice. "The news business has changed. A lot. And not for the better. I've been a reporter for ten years and I've seen the changes. Mark was in it a lot longer and he said he'd seen a dramatic change in how the news was reported."

Ryan appraised her doll-like face. "You don't look old enough to have been a reporter for ten years – I thought you just got out of college, or high school even."

Mei Lin smiled, the first time today. "Asian women are like that – we don't age." She turned serious again.

"Okay, Mei. Tell me what's happening in the news business."

"Have you ever heard of 'weather porn'?"

Ryan shook his head. "No."

"It's a term we reporters use," she continued, "among ourselves. We make a joke about it, but the fact is, it's very real and very sad."

"What is it?"

"Do you watch much network news, J.T?"

"Not really."

"Okay. Then I'll enlighten you. National news programs, the six p.m. ones, and the morning shows, spend the first ten minutes of most shows talking about the weather – storms, floods, wildfires, etc. Later in the broadcast they cover celebrity news, the latest sex scandals, silly You Tube videos of babies or dogs. That leaves maybe ten minutes for hard-hitting news – a war, terrorism, that type of thing. What I call the real news."

She paused a moment. "I can tell by the incredulous look on your face that you don't believe me. But you can prove it to yourself. Just watch the national news any day of the week."

He nodded, planning to do just that. "Is this something that's specific to one network?"

"Oh, no. They all do it, with very few exceptions."

"But why?"

She rose abruptly from the couch, rubbed her temple again. "It's been a very long and tough day. I have a headache and I'm tired. I'm having a drink. Want one?"

Wanting to keep the conversation going, he said, "Sure, I'll have whatever you're having."

She went into the kitchen and came back with a quart bottle of Smirnoff and two small tumblers. Filling the glasses, she handed one to Ryan and took a gulp from hers.

"Mark never drank," she said, sitting back down. "But I don't handle stress as well as he did. Hence the vodka."

"I understand," he said, taking a sip. "What's caused this change in the news industry? Aren't reporters paid to report the news?"

Her eyes flashed in anger. "You'd think! Mark and I used to talk about this all the time. We were both angry about it. A lot of reporters – at least the good ones – are as well."

"Why do you think all this came about?"

She waved a hand in the air. "Lots of reasons. Part of it is we don't want to offend the advertisers. If we report about shady practices at car dealerships, they won't advertise with us. Same with restaurant chains, pharmaceutical companies, you name it. The news divisions just decide not to report certain news and fill their broadcasts with weather porn and cute baby videos."

Ryan downed his drink, the hard liquor burning his throat a bit. "So, I guess you'd call it self-censorship."

"That's right." She refilled their glasses and rested the bottle on the coffee table. "But it's gotten worse than that. Much worse. Especially in recent years." She lowered her voice. "Now the government is involved."

"They're censoring the news?" Ryan asked incredulously.

The woman glanced around the room, fear evident in her eyes. "I'd rather not talk about it too much." Then she fixed her gaze on him. "You seem like a good guy, J.T. But I really don't know you that well. And you do work for a government agency."

Ryan almost laughed at this, but saw that she was deadly serious. "All right. I understand your hesitation." He sipped the vodka slowly, mulling over everything Mei Lin had told him. Then an alarming thought struck him.

"You worked closely with Mark Parker on all his stories," he said, "except this one. But it's very possible that the killers don't know this. In fact, they would assume you had knowledge of the story."

Mei Lin was a very intelligent woman and the implications of this sank in immediately. "That means I'm in danger too."

"That's right. You are in danger."

Chapter 9

Washington, D.C.

The bald, obese man noticed one of the lights on his desk phone flash. Instead of picking up the receiver, he waited, not wanting to take the call. He knew who the caller was.

He drummed his thick fingers on his desk, his breathing labored. His three-piece suit was custom made to accommodate his girth.

Finally he reached over and answered the call. "Yes."

"We have a problem," he heard the woman's harsh voice from the other end.

"What kind of problem?"

"We've been analyzing the data," she replied icily. "There may be someone else involved."

He brushed perspiration from his forehead with a handkerchief. "Who is it?"

"I can't say over the phone. I'll send you an encrypted email."

"Yes, ma'am. How shall I deal with it?"

"I don't care how you deal with it, you fucking idiot. Just eliminate the problem."

Before he could reply, he heard a click and realized the woman had hung up.

A feeling of dread settled in the pit of the man's gut.

Chapter 10

Atlanta, Georgia

"We got the results back," Erin Welch said.

J.T. Ryan, who was sitting across from her, stopped munching on the pepperoni pizza and took a sip of his Pepsi.

"The results of what?" he asked. They were having lunch in the cafeteria on the first floor of the FBI building. It was mid-afternoon and the restaurant, which was usually packed with agents, attorneys, and police officers, was mostly empty.

Erin pushed aside her almost full plate of pizza. "My guys finished the handwriting analysis of Parker's suicide note."

"And?"

"The writing is in a similar style, done by someone who knows what they're doing. But it's not a match. Someone forged it."

Ryan nodded as he finished the food on his plate. "That confirms it. Parker was murdered."

"Yeah. And it was done by pros."

"You're not eating your pizza," he stated, as he wiped the grease on his hands with paper napkins.

Erin scrunched her face. "How can you eat this crap?"

"Tastes good to me."

"Typical man."

Ryan laughed as he gazed at the attractive woman. Today she was wearing a blue Versace pants suit with Louboutin heels. Her long brunette hair cascaded past her shoulders. "It figures you wouldn't like pizza."

"What do you mean?" she replied with a puzzled look.

"Anybody who wears Versace and Hanadama pearl necklaces wouldn't like plebian food. And you only drink Starbucks coffee, while I settle for the Dunkin Donuts kind."

"Are you making fun of me, J.T.?"

"Absolutely not," he said, trying to keep from smiling.

She pointed an index finger at him. "You better not. You work for me, remember?"

"How could I forget, Erin. You remind me all the time."

She stared at him, as if trying to decide if he was joking or not. Then she let out a long sigh.

He eyed her plate of food. "Are you going to eat that?"

"You can't *still* be hungry."

He smiled. "Is that a yes or a no?"

Erin slid her platter of pizza toward him. "Here. I hope you have a heart attack."

"Just want you to know that pizza is one of the three major food groups. The other two are chocolate and beer."

The FBI woman rolled her eyes.

Ryan laughed and began to happily munch on the greasy pepperoni and cheese deep-dish, which tasted delicious to him. When he was done, he took another drink of his Pepsi.

She leaned forward in her chair. "Earlier you told me about your conversation with Mei Lin. What did you think of her?"

"It's clear she's not involved in the murder. In fact, she and Parker were in love and she was genuinely distraught over his death."

"What about this news censorship she mentioned?"

He waved a hand in the air. "Sounds far-fetched to me. I mean, we do live in the United States, one of the freest countries in the world."

"I agree, J.T. It doesn't sound plausible."

"But I know one thing for sure. Mei Lin believes it, and according to her, so did Mark Parker."

Erin tucked her long hair behind her ears. "And you think she's in danger?"

"I do. Parker's dead. The other reporter, Matthews, is also dead. They may come for Mei Lin next."

She nodded. "I'll call Atlanta PD. With all the crime in this city, they won't have the manpower to keep a uniform with her 24/7, but I'll have a black and white cruise by her apartment building and check on her periodically. I'd send a team of my agents to give her protection, but I can't spare them either. We're stretched pretty thin already."

"I appreciate anything you can do, Erin. She's a nice young woman and I'd hate for something to happen to her."

An amused look settled on her face. "Is this the softer side of the rough-and-ready Ryan seeping out?"

"Maybe." The PI rubbed his jaw. "Tell me about the NTSB investigation. How's that going?"

"It's not," she snapped, a hard edge in her voice. "I've called their regional director several times, but I can't get a straight answer. Just that they're still working the case."

"Stonewalling?"

Erin shrugged. "Not sure. But you know me. I'll keep asking until I find out."

Chapter 11

Ryan drove his Tahoe out of the FBI building's underground lot and headed north toward his midtown office. It was rush hour and traffic was heavy. As he navigated around the slower moving vehicles, he mulled over his meeting with Erin.

It was clear to him what his next step would be: question Parker's boss at WMN. But Erin had told him to back off, give her a chance to set it up. Apparently the guy was a big shot at the TV network and she was concerned Ryan would turn the questioning into an interrogation. She wanted to, as she put it, 'facilitate a productive meeting'.

He smiled, knowing the woman was right. Erin was more adept at interpersonal skills, one reason she'd risen in the ranks at the Bureau. He, on the other hand, liked to kick ass and take names.

Ryan reached his building and spent the next two hours in his office doing paperwork. When he was almost done he felt his cell phone buzz and he slipped it out of his pocket.

"It's Mei Lin," he heard her say when he answered. "Can you come to my place? Something strange is happening."

"Are you okay? Are you in danger right now?"

"No. Nothing like that."

"All right." He glanced at his watch. "I'll leave now and see you in twenty." The woman lived in midtown Atlanta not far from his office. He disconnected the call and pocketed the phone.

Taking out his revolver from a desk drawer, he checked the load and slipped the handgun into his hip holster. After putting on his blue blazer, he left the office.

A short while later he pulled his Tahoe to the curb and parked the SUV in front of Lin's apartment building. To his relief he noticed an APD cruiser parked on the street also. A uniform was inside it, smoking. Erin had come through – he realized once again that as ADIC she had a lot of juice in this town.

Ryan made his way up to Mei Lin's apartment and she let him inside. She had a worried look on her face.

"What's wrong?" the PI asked.

The young Asian woman pointed to an open laptop, which was resting on the coffee table in the living room. "Something weird is going on with my computer."

They went to it and she sat in front of it while Ryan remained standing and looked over her shoulder.

She opened her email account. "It's been happening all day – I'll write an email and right after I send it, I'll see a blip on the screen as if it had been sent twice. I didn't think anything of it at first, then I looked at my email sent file and saw that a duplicate was sent out, and right after that the duplicate vanished, like I'd never sent it." She paused a moment. "I think this happened briefly last week too, but I was very busy and didn't focus on it."

"That is strange," he said. "Maybe it's problem with the Internet."

"I thought of that too, J.T. So I checked with our computer tech guys at WMN. They said everything was okay with the net. I took my laptop down to the tech guys this afternoon so they could check it out. They said it was fine."

"So the problem stopped?"

"Yes," she said. "I've sent emails this evening, but everything looks normal. Maybe I'm overreacting. But with everything that's happened ... I'm frightened. I thought I should call you."

Ryan nodded. "I'm glad you did."

"What should we do?"

He thought about this. *Is Mei Lin overreacting? It's possible — she's just lost someone she loved — grief can mess with your head.* But then, four people are dead. The two reporters and the two flight crew, and they all died under suspicious circumstances. Knowing he didn't have other leads to follow right now, this computer situation might turn out to be something.

"I need to make a call," he said, pulling out his cell. Ryan almost tapped in Erin's number, when he got a better idea. He called someone else, explained the situation, and arranged to meet.

Chapter 12

Lauren Chase opened the door and Ryan and Mei Lin entered the foyer of Lauren's home in the northern suburbs of Atlanta.

Lauren gave the attractive Asian woman a long, appraising look as she led them into the living room. As they sat down, Lauren winked at Ryan before settling her gaze wholly on Mei Lin.

"J.T. told me you're having problems with your computer," Lauren said.

"That's right." Lin was carrying her laptop under an arm and she handed it to Lauren. "It looked to me like my emails were being copied. J.T. says you're a college professor in computer science. He also said you were really smart and that you'd be able to figure out what was wrong."

"Did he?" Lauren replied, giving Ryan an amused look. Then she said, "Let's turn this thing on and take a look." She opened the laptop and Lin gave her the password to log on. After a few minutes of scrolling through the emails and several files, Lauren looked up. "Everything looks normal. I need to take this thing apart and poke around, if that's okay with you."

Mei Lin nodded. "Of course. I want to find out what's going on."

Lauren rose from the couch, holding the laptop with one hand. "I've got coffee going in the kitchen. J.T., why don't you get a cup for our guest." Then she turned and left the room.

The PI went to the kitchen, filled two mugs and came back in the living room. After handing Lin her cup, he sat down across from her. They spent the next hour talking about the case. He questioned her in detail, trying to learn as much as he could, probing into the last couple of months of her life for details she might have left out previously.

After refilling Mei Lin's cup of coffee, Ryan went to Lauren's home office, where he found the pretty redhead hunched over the totally dismantled computer. Plastic and metal pieces were strewn all over her desk. She looked up as he came in.

"Hi, gorgeous," he said. "How's it going?"

"It's going," she replied.

Pulling up a chair across from her, he sat down. "Thank you for doing this, hon."

"Don't mention it. You know how much I like tinkering with electronics." She gave him the amused look again.

Confused, he said, "What's with the smile? And the wink earlier when we came in?"

She shook her head slowly, the grin on her face growing. "I just wonder, John Taylor Ryan, if you'd be helping Mei Lin so much if she wasn't so attractive?"

Ryan now realized what was going on. *Bringing the reporter here wasn't such a good idea*, he thought. He held up both hands. "It's not what you think. I'm just trying to solve a case."

The redhead gazed at him and said nothing, her face showing no expression.

"Look, hon – I work cases all over the world – if I wanted to stray, I'd have done it long ago. But I never have. You know that."

She stared at him stonily for another long moment, then burst out laughing. "Got you, didn't I?"

"Jesus, Lauren, cut that out," he said, relieved she had been kidding all along.

"You're the jokester, J.T. But this time I got *you*!"

The PI rose, bent over and kissed her on the lips, which she returned hungrily.

When they separated, he said, "Now back to business. Is there something wrong with the laptop?"

"Yes and no. I took the whole thing apart and found nothing wrong with the hardware. It's all working as it should."

"But?"

"There's a problem with the software."

"What kind of problem?"

She pointed to the disassembled PC. "There's a Trojan that's attached itself to her computer's programming."

"What the hell's a Trojan?"

"A virus."

"Didn't her computer have anti-virus software installed?'

"Of course. Mei Lin works for a big company. All big corporations have that type of software installed. In fact, the one she uses is the best there is."

"You would know, hon."

"Yes, I would. You're the detective and I'm good with computers."

"So – you think this virus was causing the email copying?"

Lauren nodded. "I'm sure of it. I think it was forwarding a copy of each email to a third party, then erasing the evidence immediately."

Ryan pointed to the mountain of parts strewn on the desk. "I got another question. Who was the third party? Who's behind this?"

She shrugged. "No telling. The virus is very, very sophisticated. I can tell you that no average hacker could have developed it."

"Okay," he said. "If you could bag up all these parts, I'll give them to Erin tomorrow. Hopefully, the FBI techs will be able to identity the source."

She nodded.

"Thanks, Lauren. You've been a big help. I'll take Mei Lin back to her place now."

The pretty redhead stood, went up on her tiptoes and kissed him.

"I love you, J.T."

"I love you too, hon." He glanced at his watch. "It's late. Guess after I drop her off, I'll go home. Unless you want me to come back."

She gave him a mischievous smile. "Of course."

Chapter 13

The assassin raised his binoculars as soon as he saw the Tahoe SUV pull to the curb in front of the apartment building. He was hiding in an alley across the street and he zoomed the binos for a closer look. Although it was late in the evening and dark out, streetlamps illuminated the man and woman who climbed out of the SUV.

The woman was short and Asian, and the man tall and rugged looking, ex-military the assassin guessed. The assassin's boss had told him that the FBI had hired a PI to work on the case and he figured the tall man was him.

The hired killer watched as the man and woman talked for a minute outside the building, then she went inside as he got back in the SUV and drove off. He lowered his binos and was about to cross the street toward the apartment building when he noticed a police cruiser drive by slowly, then park at the curb. No one got out of the black-and-white, but he observed a cigarette being lit inside the car.

The assassin thought through his options. His boss had given him a tight deadline, with a bonus if he delivered on time. But the killer had been in this line of work a long time. Bonus or no bonus, the job would have to wait a little longer.

Stepping back deeper into the alley, he turned and disappeared into the shadows.

Chapter 14

Erin Welch and J.T. Ryan strode out of the elevator and into the FBI building's underground parking lot.

"I'll drive," Erin said, her high heels clicking on the concrete floor. She pointed to a red Jaguar sedan parked in one of the reserved slots next to the elevator.

"Nice wheels," Ryan replied with a low whistle. "It's new right?"

"Just bought it last month." She unlocked the car with her fob, put her briefcase in the back seat, and slid in the front.

Ryan climbed into the passenger seat and admired the burl wood trim, top-notch NAV system, and rich, tan leather interior. He took in a deep breath, inhaled the intoxicating new car smell. "I wish I could afford a car this nice."

She started up the Jaguar and the engine let out a pleasant, low-throated roar. Turning toward him, she said, "What are you talking about? You drive a Tahoe. That's not cheap."

"Yeah, but I saved for years to be able to afford it. And it's the only expensive thing I own." He waved a hand in the air. "This car is just another one of your toys."

"You could always work at the Bureau," she replied as she pulled out of the lot and unto the street. "The pay's better."

"No thanks. Too many rules."

Erin grimaced. "That's the truth."

"Have your tech guys finished checking Mei Lin's laptop?"

She nodded. "Yeah. Lauren was spot on. The PC is infected with a complex virus."

"Who planted it?"

"My guys can't determine that. But it's sophisticated."

"How sophisticated?"

Erin gave him a sidelong glance. "Very. My tech guys, who have been in the Bureau for a long time, both agreed it was the work of a government."

"Which country? The Chinese? Russians?"

She shrugged as she passed a slower moving car on the road. "No way of knowing."

Ryan thought through the implications. Not coming up with a good explanation, his focus turned to the upcoming meeting. "We didn't need to interview the WMN guy together. I could've handled it by myself."

Erin pursed her lips. "Oh, no. I know how you work. Dan Marshall is a top executive at the network. I don't need a TV news story about how the FBI is harassing the press."

"Maybe you're right," he replied with a grin.

"I know I'm right."

Half an hour later they were shown into Dan Marshall's corner office on the penthouse level of the WMN building. The office had deep-pile carpeting, teak wood furnishings, and a panoramic view of downtown Atlanta. It was a bright, cloudless day, and the sunlight glinted off the glass and steel skyscrapers.

Dan Marshall, a tall, thin, balding man stood as they came in, but instead of going around his desk to shake hands, simply waved them to the deeply upholstered chairs fronting it. "Please have a seat."

"Thank you," Erin said, flashing her cred pack at the man. "I'm ADIC Erin Welch, and this is J.T. Ryan, who's assisting me on the case."

"Yes," Marshall replied as they sat down. "My secretary filled me in."

"We're sorry for your loss," Erin said.

The news executive nodded, but his face was impassive, showing no emotion. "Mark Parker was one of our best reporters."

Erin leaned forward. "As you know, Mr. Marshall, we're conducting an investigation into his death. Although it appeared at first to be a suicide, it's clear now that it was a murder."

"I see," the TV executive replied. He did not seem surprised by the news.

"Parker's death," the FBI woman continued, "may be connected to the death of another man, a prominent *New York Times* reporter."

Marshall's eyebrows arched but he said nothing.

"We think," she said, "that the two men were working on an important story together. What could you tell us about that?"

The news executive, who was dressed in a pin-stripe navy blue suit, a pink silk tie, and a pink pocket square, picked off a trace of lint from the lapel of his suit. "There's nothing I can tell you about that."

Ryan hadn't said a word since coming in, but he was getting aggravated by the man's cavalier attitude.

"Can't or won't," the PI snapped.

Erin shot Ryan a glare, then turned her gaze toward the newsman. "This is an official FBI investigation. We'd like your cooperation."

Marshall waved a hand in the air. "I wish I could be of more help. But a reporter's sources are confidential. As are the stories they work on until they're broadcast or published. It's called freedom of the press. Surely, Ms. Welch, you've heard of that."

Erin's face flushed. "Two reporters are dead," she said in a hard voice.

The executive shrugged, his face impassive.

"I can legally compel you to testify," Erin snapped.

Marshall rose abruptly. "I think this meeting is over. If you have any further questions, refer them to our corporate legal department."

"You know the difference," Ryan said in a pleasant tone, "between a pathetic asshole and you, Mr. Marshall? Absolutely nothing."

A shocked expression crossed the executive's face as his jaw dropped.

Erin tried to keep from laughing, with no success.

Grinning, Ryan and Erin left the office.

Back in the Jaguar minutes later, Erin started the car and drove away from the WMN building.

"That was a bust," Ryan said.

"Agreed," replied Erin as she stepped on the gas, the sedan surging forward. "The question is, why did he clam up?"

"Are you buying this freedom of the press bullshit? The reporters are dead."

"I don't know, J.T."

"I think it's crap."

She glanced at him and smiled. "You were pretty funny in there."

"I'm humorous all the time. You just don't always appreciate my jokes."

"Well, J.T., that guy deserved it."

"He did. By the way, I'm glad you were with me – I would have ripped his head off if I'd been on my own."

"I know."

Ryan watched as the FBI agent deftly navigated the heavy traffic. "Something else bothers me about the meeting," he said. "Marshall didn't seem surprised that Parker's death was not a suicide."

"I caught that too."

"And something else, Erin. He didn't react to the apparent connection between the two dead reporters."

"Yeah, that bothers me also."

"So, where do we go from here?" he said.

"I'll talk to the ADA – have him contact WMN's lawyers – we need answers, and by God, I'm not going to let an empty suit like Marshall stonewall us."

"I like the sound of that, Erin."

"What's your next move?"

"I'm going to check on Mei Lin – I think she's in danger, and I want to make sure she's okay."

"You better watch out," Erin said with a grin, "your girlfriend's going to think you have the hots for Ms. Lin."

Ryan shook his head slowly. "Tell me about it. You should have seen Lauren's face when she saw her the other day."

"Well, Mei Lin *is* cute."

"Please stop," Ryan said seriously. "I've got enough problems handling one woman. The last thing I need is to complicate my life with more. Women! Can't live with them and can't live without them."

Erin laughed and sped up the car.

Chapter 15

Ryan drove slowly by Mei Lin's apartment building, looking for the police cruiser that had been stationed there last time. He didn't spot it, but was not completely surprised. It was difficult for cops to provide 24/7 protection with the limited resources they had.

Parking his car at the curb, he climbed out and made his way up to her apartment.

When he knocked at her door, he heard a woman's muffled scream from inside, "Help! He's got a gun!"

His heartbeat racing, Ryan pulled his pistol and kicked the door hard. Splinters flew as the lock gave way and the door swung open. He went to one knee and trained his revolver forward.

A man dressed in a black ski mask and black clothing had his arm locked around Mei Lin's neck. He was holding a gun to her head. Lin was standing in front of him, her body trembling, her face ashen and her eyes wide with fear.

"Drop the gun!" the man in black shouted. "Or I kill her!"

Ryan lined up his sight for the man's head. He almost pulled the trigger, but Lin was shaking uncontrollably and he feared shooting her.

"Drop it!" the man yelled again, this time pressing the muzzle of his semi-automatic to her temple.

Ryan aimed for a spot three inches over the man's head and fired one round.

The masked man flinched from the sound of the blast, pushed Mei Lin aside and pointed his weapon at the PI.

In the same instant Ryan pulled the trigger and fired two rounds, the man's head exploding as the .357 Magnum bullets made contact. His body dropped to the floor as blood and brain matter splattered the wall.

With the roar of the gunfire ringing in his ears, Ryan cautiously approached the collapsed body and crouched next to it. *No need to check for a pulse*, he thought. *The guy's clearly dead.*

Mei Lin, sobbing hysterically, huddled on the floor by the sofa, her head in her hands. After making sure she hadn't been hurt, the PI searched the other rooms, but found no one else in the apartment.

Holstering his revolver, Ryan kneeled by the dead man and pulled off his ski mask. Not much of his face was left – just a bloody pulp. He checked the rest of the body and found no ID. As he had suspected, the man was wearing a bullet-proof vest. *Good thing I aimed for the head*, he thought.

Standing, Ryan pulled out his cell phone and called Erin to let her know what had happened.

Then he went over to Mei Lin and tried to comfort her. With the smell of blood and gunpowder still thick in the room, he sat next to the woman and waited for the FBI to arrive.

***

Erin Welch looked down at the bloody corpse. "You found no ID?"

"None," replied Ryan, who was standing next to her in the living room of Mei Lin's apartment.

An FBI forensics team was also in the room colleting trace evidence. Lin was on the sofa. She had stopped sobbing and was now sitting silently, a stunned expression on her face.

"Any idea who the perp was?" Erin asked.

Ryan shook his head. "No. But he was a pro. He was wearing body armor and his Glock 9 mil had a suppressor. He was also carrying a switchblade and a garrote. He was prepared for any contingency. This wasn't his first rodeo."

"I agree. Looks like he was a contract killer." Erin glanced at Mei Lin. "Lucky for her you came by when you did, J.T."

Ryan nodded.

Erin turned her gaze back to the dead body. "We'll run the guy's prints through the NCIC database. If he's a paid assassin, he's bound to be in the system for something."

The PI pointed to the corpse's bloody face. "I guess facial recognition is out of the question."

"Gallows humor, J.T.? Really?" Erin snapped, aggravated at his attempt at a joke.

Ryan shrugged. "What can I say – it's been a tough day. Sometimes humor gets me through the life-and-death situations we have to handle."

Erin nodded, knowing what he was saying was true. She'd met many cops, coroners, and EMTs who felt the same way. She glanced at Lin, who hadn't said a word since the FBI agent had come into the apartment. "She's in shock."

"Yeah," said Ryan. "She's scared to death. You need to put her in protective custody."

"I'll arrange it. Whoever tried to assassinate her will probably try again."

Chapter 16

Washington, D.C.

"We have a problem," the woman with the hard, angular face said into the phone. "A big problem."

"Is this an encrypted call?" the man on the other end snapped.

"Of course. All my calls to you are encrypted."

"What's the problem?"

The woman glanced around the sparse office before answering, trying to frame her response. She didn't want to deliver the bad news, but it was unavoidable. "Do you remember the last conversation we had?"

"Yes," he groused. "Just tell me the problem, damn it."

"The contractor we hired failed."

"What?" the man screamed into the phone. "You told me you were handling it! You told me you had everything under control."

She didn't reply and waited a moment for the man to calm down a bit. "And we've run into some other unforeseen complications," she said.

"Such as?"

"The FBI office in Atlanta has opened an investigation."

"What the fuck!" he yelled. "This is unacceptable!"

"I agree. And I'm addressing the situation."

"You'd better," the man said angrily. "We both have a lot to lose if our operation is exposed."

"Don't worry. I'll handle it. I've always taken care of problems in the past."

"Okay," he replied, sounding somewhat calmer. "You are good at what you do. That's why we make such a good team."

"I want to see you again soon," the woman said, her voice less business-like now. "It's been too long."

"I know. I want that too. But you know it's more difficult now that we've ramped up the operation." He paused. "Take care of these problems and I'll see what I can arrange. I'll be making a trip to the States soon."

Pleased by his response, she said, "We speak with one voice."

"Yes. We speak with one voice," the man replied and hung up.

She replaced the phone receiver and sat quietly at her desk for a long moment, thinking about the call.

Her office was small and sparsely furnished, which was unusual for someone who wielded substantial power. The room had no windows, the metal desk and cabinets were utilitarian. The walls, painted a dull gray, were bare.

Like her office, the clothes the woman was wearing were simple and inexpensive – she favored off-the-rack, non-descript business suits from big-box stores. She wore no makeup, which would have softened the hard, angular features of her unattractive face. The woman kept her blonde hair cropped very short. She'd always thought women spent way too much time obsessing over their clothes and hair. And although she was in her mid-fifties, she had never been married. She deeply admired her boss, and she had only been in love with one man in her life. That was her business partner, the man she'd just spoken with on the phone.

Her job, she mused, was her true obsession. And the current operation, was the ultimate prize.

"We speak with one voice," she said to herself.

Chapter 17

Atlanta, Georgia

J.T. Ryan drove north on Interstate 575, his thoughts focused on the day ahead.

Erin Welch had run the prints of the man he'd shot through NCIC, the National Crime Information Center database and had found a match. The contract killer's last known was an address in Blue Ridge, a small town in the mountainous region of north Georgia.

Traffic thinned the farther Ryan got from Atlanta. The Interstate merged into a highway, and then to a state road as the scenery changed from high-density urban sprawl to rural, with an occasional gas station and mini-mart along the road.

It was an overcast day, the dark gray clouds threatening rain. It was also chilly so he turned up the heater in his SUV. He scanned the gray sky, and as if on cue, large raindrops splat on his windshield. The splats turned into a torrent and he clicked on his wipers.

Slowing the vehicle to adjust for the poor visibility, his mind went back to the info Erin had supplied. It wasn't much. Just the guy's name, an address, and the two vehicles registered in his name. There was no record of employment – which made sense – as a rule, contract killers didn't do 9-to-5 jobs. But it bothered Ryan that not much else had popped from the NCIC database. The guy had one arrest on an illegal gun purchase, which was the reason he was added to the database. The PI figured the man went by several aliases, also common for hit men.

The state road curved around the heavily-wooded, hilly terrain, the elevation climbing with every mile. By the time he reached the outskirts of Blue Ridge, the hilly terrain became mountainous.

He drove slowly through the town's main street, observing the quaint antique shops, fashionable restaurants, and art galleries. Interspersed among the upscale places were barbecue joints, pubs, and taverns. A historic train station was situated in the middle of the town, with a century old train making daily runs through the scenic mountains. The railroad cars were usually filled with tourists, but today the train sat empty on the tracks. No doubt the bad weather was keeping people away.

Ryan had been to the town several times before, in fact had rented cabins there with Lauren for long weekends. The area, only a few hours drive from Atlanta, was a haven for tourists and city dwellers who kept second homes there.

After grabbing lunch at *Harvest on Main* restaurant, he stopped at a local realty office to get directions. The realty agent had never heard of the man he'd shot – confirming what the PI had suspected – that the name in NCIC was an alias. But the realty guy knew the area well and gave him directions to the location of the house.

Ryan took the two-lane road out of town and headed east, through even more remote areas. Other than a few homes situated high-up the wooded cliffs along the road, there was nothing else. Eventually he came to an unmarked gravel and dirt path leading up a steep hill. A rural mailbox with the right house number was at the foot of the hill. The heavy rain had washed away much of the gravel, turning the trail into a soupy, mud path. Wanting to make a stealthy approach to the house, Ryan decided to continue on foot. He parked his Tahoe off the main road at the foot of the hill.

After checking the load in his pistol, he zipped up his windbreaker, put on a ball cap, and grabbed his backpack from the rear seat. Climbing out, he was instantly pelted by the heavy downpour. Brushing water from his face, he slung the bag over one shoulder, then began climbing up the steep, muddy, and winding trail.

Fifteen minutes later he spotted it through the trees: a large two-story cabin sitting at the end of the gravel driveway. It was midday, but it was so overcast that it appeared to be dusk. He noted no lights in the home.

Parked in the driveway was a late-model Ford pickup truck with oversized wheels. It was one of the vehicles registered in the man's name. The FBI had found his other vehicle, a Jeep, in a parking lot close to Mei Lin's building.

Crouching behind a tree, he watched for activity at the place and saw none. Listening closely, he only heard the drumming of the rain on the cabin's metal roof and the baying of dogs in the distance.

The PI was drenched from the downpour – his clothes were clinging to him and his boots were caked with mud up to his ankles.

After strapping his backpack on tighter, he pulled the revolver from his hip holster and cautiously approached the cabin, using the heavy vegetation for cover. It was possible the man had accomplices and he half expected gunfire to erupt at any moment.

Going around to the back of the house, he sprinted the last fifteen feet, his boots sloshing over the muddy ground. He hugged the wall by the rear door and scanned the dim interior through the door's window. Seeing no activity, he took out his lock-pick set and fiddled with the lock. Putting away the tool, he turned the knob and slipped inside.

Tense, he held the pistol in front of him with both hands as he gazed around the kitchen and dinette area. No one was there and no sounds emanated from the other rooms.

Closing the door behind him, he carefully searched each of the rooms on the first floor. Along the way he pocketed several items that might provide clues to the man's activities or associates. The place was a mess, Ryan noted – empty beer cans, crumpled food wrappers, pizza cartons, and magazines, were strewn haphazardly on the furniture and the floor.

Finished searching the lower level, he stood by the banister and gazed up the wooden staircase leading to the second story. It appeared to be just as dim and quiet as downstairs.

Ryan began climbing the stairs, but when he reached the third step, he heard a metallic click and his heart stopped.

It was sound he'd never forget – a noise he'd heard when serving in the Army's Special Forces in Afghanistan. Two soldiers in his squad had been killed instantly by the IED, an improvised explosive device. Ryan, who luckily had been ten feet away, had only been knocked out by the blast.

His mouth dry, he knew that once he took his foot off the pressure plate under the stair step, the IED or Claymore mine would explode. Staying perfectly still, the PI's heart raced as his eyes darted around the room, looking for a way to escape. There was a window next to the front door, but it was ten feet away.

Knowing the bomb could go off at any instant, he lunged off the stairs, raced to the window and crashed through it, glass and wood splinters cutting into his skin. He landed in a rutted pool of mud and gravel, just as he heard the roar of the explosion and felt the concussion shock of the blast.

Laying there on the muddy ground, drenched by the heavy downpour, he felt the pain from the cuts on his arms and face. Looking back toward the house, he heard and felt the concussion from a secondary, much larger explosion. The door, windows, and parts of the roof were blown out as the cabin erupted into a huge fireball.

Ryan felt a blinding pain and everything went black.

Chapter 18

Langley, Virginia

"So what's next?" Rachel West asked, sitting across from her boss Alex Miller.

"Now that you've completed your assignment in Argentina," Miller replied, "I've got something else for you."

The two people were in Miller's office at the CIA. He was the director of the Agency's Special Operations Division. He pulled a file from a desk drawer and slid it across his desk.

Rachel picked it up, opened it and scanned it quickly.

"Two deaths," she said, "one in Venice, the other in Paris." She closed the file. "People die all the time, Alex. Why do you need me on this?"

Miller tented his fingers on the desk. "It's who they were and how they died."

"Okay," Rachel said. She was a field operative at the Agency and had solved several big cases over the years. In her mid-thirties, she was 5'-9", tall for a woman, athletic, and curvaceous. She was also very attractive, with long blonde hair and piercing blue eyes. Today she was dressed in a long-sleeve blue denim shirt and jeans, but the simple clothes didn't hide her beauty.

"I got a call recently," Miller continued, "from a friend of mine at the FBI, Erin Welch. She's working on a case involving the suspicious deaths of several reporters in the U.S." He leaned forward in his seat. "When I read about the death of an American reporter in Italy yesterday, I got curious and started checking. Another American journalist, this one located in France, died last week also."

Rachel nodded. "Too many coincidences."

"Agreed. The man in Venice died of a drug overdose. The Paris journalist was run over by a truck. No signs of foul play. But still."

Rachel opened the file and read through it again. "It says here the reporters worked at different news organizations. Any connection between these two and the reporters who died in the U.S.?"

"None that I could see. That's why I want you involved, Rachel. You've got a good track record solving these complex cases. And you're one of my best operatives."

She smiled. "Admit it, I'm your best agent."

He didn't reply, simply gave her a hard stare.

"When do you want me to start, Alex?"

Miller opened a drawer, took out an envelope and handed it to her. "Now. You're booked on a flight tonight to Venice."

Chapter 19

Blue Ridge, Georgia

Erin Welch trudged over the muddy ground, glad she'd changed her high heels for sensible flats. The rain was coming down in sheets, her Burberry raincoat doing its best to keep her dress from getting soaked; she'd pulled the hood up on the coat, but even so her long hair was wringing-wet and plastered to her scalp.

She stopped, gazed at what was left of the mountain-top cabin. It was a smoldering ruin, the fire from the explosion burning most of the wooden structure. Only charred logs, pieces of the blackened metal roof, and a stone fireplace remained. Acrid smoke hung in the air and she coughed as it filled her lungs.

Erin slowly turned around 360 degrees to survey the scene. Her FBI forensics team was busy at work, collecting whatever evidence they could find, which didn't appear to be much. The first responders, Fannin County police and fire department personnel, were here as well, their vehicles parked haphazardly on the gravel area around the house. An EMT truck was off to one side, its lights still flashing, lighting up the nighttime scene with an eerie glow.

Brushing rain from her face, she marched toward the truck, her shoes sinking into the mud. A paramedic was climbing out of the back of the vehicle as she reached it.

"Is he conscious now?" Erin asked the man.

"Yeah," the EMT guy said, "you can talk to him."

She clambered up the steps and sat on the bench by the stretcher. J.T. Ryan, his face and arms covered with bandages, was laying on it.

"You're a lucky man," Erin said, pulling off her hood.

"I don't feel lucky, he replied, grimacing. "I feel like shit."

"You're alive. The EMTs told me you suffered a concussion and serious burns and cuts."

He turned his head towards her. "Yeah. You're right, I am lucky to be alive."

"The explosion was extremely loud," she said. "The sound carried for miles. Neighbors reported it to the police. The local cops found you unconscious by the house, or what's left of it. They saw your ID and called me. Tell me what happened."

Ryan grimaced again. "I was searching the place. One of the stair steps was rigged with an IED. My only way out was through a window. When I stepped off, the device was triggered as I jumped out."

Erin nodded. "Another sign that the guy was a pro. Probably figured someone would track him down eventually. I wonder what he was hiding in the place?"

"We'll never know," Ryan said. He stared at her for a long moment, taking in her wet hair, soaked clothing, and muddy shoes. "You look like a drowned rat, Erin."

"Thanks," she snapped. "You really know how to perk up my day."

After talking with Ryan for another few minutes, Erin climbed out of the EMT truck, met with her forensics team, then trudged to her Jaguar. Getting in, she fired it up, turned on her headlights and slowly made her way down the dark, muddy trail. By the time she got back to Atlanta it was four a.m.

Going home to her townhouse in Buckhead, she tried to get some sleep. But she was too wired, and after an hour of tossing and turning restlessly in bed, she got up. She took a long, hot shower, dressed, and drove to work.

As soon as she walked into her FBI office downtown, her assistant came into the room. "There's someone here to see you," the young man said.

Erin glanced at her watch. It was only seven a.m. "I don't have any appointments this morning. Who is it?"

"DHS."

Her brows arched, wondering what this could be about.

"He's in the conference room, Erin," her assistant said and left.

Placing her briefcase on the floor, she took off her raincoat and went into the bullpen, the open office area full of desks that fronted her office. Several of her agents were already at their desks, on the phone or on their laptops, and she saw a few more walking in. The area was quiet now, but within an hour when the bullpen was full, the place would be a beehive of activity.

After grabbing a cup of coffee from the vending machine in the break room, she entered the glass-walled conference room and closed the door behind her.

A tall, thin man with a mustache and wearing a dark suit was sitting at the conference table. Seeing her, he rose and showed her his cred pack. "Agent Castillo, DHS."

After shaking hands, she said, "Have a seat, Agent Castillo." They sat across from each other at the table.

"It's not often I get a visit from Homeland Security," she said, taking a sip of the hot but watery coffee.

Castillo nodded. "Considering both our agencies work for the same side, you'd think DHS and the FBI would have a closer working relationship."

"You'd think," she said skeptically, eying him with suspicion. "But in my experience, it hasn't always worked that way."

After the tragic events of September 11, 2001, she recalled, the Department of Homeland Security had been created to thwart future terrorist attacks. The FBI, along with every other U.S. federal law enforcement agency, now worked under the umbrella of DHS. Sometimes with mediocre results, Erin thought.

"That's true, Erin."

"That's ADIC Welch to you," she snapped, irritated at the man's use of her first name.

Castillo waved a hand in the air. "I stand corrected, ADIC Welch." A thin smile crossed his lips. "But remember one thing. The FBI may be the 800 pound gorilla. But DHS is the 1,000 pound one."

Erin grit her teeth, knowing the man was right. "I don't have time for word games, Agent Castillo. Let's get down to business. What's this meeting about?"

The man leaned forward in his chair. "You've been working a case regarding the deaths of two reporters and several other people. I'm here to inform you that Homeland Security is now in charge of this investigation, with full jurisdictional control."

"What?" she snarled. "I work for the FBI director in D.C. He hasn't said anything to me about this."

"He's being informed this morning as well."

Erin's face reddened and she gave him a piercing glare. "Why the hell is this happening?"

"This is now an active DHS investigation, ADIC Welch. Since you're no longer working the case, that's none of your concern."

The man abruptly rose and handed her his card. "We'll need copies of all your case files on this investigation within 24 hours. Please have them delivered to my office." Then, before she could protest, he turned and left the conference room.

Chapter 20

Atlanta, Georgia

J.T. Ryan was sitting up on the hospital bed, a food tray in front of him. Still in pain from his recent injuries, he took a spoonful of the tapioca pudding and almost gagged. Grady Memorial was a good medical facility but its culinary expertise was nonexistent. He pushed the tray aside and tried to watch the mindless game show on the TV mounted on the wall.

Just then Lauren Chase strode into the hospital room, a frown on her face. She gazed around the small, semi-private room and noticed the old, frail man on the bed next to Ryan's. Without saying a word, she pulled the cloth partition closed, separating the room into two and giving them some privacy.

"Hi, hon," Ryan said, noting her red-rimmed eyes. "Is everything okay?"

She stood by his bed, her arms crossed in front of her. "I'm so mad at you right now, John Taylor Ryan."

He studied the petite, pretty redhead, trying to figure out what was happening. Her long auburn hair was pulled back carelessly into a ponytail and it was obvious she had dressed quickly, wearing a Georgia Tech sweatshirt and jeans.

"Why are you mad, Lauren?"

She waved a hand in the air. "This place. You. Again. I almost had a heart attack when Welch called me and told me what happened and where you were."

"Have you been crying, hon?"

Her hazel eyes welled up. "What do you think?"

"I'm sorry. I would have called you myself, but they sedated me for the pain – I had trouble dialing your number."

She brushed aside a tear. "It's not that, J.T. It's that you almost got killed. Again. I've lost track of how many calls I've gotten in the middle of the night ... I love you very much, J.T ... I don't want to lose you ...."

"I know. But I'm okay. Nothing's wrong with me. Just some minor cuts."

She stabbed a finger in the air at him. "Bullshit. Those bandages on your face say different. The nurse I just talked to says different."

Ryan tried smiling, but it hurt his face too much. "What does she know? I love you, Lauren. That's what's important. Now, please, hon, sit and calm down."

She gave him a long, hard look, then her features softened. "Okay." She sat on the metal chair next to the bed and reached out and held one of his hands.

"I'm fine, really," he said, squeezing her palm. "I'll be out of here in no time."

Lauren brushed away another tear and smiled. "All right."

"Are you teaching classes today?" he asked, trying to change the subject.

"Yes. It's Tuesday. You know I teach Monday through Friday."

"Yeah, of course. But you're not wearing your office clothes."

"I just threw these on and rushed over as soon as I got Erin's call."

He caressed her face, traced his fingers over her soft, delicate skin. "I love you, babe."

Her face lit up with a wide smile. "I love you, too."

"I can't wait to get you home," he said, his voice low. "I want to do some nasty things to you."

Lauren blushed, the reddish hue accentuating her cute freckles. "J.T.," she whispered, "cut that out. The other man in the room is going to hear us."

"Don't worry. He's old and hard of hearing."

"You're incorrigible, you know that?" she replied, but he could tell she was enjoying the banter. It made him feel good to see her mood had lightened.

Ryan patted the bed. "Why don't you sit here," he whispered. "I want to give you a big hug."

"That's not the only thing you want to do," Lauren replied with a grin. "And the answer is no. This is a hospital, remember?"

"The young lady is right," a matronly nurse said sternly as she marched into the room. "This isn't a hotel, Mr. Ryan. We have rules around here." It was obvious the woman had overheard their conversation. The nurse stuck her hands on her wide hips. "And I'm here to enforce those rules."

Lauren's face turned bright crimson from embarrassment and she lowered her head and faced the floor.

"You seem like a sweet young lady, miss," the nurse said to Lauren. "I suggest you conclude your visit before this ... ruffian here ... talks you into something *inappropriate*."

Ryan almost burst out laughing at this, but he stopped himself. His girlfriend was already embarrassed enough and he didn't need to make it worse.

Lauren rose quickly from the chair, and still blushing, mumbled "I love you" to Ryan, then fled the room.

Chapter 21

Langley, Virginia

Erin Welch was driving the rental car they'd picked up when they landed at D.C.'s Reagan Airport earlier in the day. J.T. Ryan was in the passenger seat. Unaccustomed to having a woman drive, he was itching to get behind the wheel. But Erin, who knew exactly where they were headed, had won that argument.

"I still can't believe what happened," Ryan said.

Erin gave him a sidelong glance. "Believe it. Like I told you, DHS just came in and took over the case. I had sent one of my agents to New York City to investigate the death of the *Times* reporter, and I had to recall him."

The PI shook his head slowly. "And the FBI Director was okay with all this?"

"Hell, no. He was angry like I was. But he had no choice. The Department of Homeland Security trumps the Bureau. This kind of crap happens all the time in government." She stepped on the gas and the Chevy Impala surged forward, passing a slower moving vehicle on the highway. "But it's never happened to me before," she added bitterly.

"Did DHS explain why they were taking over?"

"Again, hell no. To say I'm pissed is an understatement."

Ryan chuckled, admiring the woman's moxie. "So, now that you're officially off the case, you're FBI agents in Atlanta can't work it."

"That's right," she replied with a sly smile. "But nothing's stopping me from *un-officially* working it. Just because I can't assign my guys, doesn't mean I can't pursue it on my own."

"And that's where I come in," Ryan said.

"Bingo."

"So how do I get paid?"

"Don't worry, J.T. I've got a big budget. It's one of the perks of having a bloated, big-government system. I can always find money to hire contractors like yourself."

"Our tax dollars at work."

She nodded. "You got it. Our taxes at work. And this time for a good cause. First, because I don't like getting pushed around. And second, I want to solve this case. Mark Parker was a good friend of mine and I want to make sure his killer is caught."

"So what's this trip about?"

A truck cut in front of them and Erin slammed on the brakes and leaned on the horn. "I couldn't talk about it before. The walls in my office probably have ears. But I've got a contact at another agency. We're headed there right now." She got off the highway went on a local road.

"The only government agency I know in Langley," Ryan said, "is the CIA."

She glanced at him. "I always knew you were a good detective."

He pointed back toward the direction they had come from. "I was at the Agency's headquarters a few times, when I was doing covert ops with Delta Force. And they're back there."

"We're not going to the glass palace," Erin said, referring to the CIA employee's nickname for their headquarters. "We're going to a different location."

"Okay."

They drove in silence the rest of the way.

Eventually they reached a two-story, non-descript gray cinder block building. There was no sign on the structure, just a street number. Except for the razor-wire-topped fence that ringed the facility and the security cameras everywhere, the building looked like a squat, ugly warehouse.

"What the hell is this place?" Ryan asked, as Erin drove up to the gate.

"CIA people refer to it as the 'Factory'," she replied, pulling out her cred pack from her jacket. "Officially, it's the Agency's Special Operations Division. They do all the dirty work. Black ops, wet-work, assassination if it's needed. My friend, Alex Miller, is the Director here. He runs the operation."

"That name rings a bell."

"It should, J.T. One of his agents saved your life in Colombia when we were working a case there."

"Yeah, I remember. This Miller guy going to help us?"

"I sure hope so," she said. "Because we need his help. We can't go around DHS all on our own. I called Miller and described the situation. He said he was willing to listen."

Erin stopped at the guard shack and two armed men stepped out.

"FBI ADIC Welch and J.T. Ryan to see Director Miller," Erin said, handing one of the guards her cred pack.

The guard examined it closely, then using his cell phone, made a call. After putting his phone away and returning her cred pack, he said, "Assistant Director Welch, you'll have to leave your car here – we need to search it. My partner will escort you into the building. Sorry for the inconvenience, but we can't afford to take any chances."

"Understood," Erin replied, grabbing her briefcase from the back seat, then along with Ryan, climbed out of the car. After Ryan and Erin were scanned with an electronic device, they followed the guard toward the building.

As they made their way into the structure, Ryan noted the tight security measures. A K-9 officer and his German Shepherd began inspecting their Chevrolet rental car, while another guard popped the trunk and hood, and ran a scanner under the car. The PI also noticed that the guards were all armed with MP-5 submachine guns, the weapon of choice for Special Forces units like the U.S. Navy SEALS and the Army's Delta Force.

"Impressive," Ryan said under his breath to Erin. "These guys are good."

After entering the building, the two surrendered their personal weapons and went through a metal detector before being handed visitor's badges. Then they were led down a long corridor and shown into a small, non-descript office. The guard left and closed the door behind him.

After welcoming them, Alex Miller sat behind his desk while Erin and Ryan sat across from him on hard-plastic chairs. Miller was a balding, dour-looking man in his sixties. To the PI, the man looked like an accountant, rather than the head of the Agency's most lethal department. But from what Erin had told him, Miller was a highly-decorated operative himself who had risen up the ranks over the years.

Miller leaned forward in his seat. "So, Erin, on the phone you gave me a brief description of what happened. I find it peculiar that Homeland Security took over your investigation."

"Peculiar is not the word I would use," she responded. "I think it's suspicious."

Miller nodded. "Has this ever happened to you before?"

"Never."

"What did the Director of the FBI say about it?"

Erin shrugged. "My boss's hands are tied. He's got a pension to protect. Go along to get along."

"It's not uncommon," Miller said, "in the higher ranks of government."

"Well I think it sucks," Erin snapped.

Ryan smiled at her comment, while Miller's only expression was an arching of a brow. By his demeanor, he was clearly a very serious man.

"That's probably true," Miller said. "But it is a reality." He tented his fingers on the desk. "Were you making progress in solving the case?"

"Yes, absolutely. With Ryan's help, we've been generating good leads."

Miller turned his gaze toward the PI. "Erin filled me in on your background. Being a thorough person, I checked you out as well. You have good credentials, Ryan. U.S. Army Airborne, 75th Ranger Regiment, Green Beret, then the best of the best in Special Forces: Delta Force, Tier 1. Very difficult to achieve. You rose to the rank of Army Captain, then turned PI. You've got a good reputation there as well. A tough, aggressive investigator, from what I could tell. But also a smart-ass and prone to breaking the rules at times."

Ryan grinned. "That would be me."

"I don't like smart-asses," Miller stated.

"I vouch for him," Erin interjected forcefully.

Miller stared at the FBI woman. "That's what counts." After a moment, he said, "Getting back to the case. Since you were making progress on the investigation, it is suspicious that the Bureau, the premier investigative agency in the U.S., would be sidelined."

"There's something else, Alex," the woman said.

"What?"

"I haven't been able to get a straight answer from the NTSB. They're investigating the plane crash that killed the New York reporter."

Miller nodded. "I see. It would take someone high up to handcuff both the FBI and the NTSB."

"Agreed."

The CIA man went quiet, took off his eyeglasses and began to methodically clean them with a handkerchief. It was obvious to Ryan that the man was processing everything he'd heard.

"And you want my help on this," Miller finally said.

"Yes," Erin replied. "Ryan and I can do a lot on our own, but as you know, Homeland Security is a powerful agency. I'm sure we'll need certain resources to solve this. Resources you have at your disposal."

Miller gave her a hard stare. "We've known each other a long time. But you're asking a lot. I also have a pension to protect."

"DHS is going to slow-walk this investigation," Ryan snapped. "They may bury this as a cold-case. We'll never know why these reporters were killed. Don't you want the damn truth?"

The CIA man seemed taken back by Ryan's outburst. He put his eyeglasses back on and sat there a moment, pensive. Then he pointed to the numerous plaques on the wall. "I received those commendations for serving my country. I risked my life more than once. And I was always proud of what I did. The United States is the best country in the world, and I'll do anything it takes to keep it that way. Yes, Ryan, I do want the truth." He turned his gaze back to Erin. "I'll help you. Whatever it takes."

Erin grinned. "Thank you, Alex."

"You'll owe me a bottle of scotch for this, young lady."

"I'll buy you a case," the FBI Assistant Director said.

Miller didn't smile, simply shook his head. "One bottle will do. By the way, Erin, ever since your initial call I've been keeping an eye out for similar incidents. A reporter died in Venice recently, and one in Paris. Both were Americans. And although both deaths appeared accidental, I've been in this business a long time. Something smells." He tented his fingers on his desk again. "I've assigned one of my operatives to look into it." He looked at Ryan. "You may remember her. Rachel West."

"The blonde who saved my life in Cartagena," Ryan said.

Miller's lips pressed into a thin line and he frowned. "She's not just a 'blonde', Ryan. She's one of my best agents."

Ryan nodded, realizing Miller had absolutely no sense of humor. "I'm sure she is. She saved my life under very difficult circumstances."

"I'd like to meet her today, while we're here," Erin said. "I want to brief her on what we have so far on the case."

Miller leaned forward in his chair. "That won't be possible. Rachel is out of the country. I'll call her and bring her up to date."

"Where is she?"

"Venice," Miller replied.

Chapter 22

Venice, Italy

Rachel West paid the fare and stepped onto the water taxi.

After a few more passengers came aboard, the small ferry boat cranked up its engine and plowed its way over the choppy waters. It was a windy day and the usually calm canals that separated the island of Venice from the Italian mainland were turbulent.

The CIA operative held on to the railing to steady herself as the boat dipped and rose with the waves, the salt-water spray coating her face and long blonde hair, which was pulled into a ponytail. She zipped up her jacket to shield herself from the cool temperatures. As she watched the dark, industrial-gray waves, she mused that the canals contained none of the sparkling aquamarine water described in the Venice tourist brochures.

Rachel's thoughts focused on her upcoming day. She'd be meeting the police inspector assigned to show her the scene where the American reporter had died. She would have preferred to do this alone, but her boss Alex Miller had insisted she follow protocol. Since there was no evidence that a crime had been committed, it was his opinion that it was best to work with the local PD.

The tower of St. Mark's Square loomed in the distance, dominating the Venice skyline. It grew in size as they approached the city. Ten minutes later the water taxi reached the dock and she stepped off the boat. Rachel began walking toward the *Piazza San Marco*, how the locals referred to their main square. She passed the long row of *traghettis* that were tethered at the dock, surprised more of the gondolas were not in use. Tourists usually flocked to them, but today not many people seemed to be out. As soon as she neared the main square, she knew the reason. The historic city of Venice, which had been built on low mud banks during the Middle ages, often flooded during certain times of the year. The problem had become worse in recent years and now wooden boardwalks were erected about a foot off the ground to facilitate pedestrian movement. The area of St. Marks's Square was particularly low and much more prone to flooding than other parts of the city. This morning pools of water already covered much of the square, and the boardwalks were in place in the area.

Striding over the wooden walkways, she entered the massive *Piazza San Marco*. Although Rachel had been here several times before, she was still impressed by the sight. To her left rose the *Campanile*, the 323 foot tall red brick tower that dominated the skyline. Originally built by the Romans in the 9th century as a watch tower, the structure had been rebuilt and enhanced over the centuries, with a marble belfry and gold leaf spire added. Its last restoration had taken place in 1902.

To Rachel's right was the *Palazzo Ducale*, the gothic Doges Palace that was once home to the Venice rulers, and straight ahead was the *Basilica di San Marco*, the 13th century church with its Byzantine arches and opulent gold and bronze mosaic facade. Napoleon had once described the *Piazza San Marco* as the "most elegant drawing room in Europe" and she could see why.

Rachel walked toward the church as she gazed around the square, looking for her assigned contact. They had agreed to meet at ten in the morning in front of the Basilica. Not seeing him, she leaned against a wall to wait.

Thirty minutes later a short, pudgy man with slicked-back hair and wearing a black shark-skin suit casually strolled up to her. "You must be Agent West," he said with a flourish and a wide grin. "Inspector Tortoli at your service."

She flashed her CIA cred pack, then pointed to her watch. "You're late, Tortoli."

"Ha," he replied, the smile still on his pock-marked face. "What can I say? This is Italy."

The police inspector looked her up and down carefully, taking in her curvaceous figure, attractive features, long blonde hair and vivid blue eyes. Rachel felt like he was undressing her with his eyes.

"My first name is Anthony," he said, "but my friends call me Tony."

She sighed, used to men coming on to her. "Let's get one thing straight, Inspector. I'm here to do a job. Plain and simple. I didn't come to Venice to hook up."

The smirk didn't leave his face. "You are a beautiful woman, *signorina*. After we conclude our business today, I'd be delighted to show you the sights of my city."

Aggravated by the man's attitude, Rachel unzipped her jacket, revealing the Glock pistol holstered on the hip of her jeans. "As you can see, Tortoli, I'm armed. And I'm not afraid to use it. I suggest we get going. I don't have time to waste."

Tortoli glanced at the weapon and the leer left his face. "Such a pity. We could have made beautiful music together, *signorina*."

Then he pointed toward the left of the Basilica. "The apartment is that way."

She followed him for the next twenty minutes as they made their way through the well-worn cobblestone streets. Venice was a pedestrian-only city; no cars were allowed and the only engine sounds she heard were the motor boats that plied the waters of the canals.

The streets were narrow and winding. They traversed the labyrinth maze of roads and crossed over numerous stone bridges that connected the districts. She noticed the trash and flotsam that floated on the oily black water of the canals. And she breathed in the acrid scent. *They don't mention the smell in the tourist brochures*, she mused.

Eventually they reached a soot-covered, four-story apartment building deep in the heart of one of the shabbier districts.

"This is where he lived," Tortoli said.

Rachel appraised the structure. "Not fancy, that's for sure."

The inspector shrugged. "Venice is an expensive place. Only the rich can afford apartments overlooking the Grand Canal."

They entered the building, and since there was no elevator, they climbed the narrow stairs to the fourth floor. Tortoli unlocked the apartment door to let them in, then flicked on the light switch. A naked bulb hung from the ceiling, giving off dim, flickering light.

Rachel gazed around the small, one room flat with a kitchenette in a corner. There wasn't much in the apartment: a sofa, a narrow bed, a kitchen table, and a scarred wooden chest of drawers. The only decoration in the place was a small crucifix which hung on a wall. The dead reporter was a stringer for Reuters and didn't make much money, which explained his shabby living conditions. Before leaving for Italy, Rachel had researched the man's background.

"Where's the body now?" the CIA operative asked.

"At the morgue," Tortoli replied.

"They do an autopsy?"

"Yes, *signorina*. They found a large amount of heroin and alcohol in his bloodstream. It's obvious he died of a drug overdose."

"Where was the body found?"

He pointed to the messy, unmade bed. The soiled sheets were rumpled and half-off the mattress. "Right there."

Walking over, she inspected the area. Spent needles littered the floor and a couple of empty wine bottles stood on the night table.

"You sure they found heroin in his system, Inspector?"

"Of course."

"This doesn't track, Tortoli."

"What do you mean?"

Rachel shook her head. "I did a background check on this guy. By all accounts he was deeply religious. And he never drank. And he definitely did not do drugs."

Chapter 23

Atlanta, Georgia

J.T. Ryan was driving north on Peachtree Street, his eyes trained on the Mercedes sedan just ahead. It was past eleven in the evening and traffic was light.

In the Mercedes was Dan Marshall, the executive at World Media Network that he and Erin had questioned recently. The man and his extensive legal team had been successful in evading further questioning, much to Ryan's chagrin. And since DHS had taken over the investigation from the FBI, the PI had decided to pursue the case on his own.

Marshall and his bodyguard had left the WMN building a few minutes ago, and considering the lateness of the hour, Ryan assumed they were on the way home. The TV executive lived in Dunwoody, an exclusive area north of the city. The man's estate was in a gated community with extensive security. Security that included, Ryan was sure, numerous surveillance cameras, something he wanted to avoid at all costs. The PI had to make his move, and do it soon, before Marshall got home.

Ryan knew this part of Peachtree Street well. Up ahead, past the Fox Theatre, there was a large, empty lot on the right hand side of the road. After checking his rearview to make sure there were no cars following, he stepped on the gas and flicked the wheel left. His Tahoe had a big V-8 engine and the vehicle shot forward and came alongside the Mercedes. The PI, his hands gripping the wheel tightly, edged closer to the sedan until both vehicles were almost touching.

Out of the corner of his eye Ryan could see the other driver, a crew-cut bodyguard, yelling at him while gesturing frantically and leaning on his horn.

His adrenaline pumping, the PI flicked the wheel a bit more to his right so that the vehicles touched, metal scraping on metal.

Suddenly the Mercedes jerked right as the bodyguard drove off the road to evade collision. The large sedan bumped over the curb, crossed the sidewalk and went into the vacant lot.

The Tahoe followed and both vehicles came to a screeching halt in the dimly lit lot. Jumping out of his SUV, Ryan sprinted to the sedan just as the bodyguard climbed out, his pistol drawn.

Ryan lashed out with a martial-arts side-kick, the blow sending the gun flying in the air. Not wanting to risk the sound of gunfire alerting the police, the PI left his own pistol holstered, and instead spun around in a round kick, which caught the man in the face.

The bodyguard staggered back, went to one knee, then, his eyes full of hate, charged toward Ryan. The PI punched him hard in the solar plexus, then hit him with a fierce upper cut to his chin, and this time the man went down and stayed down.

Ryan spotted Marshall fleeing toward the street; racing over, he grabbed the executive by the shoulder, spun him around and threw him to the ground.

"You!" Marshall yelled. "You're crazy!"

"Stop screaming, Marshall!"

The man shouted out again and the PI struck him on the face, knocking him unconscious. Then he strode back to the bodyguard, who was still unconscious as well. He bound his hands and feet with flexi-cuffs and stuffed a handkerchief into the man's mouth.

Ryan gazed around the dimly-lit vacant lot, which was nestled between two buildings. By the painted markings on the asphalt it was clear the area served as a parking lot during the day. He sprinted back to Marshall, grabbed the man by his shoulders and dragged him deeper into the dark lot. Then he pushed him up into a sitting position against a wall. He slapped him lightly until he came to.

"Do you know who I am, Marshall?"

His eyes wide, the man said, "You're the guy who came with the FBI woman to ask me questions."

"You have a good memory."

"You're crazy, Ryan."

"I've been called worse."

Marshall was bleeding from his nostrils. As he wiped the blood with his hand, the gore stained his blue suit, white shirt, and Hermes pink tie.

"Sorry about the mess," Ryan said with a grin. "You can send me the cleaning bill later."

The man's eyes, which were already wide from fear, turned into saucers. "You *are* crazy!"

Ryan didn't intend to kill or even seriously hurt him. But having been a trained interrogator in Delta Force, he knew it was essential to break down a man and make him feel vulnerable so he would talk.

"You can hide behind your fancy lawyers," Ryan growled, "but they can't help you here."

"What you're doing is illegal!" the man gasped, as more blood trickled down his nose.

"Yes, it is."

"Why are you doing this, Ryan?"

"Two reasons. First, you were rude to Erin Welch. I'm old-school. I hate men who are rude to women. Especially women I admire. And second, you didn't answer our questions."

Marshall gazed wildly around the dark lot as if trying to figure a way out.

Ryan slapped the man hard across the face. "Nobody's coming to help you, friend. It's just you and me here."

The TV executive flinched away from him and tried to get up, but the PI held him down. "You're not going anywhere. Not until you talk."

"You're FBI. You know news sources are privileged information. I don't have to talk to you!"

"You're right, you don't have to talk. But before I get through with you, you'll be begging to talk."

"I know my rights, damn it!" Marshall said defiantly.

Ryan grabbed the man's pink tie and began pulling on the short end, the tie closing tighter around his neck. Marshall's eyes went wide again and he clutched his throat, but the PI kept pulling even tighter.

The WMN executive's face turned bright red and his eyes bulged. He tried fighting back with his arms and legs but the PI was much bigger and stronger and the blows were ineffectual.

Ryan didn't stop, but rather kept pulling even tighter on the tie.

A few seconds later he let go.

Marshall gasped for air as he frantically pulled his tie loose and then began coughing uncontrollably.

The PI waited a minute for the man to catch his breath.

The executive massaged his neck as he took in lungfuls of air. "I'll ... talk," he croaked.

"It's about time."

"What ... what ... do you want ... to know ...." he said in between gasps.

"What was your reporter, Parker, working on when he died?"

"I don't know ... for sure ...."

Ryan slapped the man hard, and more blood spurted from his nose.

"It's ... true!"

"Talk, you bastard. I've taken it easy on you so far. But you keep stonewalling and it's no more mister nice guy."

Marshall's eyes went wide again. "No ... please no ... I'll tell you ... everything ... I know ...."

"I'm listening, Marshall."

"Parker told me ... he was working ... on a big story ... the biggest of his career ... it had to do with censorship ... he never told me ... the exact details ...."

"So why didn't you tell us this when Erin and I talked to you?"

"I was afraid the ... info would leak out ... the news business is cut-throat ... if Parker had a great story ... I wanted to break it ... not some other ... TV network ... I figured my lawyers would stall you guys until ... I could find out what ... it was all about ...."

"Okay, I guess I buy that. What did Parker tell you? He must have given you some information."

Marshall nodded as he continued to massage his neck. By now his white shirt was covered with blood.

"That's right, Ryan ... he said ... it had to do ... with something ... called O.O.V."

"O.O.V.? What the hell's that?"

The executive shook his head. "I don't know ... Parker committed suicide ... before ... I could find out ...."

Chapter 24

Atlanta, Georgia

"It looks like we got lucky," Erin Welch said, leaning forward and placing her palms flat on her desk.

"What do you mean?" J.T. Ryan replied. They were sitting in Erin's FBI office downtown.

"It's been two days since you roughed up Marshall. If he was going to call the cops, he would have done it by now."

Ryan grinned. "Yeah. Sometimes it's better to be lucky than good."

She gave him a stern look. "Be careful, J.T. Now that Homeland Security has taken over this investigation, I may not be able to pull your ass out of the fire."

"I know that."

Erin rose, crossed her arms over her chest and stared out the wall-to-ceiling windows. "I'm still pissed DHS took over this case."

"Have you heard anything from them, Erin?"

She faced him. "Not a damn word."

"So, I'm assuming you didn't share the lead I got with them."

"Hell, no," she said with a glare.

Ryan nodded. "Any progress on what this O.O.V. is all about?"

She went back to her desk and sat down. "Not yet. I'm still working on that." Her features softened and she gave him a brief smile. "Good work on getting that out of Marshall. I don't like your methods but I like your results."

Ryan grinned. "Kind of why you hire me, isn't it?"

"I got a call from the CIA. Alex Miller's agent went to Venice and looked into the death of the American reporter there. The Venice cops chalked it up to an accidental drug overdose, but it looks likely that it was staged."

Ryan nodded. "Fits the pattern."

"Yes, it does. So far there's been three suspicious deaths of journalists – the New York guy who died in the plane crash, the WMN reporter who 'committed suicide', and now this guy in Venice. There's also the attempted murder of Mei Lin, another WMN journalist." She paused and looked pensive, as if trying to figure out the mechanics of what was happening.

Ryan stood. "While you're working on the O.O.V. lead, I've got something important to handle."

"On the case?"

"No," he replied. "This is personal."

***

Stone Mountain is the single largest piece of exposed granite in the world. The massive rock outcropping towers 825 feet over the ground, with a breathtaking view of the Atlanta skyline. Only a thirty minute ride from downtown, the mountain and the surrounding 3,200 acre Stone Mountain Park is one of the most visited attractions in the U.S. You can reach the summit of the mountain two ways – hiking up the miles-long trail, or by taking the cable car.

Ryan and his girlfriend Lauren Chase were on top of the mountain now, having just exited the cable car called the *Summit Skyride*. Usually the area at the peak was crowded, but it was an extremely windy day and only a few people were there.

As they walked over the flat granite surface of the mountain, they held hands.

"You're being very mysterious, John Taylor Ryan," Lauren said with a smile. "Wanting to come up here. What's going on?"

"You'll see," he replied enigmatically. "Can't a guy take his girl sightseeing?"

"It's the middle of a workday, J.T. When do you ever take time off for that?"

"I love you, Lauren."

"I love you too."

A blast of wind buffeted them and her long auburn hair swirled around her pretty face. Lauren was wearing a windbreaker, jeans, and sneakers, what he'd recommended, considering the terrain and breezy conditions on top of the mountain.

When they reached the center of the peak, Ryan gazed around at the amazing scenery below. The vast forest of the Georgia Piedmont, the Atlanta skyline, and Kennesaw Mountain in the distance all stretched out for miles around. *It's a majestic sight*, he thought. *Perfect for the occasion.*

"We're here," Ryan said.

She looked around, a confused expression on her face. "There's nothing up here, J.T. Just a flat rock."

"Look around you, hon. It's beautiful up here."

She gazed around once more. "Okay. I agree. It is beautiful. But we've been up here lots of times before. What's so different this time?"

He reached out and gently caressed her face and traced her freckles. "I love you very much, Lauren Chase."

She looked suspicious, then she smiled. "What's going on? Are you going to push me off the cliff?"

"I love you," he repeated, feeling nervous now.

"I'll have you know," she said with a giggle, "that I don't have that much life insurance. Unless you took out a new policy, you're going to be seriously disappointed if you throw me off this mountain."

Still nervous, but knowing he'd stalled long enough, Ryan sank to one knee. Reaching into a pocket, he pulled out a small, fabric covered box. He held it out to her.

A dawning realization came over her face and she covered her mouth with one hand. "Is that what I think it is?"

"I love you, Lauren. Please take it."

She reached out, took the box and opened it.

"Will you marry me, Lauren?"

"Oh, my God," she whispered, tears welling up in her hazel eyes. "I can't believe you did this."

"Put the ring on," he said.

She stared at him, the tears flowing freely now. "I love you more than life, J.T. You know that. But ...."

"I know we've talked about getting married before," he said, "but this time I'm not taking no for an answer."

Lauren pulled the large diamond ring out of the box and tried it on. The bright sunshine glinted off the diamond. "This is a huge stone, J.T. You can't afford this."

"You're worth it, hon."

She gazed at him, her eyes full of love but also apprehension. She slowly took the ring off her finger and with a sad expression handed it back to him. "I'm not ready, J.T. I want us to get married. But I want our children to have a father around ...."

"I can't quit what I do, Lauren. It's who I am."

She lowered her head and covered her face with both hands. She began crying, the sobs coming in jagged bursts.

After another minute, with the tears still flowing, she abruptly turned and ran away, fleeing in the direction of the cable car station.

Heartbroken, Ryan watched her go. It was one of the darkest days of his life.

Chapter 25

Washington, D.C.

The woman with the hard, angular face was in the back of the Cadillac limousine, reading the morning newspapers. It was a routine she followed religiously on her commute to work.

It was still early, but D.C. traffic was already snarled. Although she was an influential power broker, she still had to sit in traffic every day and it irritated her to no end.

As usual the woman was wearing a drab, off-the-rack business suit, plain black pumps, and no jewelry of any kind. Her blonde hair was cropped short and she had applied no makeup, which might have softened her hard features. Behind her back, her staff referred to her as the 'Dragon Lady', but she didn't care about the name, as long as they did their jobs. And did them well. A no-nonsense woman, she didn't tolerate incompetence. She only cared about the two important men in her life; her boss and her business partner.

The woman's name was Victoria Stark. Vicka to her friends, which were very few. But she preferred being called Ms. Stark.

She finished scanning *The Washington Post*, folded it neatly, and placed it on the thick stack of other newspapers on the leather seat next to her.

Vicka glanced at her watch, then lowered the opaque window which separated the rear and front compartments of the limousine.

"Yes, Ms. Stark?" her chauffeur said from behind the wheel, glancing back towards her. An elderly black man with graying hair, he had been her driver for years.

"I want to stop at the building this morning before I go to the office."

"Yes, ma'am."

She raised the window up, then settled back on the seat.

Half an hour later the limousine stopped in front of a residential brownstone building on a quiet, tree-shaded street of similar brownstones. The only thing that distinguished the building from the others were the multiple satellite dishes completely covering the roof.

Vicka grabbed her briefcase, exited the car, and walked up the steps to the entrance of the structure. She inserted her ID card in the entry device by the door, had her retina scanned by the device, and keyed in her passcode. The heavy wooden door clicked open and she stepped inside. The residential brownstone appearance on the outside of the building was only a facade – the inside of the structure had been converted into a modern office complex, full of work areas, offices, conference rooms, and a large auditorium which served as the main operations room.

Making her way along a wide corridor, she went past several closed doors. Instead of going into the main operations room, she entered the office at the very end of the corridor.

"Ms. Stark," the bald, overweight man behind the desk said, rising. "I wasn't expecting you today."

"That's best," she replied with a cold smile, "don't you think, Harold? Keeps you on your toes."

"Yes, Ms. Stark."

"Sit down, for Christ sakes," she said gruffly, as she perched on the chair in front of the desk.

His name was Harold Meeks and he was Vicka's operations manager. *A cog in my machine*, she thought idly. *But an important cog.* She gazed at him, once more noticing his girth. He had his suits custom made to accommodate his grossly overweight frame, but even these clothes could not camouflage his rotund belly, fat fingers, and rolls on his flabby neck.

"You need to lose some weight, Harold. I can't have you dying of a heart attack."

"Yes, ma'am."

Vicka had admonished him about this before, but deep down knew she was wasting her breath. The man had a huge appetite and ate ravenously at every meal.

"Enough chit-chat," she snapped. "How's the operation going?"

"Fine, Ms. Stark."

"Fine? What does that mean, *exactly*?"

Harold Meeks appeared nervous and he ran his thick fingers over his bald head.

"How many items did you flag yesterday, Harold?"

"Only four."

She gave him a hard look. "Tell me the truth. How many?"

"Ha ... ten ...."

"Ten!" she snapped, her blood pressure spiking. "That's totally unacceptable."

"Yes, ma'am."

"Have the flagged sources been contacted?"

"Of course, Ms. Stark. I called them myself."

"Good." She opened her aluminum briefcase, took out a folder and scanned the Excel spreadsheets. "There's a disturbing upward trend in offenses in the last month. To what do you attribute the rise?"

"I'm not sure," he replied, a tremor in his voice.

She tapped the folder forcefully. "I'm not pleased. Not pleased at all." She lowered her voice for emphasis. "I depend on you, Harold, to handle these issues. You've done an adequate job in the past. But if you can't do your job, I'll have to find someone else who can. I've done that before, and I'll do it again."

Beads of sweat formed on the man's fleshy face.

She pointed her index finger at him. "And you know I mean business. I'm not talking about a demotion, or reassigning you to another department, or even a forced retirement. You know too much, Harold. There's only one solution for you if you don't do your job."

"Yes, ma'am," he croaked. He unbuttoned the top button of his shirt and loosened his tie. "I understand."

Vicka placed the folder back in the briefcase and clicked it shut. Then she gave the man an icy glare. "I want you on the phone this morning calling every source that had a flagged item in the last month. I want you to read them the riot act. Tell them if they don't change their behavior, I'm going to come down on them like a ton of bricks. I have a lot of resources at my disposal, Harold, and I'm not afraid to use them. Is that understood?"

Chapter 26

Atlanta, Georgia

"You're awfully quiet today," Erin Welch said, glancing at J.T. Ryan. Erin was driving her Jaguar and Ryan was in the passenger seat. "Something wrong?"

"Women," he said with a shrug.

"That's a big topic. Any woman in particular?"

Ryan stared through the windshield. They were in a rural area east of the city – it was sparsely populated, with occasional farmhouses sitting on large plots of land. "Lauren and I," he said morosely, "we ... it's complicated ... I don't want to talk about it ...."

"Okay, J.T. Been there myself, once or twice. But I need you to get your head in the game. We have a job to do. There are some dangerous people out there and they don't play nice."

Ryan nodded, her words sinking in. Shaking off his depressed mood, he said, "How soon before we get there?"

"We're not far. A few more miles. Here are the ground rules. You can spend two hours talking with Mei Lin. No phone calls, in or out. I'll drop you off and pick you up when the time's up. I spent a lot time and effort setting up this safe house for her and I don't want it compromised."

"Understood. Where will you be?"

"I'll park my car out of sight where I can keep a close watch on the house. I took precautions getting here. I don't think we were followed, but you never know."

"Okay, Erin. You carrying?"

In response she zipped down her jacket and he noticed the Glock 9mm on her hip.

"You know how to use that thing?" he joked.

"Of course. I go to the shooting range once a month."

He chuckled. "Just checking. I'm so used to you being an Assistant Director, it's tough for me to visualize you as FBI special agent Welch, woman of action."

"I'm both, wise guy – ADIC and Agent. And if you don't quit being a smart-ass," she added with a grin, "I'm going to pull this pistol and show you how proficient I am."

Ryan laughed.

Soon after they reached a rundown farmhouse sitting on a large, wooded lot. The home had a sagging roof and was badly in need of some paint. Erin drove to the front of the place. He got out of the car and she drove away.

The PI climbed the creaky wooden steps and knocked on the door. After a moment he heard the clicking of several locks and the door opened partway.

Mei Lin stood there, a worried look on her face. "Come in, J.T.," the young Asian woman said, opening the door fully. "Where's Erin?"

"Nearby," Ryan replied.

Mei Lin closed the door behind them, reapplied the locks and led them into the dingy living room, where they sat. The room was filled with cheap knockoffs of Early American furniture. The squeaky wooden floors were worn and the dated wallpaper was peeling in places.

"Anybody else here, Mei?"

"Not anymore," she said. "Now that DHS took over the investigation, Erin told me she had to pull her agents off. And she never told Homeland Security about this safe house. She has one Bureau agent she trusts who comes once a day to check on me and brings me anything I need."

Ryan nodded. "Erin told you why I'm here?"

"Yes. You had more questions for me."

"That's right. I got a lead from your boss at WMN."

"I'm surprised he talked with you."

The PI smiled. "He needed a little encouragement, but, yeah, he was cooperative in the end."

"I was having tea. Would you like some, J.T.?"

"No, I'm good."

"What did you want to ask me?"

Ryan leaned forward on the ancient rocking chair. "Have you ever heard of something called O.O.V.?"

The young woman shook her head. "No. Erin asked me the same thing."

"You're sure, Mei Lin? It's apparently connected to the story Parker was working on."

"I'm sorry. But he didn't confide in me on that story. He thought it would be safer if I didn't know about it."

"Okay. I've got a couple of more things to go over." Ryan asked her additional questions over the next hour, things he'd asked before, hoping to jar her memory.

It was clear she was being cooperative and truthful. It was also clear Parker had kept her in the dark, and Ryan didn't learn much new information.

"I'm sorry I'm not much help, J.T."

"It's not your fault."

Suddenly her expression brightened. "I just thought of something. Parker has a brother. A half-brother, actually. He lives in the Atlanta area. It's possible he may have confided in him."

"That's good, Mei." Ryan took out a notepad and a pen and handed them to her. "Write down his contact information."

The woman did so and he put away the notebook. Then he glanced at his watch. He still had time before Erin came back.

"It's almost dinner time, J.T. If you can stay, I can fix us something to eat."

"I'm not hungry, but thanks anyway."

"Okay," she said. "By the way, remember what I told you about what's happening in the news business?"

"Sure, that news reporting, in particular by the major TV networks, was being censored."

"That's right, J.T. Have you checked into that?"

Ryan shook his head. "No. I had more urgent things I was working on." It was true he had been busy, but he'd also been skeptical of her theory. It sounded far-fetched.

She waved a hand in the air. "I've had a lot of time on my hands, being cooped up in here. I spend much of it reading or surfing the Net. But since I'm a reporter, I watch a lot of news too. A lot more than when I was at WMN working full time."

"You're here for your own safety, Mei Lin."

"I know. And I appreciate what you and Erin have done for me. I'd be dead right now if it wasn't for you." She leaned forward on the sofa. "If you have time, I want to show you something."

Ryan nodded. "Erin won't be back for awhile. Go ahead."

"Let's go to the kitchen."

She rose and strode out of the room and Ryan followed.

Resting on the worn, butcher-block kitchen table was a laptop. She sat down in front of it and powered up the computer while the PI looked over her shoulder.

"I'll show you the Internet news sites first," she said, as she clicked the keys, going to CNN, WMN, Fox News, and several other cable news websites. She stayed on each for several minutes, asking him to read the various news stories that appeared there. After fifteen minutes of this she turned toward him. "What's happening today in the world, J.T.?"

Ryan thought about this a moment, remembering the various headlines he'd just read. "Lots of things. Mostly bad. The war in Syria is getting worse; the U.S. stock market hit a new yearly low; Chinese hackers stole the identities of millions of U.S. government workers; the American embassy in Nigeria was ransacked; a Russian warship was spotted just a few miles from the North Carolina coast; a riot in Detroit. It's a long, ugly list."

"That's right," she replied with a glint in her eyes. She pointed to a stack of thick notebooks sitting next to the laptop. "I've been keeping a log to track my theory."

"Okay," he said, not sure where she was headed with this.

She glanced at her watch. "Let me show you something else. It's almost six p.m. The evening TV news casts will be coming on soon." Rising from the chair, she went to the portable television that was on the kitchen counter and turned it on. She changed the channel until she found one of the major TV network news programs. The anchor, a Brad Pitt look-alike in a thousand-dollar suit and perfectly coiffed hair, began talking about a new weather pattern developing in California – heavy rains were expected for the next two days.

"This is called 'weather porn'," Mei Lin said. "Most national news programs talk about weather for the first five or ten minutes." To prove her point, she changed to the other evening news casts, and to his surprise, it was true.

She flipped to another news cast, in which the anchor was showing a cute baby video that had gone viral on the Internet that day. Then the anchor briefly talked about the problems in the U.S. stock market, before turning to a human interest story about a new weight loss program.

Ryan was about to say something when she pointed to the screen and changed the channel again. "Just watch," she said. The anchor in another news program was talking about a sex scandal involving a Hollywood actress. The anchor briefly mentioned the war in Syria, before devoting the next ten minutes to a plane crash story in Indonesia.

Ryan shook his head, perplexed. "They're not covering the news we just saw on the Internet. Why is that?"

"A lot of the real news," she said, "what's actually happening in the U.S. and around the world, doesn't fit the 'narrative'."

" 'Narrative'? What the hell's that?"

"It's an approved list of topics. Topics deemed safe to talk about, J.T."

Ryan was still skeptical, but much less so than half an hour ago. "Maybe it's coincidence."

Mei Lin turned off the TV and picked up one of the thick notebooks by the computer and handed it to him. "Look through this. It's a log I've been keeping of national TV news; the evening and morning shows."

The PI opened the notebook and scanned the pages. It was filled with very detailed handwritten notes listing times, dates, and news sites for the last week. It was clear the young woman was very thorough, listing exact sources for each note, much like a reference book or encyclopedia.

He looked up at her, realizing her theory wasn't so far-fetched after all. *Maybe the news is being censored, or at least being sanitized.* He placed the notebook on the table. "If this is true, then the American people don't really know what's going on in the world."

"That's right, J.T."

"What about the local news stations? Is that being censored too?"

"Not as much," she replied. "There's hundreds and hundreds of local networks and those are owned by a large number of companies. So the local news outlets are more difficult to control. But there's only a few of the major networks and newspapers. It's easier to manipulate those."

Ryan pointed to the laptop. "People can still find the news, but they really have to search for it on the Internet."

"For now," Mei Lin said with a frown.

"What do you mean?"

"I think the censorship of the networks is just the first step. I believe it'll spread to the Internet too. It's possible that eventually every news item you read or watch will be 'sanitized' if it doesn't fit the 'narrative'."

"So the U.S. would become just like Russia or China or North Korea, where the news is controlled."

"That's right, J.T."

Ryan mulled this over and a feeling of dread settled in the pit of his stomach.

Chapter 27

Paris, France

Frustrated by the incompetence of the Italian police in Venice, Rachel West had decided to try a different approach in Paris and go it alone. The American reporter who had died in France recently had been killed in a hit-and-run. Rachel had read the police report at the local *gendarmerie* station, and was on her way now to the scene of the accident.

She was driving the rented Peugeot along the *Champs-Elysees* avenue, having just passed the *Arc de Triomphe*. It was a blustery, rainy day and the windshield wipers were struggling to clear the sheets of water from the heavy downpour. The accident had happened on a busy stretch of the *Quai des Tuileries*, a road bordered on one side by the Seine River and on the other by the Louvre Museum.

Rachel found a place to park along the *Quai* and waited a few minutes in the car for the rain to abate. Zipping up her jacket, she pulled her long blonde hair into a ponytail and covered her head with a ball cap.

Climbing out, she strode on the wet sidewalk that bordered the wide, meandering river, stopping at the intersection where the journalist had been run over.

Traffic was heavy today, just as it had been the day of the accident, she recalled from the police report. The American reporter had been crossing the street in the pedestrian crosswalk. All of a sudden a truck, ignoring the red light, had barreled through the intersection, plowing into the man, sending him flying through the air. His mangled, bloody body crash landed fifteen feet away. Death had been instantaneous. The truck had kept going, and eyewitness reports as to the type of truck or its plate number were conflicting.

Paris is a large city with a population of over two million people, with its share of serious crimes. After spending one day looking into the hit-and-run, the *gendarmes* had moved on to more urgent matters.

Rachel gazed at the intersection from the sidewalk, watched the flow of traffic as the street light changed several times from green to red and back to green again. It's a perfect spot, she thought, for a hit-and-run. The busy avenue was full of fast moving traffic of all types – cars, motorcycles, mopeds, buses, trucks, all jockeying to get one lane ahead, horns blaring, engines roaring, the cacophony of noise almost deafening.

The rain began in earnest again and she glanced up at the ominous clouds overhead. It had been raining from the moment she'd landed at Charles de Gaulle Airport, and from the looks of the sky, the foul weather would hang over the city for days.

Finished checking out the scene, Rachel strode along the avenue, looking for a cafe where she could eat before her next stop. She'd only had crappy airline food today and was starved.

***

The man lived in an upscale apartment building in the Latin Quarter, a tony riverside district of Paris. Rachel was there now, knocking on is door.

A moment later a stooped, gray-haired man wearing a bathrobe opened the apartment's door.

"I'm Rachel West," she said in French, holding up her cred pack. "I'm with the American CIA."

The man took the wallet, inspected her ID carefully, and handed it back. He coughed a few times.

"Yes," he replied in French, "my office called me and told me you were coming by."

"May I come in, Mr. Arnaud?"

Arnaud coughed again and nodded. "Yes, yes, of course."

Rachel entered the tastefully appointed but tiny living room. Paris was an expensive city; even the well-off lived in small flats.

The stooped man closed the door behind them, and leaning on a cane, shuffled to an armchair and sagged onto it.

Sitting across from him, Rachel studied the frail, sickly-looking man. His eyes were sunk into the sockets and his face had a gray pallor.

"When I visited the Associated Press news office today, Mr. Arnaud, they told me you were home sick."

He coughed again. "Yes ... I've been sick for weeks and weeks ...."

"Nothing contagious, I hope," she replied with a cautious smile.

"No, it's nothing like that ... you don't have to worry, miss. I went to my doctor ... he couldn't figure out what was wrong ... he said it wasn't contagious ... but told me to get some rest ...." He coughed again, a hacking cough that lasted several minutes. After he composed himself, he said, "You must be here ... about the death ... of my reporter, Jonas."

"That's right, Mr. Arnaud."

"I've already ... talked with the police. Why would the American CIA ... be interested in a hit-and-run accident?"

Rachel leaned forward. "It's very possible it was no accident."

The man frowned. "You think ... he was run over on purpose?"

"Yes."

"But why?"

"That's unclear, Mr. Arnaud. What is clear is that several reporters have died recently under suspicious circumstances."

The man's facial expression changed from a concerned frown to alarm. "What? I'm not aware of that."

"Several took place in the U.S.; also one in Venice, and now this one in Paris. It's too coincidental."

He nodded, then coughed again.

"Mr. Arnaud, since you're one of the top editors at the Associated Press office in Paris, you're probably familiar with the stories your journalist was investigating."

"Yes. In fact Jonas was looking into a story I had assigned him ... it was regarding possible corruption among newspapers here in the city ...." He coughed again, then continued, "I sensed that several of them ... were coordinating their daily coverage, which is the opposite of what good journalists do ... it's always been my policy to break a story first ... and get the scoop ... on our competitors."

"Of course. That makes sense."

"My suspicions intensified," the man continued, "after I received a call ... from a man about a month ago ... he said he was representing a wealthy benefactor who wanted, as he said, "to donate ten million Euros toward my retirement."

"Did he say why he wanted to 'donate' this money?"

"In a roundabout way ... he said I should stop digging into the story ... the story that I had assigned ... to Jonas."

Rachel nodded. "I see. What did you tell this man?"

Arnaud laughed, but then started coughing again. "I told him, as you Americans ... would say ... to go fly a kite ...."

She smiled. "Okay. What happened then?"

"The man hung up ... and I've heard nothing since."

"Do you know who the man was who called you, Mr. Arnaud?"

The stooped, sickly man shook his head. "No clue ... I tried to have the call traced ... but it was made ... from one of those ... disposable cell phones ...."

"A burner."

"That's right. I've heard that term for them."

Rachel thought through what Arnaud had just told her. After a moment she said, "What did your reporter Jonas find out in his investigation?"

"The journalists at the newspapers he contacted wouldn't talk with him ... but he was a good reporter ... and was pursuing ... several angles ... in fact, we had a meeting set up ... to go over his findings ... but then ... he died."

Rachel nodded. "I see. Did Jonas mention the initials O.O.V. to you?"

Arnaud coughed again, then shook his head. "No."

"Is there any other information you can tell me about the story Jonas was working on?"

The man began hacking again, the pallor on his face growing grayer. When he caught his breath, he said, "Jonas did mention ... one thing ...."

"What's that, Mr. Arnaud?"

"He said ... it all starts ... in Spain ...."

"What does that mean?"

"I ... don't know ...." Arnaud started coughing again, and in between hacks, he said hoarsely, "Please ... get me ... some water ...."

Alarmed by the man's condition, Rachel jumped up from the chair, but before she could run to the kitchen, the man's eyes rolled white, his body sagged and he slumped to the floor.

The CIA agent rushed to his side, and realizing he was unconscious, tried to revive him. She gave him mouth-to-mouth and desperately pressed on his chest for several minutes, but he remained unresponsive.

She checked his pulse.

Arnaud was dead.

Chapter 28

Atlanta, Georgia

J.T. Ryan had finally tracked down Mark Parker's half-brother, although it hadn't been easy. The man, a homeless veteran from the Afghan war, had no permanent address.

Ryan parked his SUV in the lot and strode into the downtown branch of the Atlanta library. He glanced around the library's sitting area looking for the man. It was a cold morning, and as Ryan expected, the place had its share of poorly-dressed, obviously homeless people. Libraries, he knew, were shelter for them, a place to get warm.

He spotted a man in a wheelchair wearing a soiled Marine field jacket at one of the tables. He had long hair and a shaggy beard. The PI approached, figuring this was probably him.

"Are you Tom Parker?" Ryan asked.

The man in the wheelchair looked up from the newspaper he was reading, a suspicious look on his face. "Who wants to know?"

"My name's John Ryan. I'm working a case involving your half-brother, Mark Parker."

"You a cop, Ryan?"

"No."

"You look like a cop."

Ryan smiled, hoping to disarm the man's suspicion. "I get that a lot. I'm a private investigator. Mind if I sit down?"

Folding his arms across his chest, the homeless man said, "It's a free country. I can't stop you."

Ryan sat across from him. He pulled out his PI license and showed it to the veteran. "Like I said, my name's J.T. Ryan. I'm helping the FBI with a case involving Mark Parker. I'm sorry to tell you this, but you're brother's dead."

The veteran's face reddened. "Just because I'm in this fucking wheelchair doesn't mean I'm an idiot. I read the papers. I know he's dead, God bless his soul."

Ryan studied the long-haired, shabbily-dressed guy, trying to figure out a way to calm him down and ease his suspicions. He recalled the info Erin had been able to find out about him. "I understand you were wounded serving in Afghanistan. You received a Purple Heart and a Bronze Star."

"Yeah. Lost both my fucking legs over there, too."

"I'm sorry," Ryan replied. "I lost several buddies in Kandahar, when I served over there a few years back."

Tom Parker's eyes brightened. "You were in the Marines too?"

"Army. Special Forces."

Parker nodded as he stroked his shabby beard with a hand. "You said you're investigating Mark's death? The paper said he jumped off a building. Wasn't it a suicide?"

"We don't think so."

"What do you mean?"

Ryan lowered his voice. "It's pretty clear he was murdered."

"Fuck. Who killed him?"

"That's what I'm working on. I want to find them and see that they pay for their crimes."

"Okay, Ryan. I'll help any way I can. Mark was a good brother to me. Specially when I came home from the war. After I was discharged from the Marines, I couldn't hold down a job. Mark gave me money to survive. I was pretty messed up. I lost my legs." He pointed to his head. "I got PTSD too."

Ryan nodded, sympathetic to the man's plight. "The VA help?"

The veteran's eyes flashed in anger. "Hell, no. Half the time I can't even get an appointment at the Veteran's Hospital."

"Yeah, I've heard that before," the PI replied, knowing what the man was saying was true. It was common knowledge among veterans that the VA health system was dysfunctional.

Ryan pulled out one of his business cards and handed it to him. "Next time you have trouble with the VA, give me a call. I have a friend at the FBI, Erin Welch. She's high up in the organization. I'll get her involved and she'll read them the riot act."

"I'd really appreciate that, Ryan."

"Don't mention it. I'm always glad to help out a fellow soldier."

Parker stroked his beard again. "So, what can I do to help?"

"Your brother was working on a story about the news media. We think the story and his murder are connected. His fiancée, Mei Lin, didn't know the specifics of the story, but she's the one who gave me your name."

At the mention of Mei Lin's name, the veteran's eyes lit up. "I met her once. Cute girl."

"Did your brother tell you anything about the story he was working on?"

He rubbed his beard thoughtfully. "Mark mentioned he didn't really trust the company he worked for, WMN. That's why he was talking to that New York reporter. He felt the story was big, and if he and this other journalist broke it together it would have more credibility."

"That makes sense. Did he mention the initials O.O.V. to you?"

"O.O.V.? No."

"Damn. Did he tell you anything else?"

"Just that he thought the news industry was suppressing certain stories. I knew it made him furious – he went on rants about it."

"All right," Ryan said. "Anything else?"

"There was one other thing. Mark told me he'd found a good lead." He gave the PI a sly grin. "It had to do with high-end hookers."

"Prostitutes?"

"Yes," Parker replied wistfully. "Along with losing my legs, I lost some other body parts. I can't do anything now, but I can still dream about it ...."

"How did the hookers tie-in with his investigation?" Ryan asked.

"Mark mentioned this really rich guy, a billionaire, who was somehow behind the censorship. This rich guy liked high-end prostitutes and when he came to Atlanta he used them. My brother thought this billionaire was European and that he had a distinctive tattoo."

"Who was the rich man? Do you know his name?"

The homeless veteran shrugged. "No. Mark didn't know. But he was a damn good reporter and he would have found out if he hadn't died."

"I agree. I'm sure that's why he was killed." Ryan leaned back in the chair. "Can you think of anything else?"

Tom Parker shook his head. "No. Sorry I don't have any more information."

"Actually, you've been a really big help. I was at a dead-end and you've given me a lead."

"I hope you find the bastard who did this."

"Don't worry, I'm not going to stop looking until I do." Ryan gazed at the homeless veteran's disheveled appearance – his long, shaggy hair and beard, the soiled and torn clothing, the dilapidated wheelchair. It looked and smelled like he hadn't bathed in many days. *That could be me*, he thought. *If I had been wounded and had PTSD*. It made Ryan angry that more wasn't being done to help American disabled vets.

The PI pulled out his wallet, took out all the cash he had and handed it to him. "I want you to have this."

"Thank you, Ryan."

"You're welcome."

Ryan stood. "You have my card. If you need help with the VA, or if you get short on cash, give me a call. I want to help." Then the PI turned around and left the library.

***

Ryan drove his Tahoe into the parking lot of the strip club, found an empty slot and turned off the engine. It was eleven p.m. and the lot was almost full.

He climbed out, and after paying the cover charge at the club's door, he went into the seedy, warehouse-like building with the garish neon sign that said, 'Gentleman's Club'. The PI had been there before and knew the place was not a high-end club, but rather a sleazy strip joint, like the other sleazy strip clubs in this part of Atlanta.

Ryan shoved his way past the throng of customers, mostly blue-collar workers, and sat at an empty table far away from the stage, where nude, unattractive women gyrated to the pounding beat of the earsplitting music. Strobe lights blended with the cigarette smoke, which cast a hazy sheen over the crowded place. As Ryan inhaled the stench of stale, spilled beer, he watched topless waitresses circulating among the tables, pushing overpriced drinks.

One of the waitresses came over. "What can I get you?" she asked.

"Candy around?"

The woman nodded and moved away.

A minute later a topless, statuesque woman with dark, short hair and a face marred by acne scars walked up to him. She was wearing six-inch stilettos, a G-string, and strategically placed pasties on the nipples of her double-Ds. She was only in her twenties, Ryan knew, but she had the weary eyes of a fifty year old.

"Well, if it isn't my favorite PI," she said with a tired smile.

"How you been, Candy?" he replied. They were talking loudly, the only way to be heard over the loud, pounding music.

"I'm still here," she said with a weary laugh. "Which sucks."

"I'm sure it does."

She leaned over and smiled suggestively. "See something you like?"

"I like your twins," he replied, trying not to stare at her large breasts. "But I'm working on a case. I'm looking for information."

She smirked. "You're no fun, J.T. All you ever want is information. You marry that pretty redhead of yours yet?"

He frowned. "That's a work in progress, Candy."

"If you're looking for info, it'll cost you."

He patted his jacket. "I brought cash."

"Good. You remembered. I don't take plastic."

"I don't want to talk here. What time do you get off work?"

"Two a.m. You want to meet at my place. It's close by."

Ryan stared at the almost completely naked woman in front of him, who was good-looking in a hard-edged, rough way. He was sexually attracted to her and didn't want to be tempted. "No. I'll meet you in the parking lot outside at two. I'm driving a white Tahoe."

"Okay, sweetie," she said with a grin. Then Candy sashayed away to another table.

Ryan left the place, drove to the Varsity for a late dinner, and pulled into the strip club's parking lot a few minutes after two a.m. Candy, now dressed in black slacks and a fake-fur jacket, was waiting by the front door.

He drove up, she climbed in and he parked his SUV in the lot.

"God, I'm tired," she said hoarsely.

"I'm guessing wearing six-inch heels doesn't help."

Candy sighed. "I used to wear flats, but the tips are better with heels."

"You don't have an easy life, Candy."

She grinned. "You're a sweetie, you know that? Most guys who come to the strip club treat me like dirt. Grabbing my tits and wanting BJs. I usually have to call the bouncer over to talk sense into them. But you actually treat me like a lady."

"I try to treat all women like ladies. It's one of my rules."

"Yeah, I remember you telling me that before. So, what kind of info are your looking for this time?"

"You've been around the block a few times, Candy. You know the seamier side of our lovely city better than most people."

"I do, unfortunately."

"I'm looking," the PI said, "for the people who run the most upscale prostitution rings in Atlanta. Do you have some names for me, Candy?"

The waitress thought about this for a long moment, then she grinned. "I know who they are."

"You bullshitting me, or do you really know?"

"Listen, J.T., I interviewed with these people a few years ago. I didn't get the job – they said I wasn't 'classy' enough. Imagine that."

"I need names."

"Let me see the cash first."

The PI pulled out an envelope from his jacket pocket. "How much is this going to cost me?" Although this was a business transaction and Erin would cover the expense, he didn't want to get hosed on the deal.

"Five hundred."

"That's bullshit, Candy."

"Okay, four hundred."

"Still too much."

"I've got a five-year-old daughter, J.T.," she replied, her eyes pleading. "You know how expensive it is to raise kids these days?"

"Okay, I'll give you three-hundred and fifty, but no more."

"Deal."

Ryan took the money out of the envelope and held the wad of cash in the air. "This info better be good, Candy. Otherwise I won't be a happy man."

She rubbed his shoulder with a hand. "Haven't I always been a good CI, sweetie?"

Knowing she was one of his best confidential informants, he handed her the money.

The waitress unzipped her fake-fur jacket and tucked the cash between the ample cleavage of her low-cut blouse.

After zipping up her jacket, she began talking.

Chapter 29

Langley, Virginia

"Welcome back," Alex Miller said, as Rachel West walked into his office at the CIA's Special Operations Division.

"Thanks, boss," she replied, sitting in one of the hard-plastic chairs that fronted his desk.

"How was Paris, Rachel?"

"Wet. It rained the whole time I was there." She grinned. "I should put in for hazard duty pay."

Miller's face remained impassive. *Typical*, she mused. The guy had no sense of humor.

"Rachel, if I wanted a climate report I'd turn on the Weather Channel."

"Small joke, Alex."

"I figured as much, young lady. Now can we get down to business?"

She tucked her long blonde hair behind her ears. "What I found in Paris corroborates what I learned in Venice."

Miller tented his hands on the desk. "How so?"

"As I had told you previously, it's clear the Reuters journalist in Italy didn't die of an accidental drug overdose. He was murdered."

Miller nodded.

"And the Associated Press reporter in France," she continued, "was assassinated also. It was no simple hit-and-run accident."

"How can you be so sure, Rachel?"

"Because his boss, the editor of the AP in Paris, was murdered also."

Miller's eyebrows arched. "Explain."

"I visited the editor, Mr. Arnaud, at his home. He told me some very interesting facts, facts that relate to the case. But before I give you those, let me tell you what happened at his apartment. I noticed Arnaud was sick from the moment I walked in. He told me he'd been I'll for many weeks and hadn't been to his office for all that time. Well, Arnaud died while I was talking with him."

"He's dead?"

"That's right, Alex. I tried reviving him with no luck. I called the SAMU, the French version of our 9-1-1, and the EMTs and *gendarmes* showed up. They rushed Arnaud to the hospital, but he was DOA."

"You said he was sick. What did he die of?"

"He was poisoned. They did tests at the hospital."

"Poisoned?"

"That's right, Alex."

"Poisoned with what?"

"Polonium-210."

"What?" Miller exclaimed loudly, showing surprise.

Then he snapped his fingers. "I remember a similar situation, Rachel. It happened years ago, in 2006 I believe. Alexander Litvinenko, a Russian intelligence officer became sick after drinking tea laced with radioactive Polonium-210. He died three weeks later. Litvinenko was living in London then and was a strong critic of the Kremlin. British police named two Russian men, former KGB agents as prime suspects, but Russia refused to expedite them."

"That's right, Alex. I remember that also. Which is why I know Arnaud was murdered."

"I agree with you," Miller said. "Do you think the Russians are connected to the murders in Europe and the U.S. of the American reporters?"

Rachel thought about this for a minute. "It's possible. But something Arnaud told me makes me doubtful. The reporter he assigned to this story, the one that was killed in the hit-and-run, believed the conspiracy originated in Spain."

"I see. That is a contradiction. Did Arnaud tell you anything else before he died?"

"Yes, Alex. He said he assigned his reporter to the case because he suspected French newspapers were collaborating on news stories."

Miller tapped a pen on his desk.

"That fits the pattern," Rachel added, "of what the FBI's Erin Welch has found in the U.S. There's definitely a conspiracy going on. Arnaud told me something else. He said a man had called him a while back, offering to give him ten million Euros if he dropped the story. Arnaud refused and a month later he died from the poisoning."

Miller's lips pressed into a thin line. "Way too coincidental. Did Arnaud figure out who had called him?"

"No. He said the caller's voice was muffled and the man probably used a burner phone."

"Figures." Miller leaned forward in his chair. "I want you on this case full time, Rachel. Drop all your other assignments." He pointed to the office door. "Get out there and find out what the hell is going on."

Chapter 30

Atlanta, Georgia

Michael Connery lived on a quiet, tree-lined neighborhood in Dunwoody, an upscale community northeast of downtown.

After having breakfast with his wife and his seven-year-old twin boys, Connery kissed his spouse goodbye, grabbed his briefcase from the foyer, and stepped out of the house. The man was whistling happily, his thoughts already focused on his family's upcoming vacation the following week, a cruise to the Caribbean.

After locking the front door behind him, he strode toward the Ford Explorer parked in his driveway and climbed in. Putting his briefcase in the passenger seat next to him, he gazed out the SUVs windows, checking on the street traffic. As usual, there was little activity since most of the residents in the neighborhood were retired, and didn't need to be up early in the morning.

At 7:03 a.m., Connery inserted the key in the ignition and started the engine.

At 7:04 a.m., the Semtex plastic explosive attached beneath the vehicle ignited, creating a massive fireball, lifting the 4,400 pound SUV five feet off the ground, as it exploded into fiery shards of metal, plastic, glass, and bloody flesh and bones.

The echo from the deafening blast was heard a mile away.

***

J.T. Ryan was on his way to his office when his cell phone buzzed. Pulling the cell from his jacket, he took the call.

"It's Erin," he heard the FBI woman say. "Where are you now, J.T.?"

"Midtown, why?"

She read off an address in Dunwoody. "Meet me here. You need to see something."

"You got it."

He disconnected the call, took the next right and made his way toward the address. Twenty minutes later he turned onto the tree-lined street, which was a beehive of activity. Several fire trucks, their lights flashing, were parked in front of one of the homes, along with police cars, EMT vehicles, and a Dekalb County CSI van.

Ryan parked on the street and walked over to Erin Welch, who was standing inside a large roped-off area in front of the home.

The smoky remnants of what was once a large vehicle littered the blackened and cratered concrete driveway. The nearby grass and shrubs were charred as well. The house, which was twenty feet away, was also damaged. The front windows were shattered and the brick front wall and front door were scarred and pitted from the flying debris. The firemen, obviously done dousing the fire, were now putting away their hoses and tools. A hazy, acrid mist hung in the air.

Erin noticed Ryan and waved him over. He nodded to the uniformed cop on the sidewalk and slipped under the yellow crime-scene tape and strode up to her.

"What happened here?" Ryan asked.

Erin pointed to the charred remains of the vehicle. "I wanted you to see this. It's got to be connected to the case."

"Someone was in the car when it blew up?"

She nodded. "His wife told local PD her husband had just left for work. She was inside the home, heard their SUV start up, then a loud explosion. She ran outside, saw what happened and frantically called 9-1-1."

"Who was the DB?" he asked.

"Her husband's name is Michael Connery. He works at World Media Network."

"That's why you think this is connected," Ryan said. "Was Connery a reporter?"

"No. He was a producer at WMN."

"Was the explosion accidental?"

"No way, J.T. I talked to the CSI techs here. They confirmed the use of plastic explosives, either Semtex or C-4. The killer probably attached a brick of the explosive to the underneath of the SUV and wired the ignition."

He gave her a long look. "By the way. How'd you hear about this? I thought the FBI had turned this case over to DHS."

"The local police detective knew I had been working on this and called me."

Ryan pointed to the charred vehicle. "Does Homeland Security know about this yet?"

"Nope," she said.

"You going to tell them?"

A smile spread across her face. "Nope."

Chapter 31

Flying at 35,000 feet over the Atlantic Ocean

The man known as Scorpion settled back on the wide, deeply-upholstered leather seat of the Gulfstream G650. Considered the gold standard of business jets, the top-of-the-line plane could carry eighteen people, but as usual the man was the only passenger. That was because Scorpion owned the jet; in fact, he owned several of them.

Scorpion was impeccably dressed in a $10,000 Armani three-piece suit, the custom-made garment fitting like a second skin on his tall, lean frame. In his fifties, with stylish silver hair and a long, slender face, he looked like a prosperous banker or financier. But his ice-cold black eyes and a thin scar that ran down the length of his left cheek marred his GQ appearance.

Sitting quietly next to him on the floor of the jet was the man's dog, a very large Doberman Pinscher.

The stewardess, an attractive Nordic blonde in a tasteful blue uniform, came out of the forward galley and approached him.

"Another drink, sir?" she asked.

He sipped the last of his bourbon, then handed her the empty tumbler. "Yes."

She walked away and he admired her sensual hips and backside as he mulled over his upcoming call, which would be much less pleasant. Glancing at his diamond-studded, gold Rolex watch, he knew it was time to make the call. After the stewardess returned with his drink and placed it on the teak wood table in front of him, he said, "I'll need privacy for my call." He spoke in a very cultured voice with only a trace of an accent.

"Yes, sir."

She moved away in the direction of the rear compartment. After hearing the door open and click shut, he picked up his satellite cell phone on the table, turned on the encryption, and punched in a number.

Victoria Stark answered it on the first ring.

"How are things progressing, Vicka?" he asked.

"Very well," she replied. By her tone he could tell she was excited by his call. "I've taken care of the situation as you requested."

"Good. Very good, Vicka." He took a sip of the bourbon, relished the crisp burn of the liquor as it slid down his throat. "That should make my upcoming trip smoother."

"Are you coming to Washington, also?" she asked eagerly. "I want to see you. To hold you. It's been so long."

"I agree, Vicka. It has been too long. I'll see if I can arrange it after I've concluded my business."

"I'd love that." She giggled like a schoolgirl, which he thought was silly, considering she was a dour, unattractive, middle-aged woman. But he knew it was best to humor her and kept quiet.

After taking another sip of his drink, he said, "Have you taken care of the other issue we discussed? The one involving the Asian reporter, what's her name?"

"Mei Lin," she replied, this time in a somber tone. "I'm afraid not."

"Why the hell not, Vicka?"

"That's proving more complicated than I anticipated."

Scorpion clenched his jaw. "Why, damn it?"

"As you know, the FBI is no longer on the case. But it appears the Bureau agent in charge, a woman named Welch, is hiding Mei Lin somewhere. My people haven't been able to find her yet."

"Damn it, Vicka! Take care of this. We can't allow any loose ends. We're too close now."

"I understand."

"I've carried out my end in Europe," Scorpion said icily. "I expect you to handle things in the U.S. That was our deal, remember?"

"Yes, of course I remember. And I'll take care of it."

He took in a few deep breaths to calm down. After a moment, he said, "All right. I know this is important to you too. We're in this together for the long haul."

"We are. I can't wait to see you ...."

"Likewise, Vicka. We speak with one voice."

"Yes," she replied, "we speak with one voice."

He disconnected the call and placed the cell phone on the table.

As he thought through the details of his conversation with Vicka, he idly stroked the head of his Doberman, who continued to sit next to him on the floor, ramrod straight, silent and unmoving. The dog's eyes, always alert, stared at him.

A few minutes later he pressed a button on the leather seat's armrest.

The stewardess came out of the rear cabin and approached him. "Another drink, sir?" she asked.

"No, I've had enough."

Then he gave her a cold, hard smile. "Why don't you go into the bedroom back there and slip into something more comfortable. I'll join you in a minute."

"Yes, sir."

Scorpion's mood brightened as the young Nordic blonde turned and walked toward the back.

Chapter 32

Atlanta, Georgia

The last couple of days had been a bust, Ryan thought, as he drove into the underground parking lot of the luxury hotel. He'd spent it tracking down the list of people who ran high-end prostitution rings that Candy had given him. Unfortunately none of them had any knowledge of the mysterious billionaire implicated in the conspiracy.

Ryan found an empty slot, parked his Tahoe, and took the elevator to the lobby of the hotel.

The massive lobby of the upscale hotel was a soaring, fifty-story open atrium done in glass and chrome. He located the exclusive bar near the lobby, strode in and gazed around the elegant place. Furnished with dark, expensive wood furniture, the bar had dim mood lighting, tasteful jazz music, and distinctive appointments. It was mid-afternoon, usually a quiet time for bars, and this was no exception. Only a few well-dressed customers were seated at tables and at the long mahogany bar. Ryan spotted the woman he was looking for at one of the tables at the far back. She was sitting alone, nursing a martini as she scanned an iPad. At the table next to hers sat a very large, muscular black man with a thick neck, wearing an ill-fitting suit. The man's head was on a swivel and he noticed Ryan right away.

Ryan walked toward the woman's table, and the man, obviously her bodyguard, stood up immediately and blocked the PI's path. By the bulge in his suit, Ryan could tell the man was armed.

The PI smiled. "I'd like a word with Ms. Sable."

"Do you have an appointment?"

Ryan smiled again. "Actually, no. But this will take just a minute."

"Sable doesn't meet with anyone unless they have an appointment," the bodyguard snarled.

Ryan thought through the situation. He needed the woman's help and didn't want to start things off on a sour note. So he decided to continue with the genial approach and grinned a third time.

"My name's John Ryan. I'm a PI and I'm working with the FBI on a case. I just need a moment with Ms. Sable. If you'd let her know, I'm sure she'll talk to me."

The bodyguard unbuttoned his suit jacket giving Ryan a good view of the large Ruger semi-automatic in the man's shoulder holster. He placed a hand on the butt of the gun. "Get the fuck out of here, Ryan."

This isn't working, the PI thought.

"All right," Ryan said pleasantly. "I'll go. But at least let me leave my business card, okay?"

The man took his hand off his pistol and nodded.

The PI slowly removed his wallet, took out a business card, wrote something on the back, and handed it to the man.

The bodyguard read it quickly and looked back at Ryan with a puzzled look.

But by then it was too late, as the PI stepped closer to him and punched him savagely in the solar plexus. They guy groaned and staggered back as Ryan hit him again with a fierce right cross to his jaw and followed that with an uppercut to his Adam's apple. The bodyguard, his face bloody, collapsed to the floor.

Ryan rubbed his own knuckles to ease his pain as he gazed around the dimly-lit bar, making sure the fight hadn't drawn attention. But it had happened so quickly and quietly that no one had noticed.

Then he stared at the woman, who was standing now, a look of alarm on her face. He strode over.

"What do you want?" she said, a tremor in her voice.

Ryan smiled. "Don't worry, I just want to talk. Let's sit down, okay?"

She sat and he took the chair opposite her.

"My name's John Ryan, but everybody calls me J.T. I'm a private investigator. And you're Ms. Sable, right?" He had a physical description of her, but had never seen her before. She was a very striking, light-skinned African-American woman in her mid-forties. She was tall and slender with close-cropped, salt-and-pepper hair. The attractive woman was wearing an elegant gray Versace dress.

"That's right, my name's Sable."

"Is that your first name or last?" he asked pleasantly.

"Just Sable."

Ryan grinned. "One of those one-name people like Bono or Beyonce, huh?"

The woman didn't crack a smile. "Is he okay?"

The PI looked back toward the bodyguard, who was still slumped on the floor, unconscious. "He'll be fine." Ryan rubbed his knuckles again and noticed they were bleeding slightly. He picked up a napkin and patted the blood. "I'm the one that's sore."

"Nobody's ever gotten the upper hand on him before," Sable said. "By the way, I noticed you scribbled something on the back of the card you gave him. What did it say?"

Ryan smiled. "I wrote, *If you're reading this now, you're fucked.* It works every time."

Sable shook her head slowly and gave him a small grin. "You ever do body-guarding work?"

"No. I'm strictly a PI."

"Well, if you ever want to do it, I could use a man with your talents. I pay extremely well."

"I'm sure you do, Sable. Let me tell you why I'm here. I'm working on a case that may involve one of your clients."

"Clients? I don't know what you mean."

Ryan lowered his voice. "You run one of the most upscale call-girl operations in Atlanta."

The woman shook her head forcefully. "Prostitution is illegal. I'm not involved in anything criminal. Who told you I deal with ... such sordid activities as sex for sale?"

"I talked with one of the girls you interviewed a while back. A well-endowed brunette by the name of Candy."

She thought about this for a long moment and a flash of recognition crossed her face. "I know of no such person. However, I will admit, I do provide female escorts to men with very high standards." She paused, took a cigarette out of a pack and lit it up. Taking a puff, she let it out slowly. "I arrange dinner dates. Plain and simple. What my girls and these gentlemen do after dinner is their business."

"We're both grown-ups, Sable. I don't care what happens on these 'dinner dates'. I'm just looking for one man."

She took another puff. "What do I get out of this? I consider the identity of my clients confidential."

He leaned forward. "I'm a nice guy most of the time." He pointed back to the prone bodyguard on the floor. "But as you saw, I can play rough when I have to."

Sable's lips pressed into a thin line.

"You'd beat me up too?" she stated, her voice hard. It was clear she was used to dealing with tough guys. "What kind of man are you?"

"No, I'm not going to beat you." He took his cell phone out of his pocket and placed it on the table. "But I work closely for the head of the FBI in this city. If you don't cooperate, I'll call her and make sure your life will be a living hell from now on." He snapped his fingers. "I can see your business evaporate if you've got Bureau agents looking over your shoulder every five minutes."

Sable stared at him long and hard. Then an amused look came over her face. "All right. I can see you're persistent. Who are you looking for?"

"A very wealthy man, probably a billionaire. Not from the U.S. – possibly European."

"Does he have a name?"

"I'm sure he does, Sable. But I don't know it."

"What's he look like?"

"I don't know that either."

She took another drag of the cigarette. "I have a large business, with lots of girls and lots of male clients. And many of the men are wealthy – they have to be to afford our services."

"I know that."

"You're not giving me much to go on, Ryan. Just a rich European guy."

"There's one other thing I know about him."

"What's that?"

"He has a tattoo."

"What kind of tattoo, Ryan?"

"Don't know."

"Okay. Let me think about this." She stubbed out her cig, lit another and leaned back in her chair. After several minutes of being quiet, she said, "I may know who it is."

Ryan's optimism surged. This was the first hopeful sign in days.

"I do have a client," she said, "not a regular, but someone who comes to the States infrequently. I don't know where he's from, but he has a slight accent. He could be from Europe. I know he's rich. Very. He didn't care how much he spent. He only wanted the best girls. And I was told he had a tattoo. A small one on his forearm. Of a scorpion."

"What's his name, Sable?"

"I don't think it was his real name, but he referred to himself as Scorpion, like his tattoo."

Chapter 33

Atlanta, Georgia

Erin Welch was in her FBI office talking on the phone when a man barged in the room. Trailing behind him was Erin's assistant, who was trying to block the man's entry.

Erin recognized the intruder, hung up the phone and waved away her assistant. "I got this," she said.

She stared at the thin man with the mustache. "If it isn't my least favorite person at DHS, Agent Castillo."

"What the hell do you think you're doing, Welch?"

She rose from behind her desk. "Is that a general question or do have something specific in mind?"

Castillo stabbed an index finger in her direction. "Homeland Security took over the case! What the hell were you doing at the crime scene? And when were you planning on telling me about a related murder? I only found out about it on the news. They said a man was blown up in his car. When I heard the guy worked at WMN, I put two and two together."

"I'm glad you have basic math skills," she replied, her voice dripping with sarcasm.

Castillo's face turned beet red. "You! Damn it, Welch!"

Erin sat back down. "Have a seat before you have a heart attack."

She could tell he was about to yell out something else, but instead he plopped down on the chair fronting her desk.

"It would be a lot better," she said calmly, "if we worked this case together."

"That's not going to happen, Welch."

"Why not? We could help each other."

"Again, that's not going to happen. I have my orders."

She tented her hands on the desk. "Doesn't that make you a little suspicious, Agent Castillo?"

"What do you mean?"

"Homeland Security and the Bureau work together all the time. Isn't that right?"

"Well, yes."

"Then why is this different, Castillo?"

He looked puzzled a moment. Then he shrugged. "Because it is. I was given specific orders. It's a DHS case. The FBI has no role in this."

She tucked her long brown hair behind her ears. "Okay. I can see this isn't getting us anywhere. Are we done?" She pointed to the thick stack of folders on her desk. "I've got a lot of other work to do."

"No. We're not done yet," he said icily.

"Well?"

"You have a PI on your payroll, someone by the name of John Ryan."

"Who I hire is my business, Castillo. Not yours."

"I saw his name on the case file you gave me," the DHS agent said, "and I've talked to local PD and the NTSB. It looks to me like he was heavily involved in this investigation. If he's still working this, I demand you pull him off!"

Erin's blood pressure spiked. "You demand it? You fucking *demand* it? Who the *fuck* do you think you are? I'm ADIC of this office and I'm not taking any shit from you!"

A smug look spread on his face. "We'll see about that."

Infuriated, Erin picked up the handset on her desk phone and punched a number. "This is Welch. Send a security team to my office. There's some trash here I want thrown out of the building."

Chapter 34

Barcelona, Spain

Spain is the third largest country in Europe, covering an area of 194,000 square miles, and with a population of 47 million people.

Trying to find one man in a place this big, Rachel West thought, is going to be tough. Rachel had just landed at Barcelona's El Prat Airport, rented a SEAT sedan, and was now driving on the C31 highway toward her hotel in the city's Old Town district.

She had chosen Barcelona to start her search because the man suspected in the conspiracy was thought to be a billionaire. Barcelona, along with Madrid, was home to most of the wealthy in Spain.

She didn't have much to go on, she mused. But her marching orders from Alex Miller were clear. Find him, wherever he was. In the back of her mind she had a nagging suspicion the guy was not from Spain, but rather from Russia, but she had let that go for now, since the Spanish connection seemed clearer.

Rachel ticked off the info she had received so far: Reporters had been murdered in the U.S. and in Europe; the main suspect, an unknown billionaire, was most likely from Spain, but possibly from Russia; the initials O.O.V. were somehow connected to the case; the FBI contractor, J.T. Ryan, had just learned that the wealthy man went by the nickname of Scorpion and had a tattoo of an arachnid on one of his arms; and this Scorpion guy liked high-end hookers.

It was a jumbled mess, she thought. But she was used to working cases where she had little to go on. She relished being on her own, solving a mystery and putting bad guys behind bars. Or better yet, six feet under.

There was a slow-moving tanker truck in front of her and she stomped her foot on the accelerator pedal as she flicked the steering wheel in order to pass the truck. But the sedan's anemic engine groaned and barely picked up speed.

I could use my bike now, she thought, thinking of her powerful Kawasaki motorcycle back home. Her rental sedan finally accelerated and she passed the truck.

An hour later, after Rachel checked into a hotel in the *Las Ramblas* district, she called her Barcelona CIA field officer.

"It's Rachel," she said. "Just got in. We need to meet."

"Sure," the man replied. "The usual place? By the church?"

"See you in an hour."

***

Rachel sat on a bench across the street from the imposing neo-Gothic style cathedral as she waited for her CIA contact to arrive. The *Sagrada Familia*, Europe's most distinctive church, was architect Antoni Gaudi's masterpiece. The building of the massive cathedral had begun in 1882, she knew, but over a hundred years later it remained unfinished. Its imposing spires, depicting Nativity scenes, towered 600 feet over street level, dominating this part of the city's skyline.

A dark-complexioned, middle-aged man carrying a suitcase strolled up sometime later, and nodding, sat next to her on the bench.

"Cortez," she said, "I was wondering if you were going to make it."

"No worries, Rachel." He tapped the suitcase. "Just wanted to make sure I got all the tools you had requested."

"Any problems?"

"No, *senorita*."

"Good. Did Alex Miller brief you on why I'm here?"

The non-descript, swarthy man nodded. "*Si*. You are looking for a rich Spaniard who likes high-end prostitutes." He smiled. "But that could be a lot of men."

She didn't return the grin. "I'm aware of that, Cortez. I'm sure Miller filled you in on why we're looking for him. And now I have some additional information."

"*Bueno. Que es?*" he said, speaking in Spanish now.

Rachel was fluent in many languages and replied in kind. "We believe this billionaire speaks English with a slight accent. We think he's a Spaniard, but he could be Russian. He goes by the nickname of Scorpion. Ever heard of him?"

Cortez shook his head.

"It's believed," she continued, keeping her voice low, "that he has a tattoo of a scorpion on his arm. And one more thing – the initials O.O.V. are somehow connected to this case. Any thoughts on who he could be?"

The CIA field officer shook his head again. "No. But I will check with my informants now we know all this new information."

"Good." She picked up the suitcase and slid it towards her. "Anything else before I go?"

Cortez gave her a long, appraising look, taking in her long blonde hair, piercing blue eyes, sculpted face, and the way her curves filled out the black pants suit she was wearing. "Join me for dinner tonight, *senorita*. We could have a relaxing meal, drink some good wine."

Rachel shook her head. "Sorry. I don't mix business with pleasure."

He placed a hand on her arm and smiled. "Are you sure, Rachel?"

She gave him a hard stare, then took out the Smith & Wesson Tactical pen she always carried with her. The pen was standard issue for all CIA operatives. It worked much like a regular pen, but it also doubled as a personal defense weapon. Constructed of T6061 aircraft-grade aluminum, its sharp metal point at one end had the ability to shatter a windshield. Or cause extensive bodily harm by jabbing into a person's eye and blinding them. It was the only tool she could get through security at airports.

"Do you know what this is, Cortez?"

"Of course. Your tactical pen. I have one just like it."

"I'm trained to use it," she stated.

His grin faded. "Understood."

Rachel rose, picked up the suitcase and walked away from the church area.

Back at her hotel later, she set the suitcase on the bed and clicked it open. To her relief, Cortez had come through and supplied her with the tools she used on field operations. In the case was an MP-5 short-barreled machine pistol; a break-apart SIG Sauer snipers rifle with scope and suppressor; a compact Glock 43 nine-millimeter handgun with a suppressor; a wire garrote; and a lightweight carbon knife. She hoped she wouldn't need all these tools while in Spain, but it was always better to be over prepared.

Taking out the knife, she slipped it into a pocket.

Then she picked up the compact Glock 43, once again admiring its light weight. The small semi-automatic could easily be carried in a woman's purse. She had carried the Glock 42 for years, but upgraded to the 43 because it fired the more lethal 9mm round. She inserted a full magazine into the butt of the gun and racked the slide. Then she slipped the Glock into the holster and clipped it to her belt underneath the jacket of her pantsuit.

After closing and locking the suitcase, she stored it in the closet and headed out of the hotel room, looking for answers.

Chapter 35

Atlanta, Georgia

"I just got off the phone with Alex Miller at the CIA," Erin Welch said, as J.T. Ryan walked in her office in the FBI building. "We had an interesting conversation."

Ryan sat on one of the chairs fronting her desk. "Tell me about it."

"Miller thinks something's changed. Some new dynamic in this conspiracy."

The PI leaned forward. "How so?"

"With the initial murders," she continued, "the reporters all died in apparent suicides or accidents." She held up a hand and began ticking them off with her fingers. "Parker jumping off the roof of a building; the hit-and-run in France; the plane crash in Atlanta; the drug overdose in Italy. All could be explained away. But these latest deaths, the AP editor dying of plutonium poisoning and the bomb killing the WMN producer – those deaths were obviously murders."

Ryan nodded, picking up on the theory immediately. "I agree. Specifically in the case of the WMN guy, it was clear that Semtex was used to blow up his vehicle."

"Miller thinks," Erin said, "that the conspiracy has developed a new focus."

"By being more open," Ryan replied, "they may be sending a message."

"And the message is pretty clear. It's a threat. Don't mess with us, or you could be next."

"In the case of the AP man in Paris," Ryan said, "the threat was probably intended to intimidate European journalists. While the murder of the WMN guy was to scare reporters in the U.S."

"Exactly, J.T."

"So how does knowing this help us?"

"I'm not sure yet. But I know one thing. You need to be extra careful. Watch yourself as you continue the investigation."

Ryan grinned. "Careful is my middle name."

"Bullshit, J.T. I know you're a cowboy."

The PI smiled again. "That would be me."

Erin went quiet for a minute, deliberating. Then she said, "There's something else I need to fill you in on. I had a visit from Agent Castillo of DHS. He *demanded* I pull you off the case."

"How'd he even know I was working on this?"

"He read the case files and talked to local PD."

"What'd you tell him, Erin?"

"Since the FBI isn't supposed to be on this, I refused to acknowledge you were involved. In fact, I told him to shove it and had him escorted out of the building."

A wide grin spread across his face. "That's one of the reasons I like you, Erin. You're tough as nails when you have to be."

***

Many hours later, after running down leads on the case, Ryan called it a day and went home to his apartment. It was ten in the evening and since he'd skipped dinner, he was starved.

Going to his kitchen, he scanned the meager contents in his refrigerator. Besides a six-pack of beer, a wilted head of lettuce, and a half-dozen eggs, there wasn't much else. As usual he'd forgotten to go food shopping. Normally he would head to Lauren's house for dinner. But since things with her were on the chilly side after her refusal to marry him, going there was a bad idea.

Finally he ended up making himself a tuna sandwich. He ate that along with some chocolate doughnuts that were always a fixture at his place. After washing it all down with a bottle of Coors, he took a long, hot shower and went to bed.

He slept fitfully, his dreams alternating between the case he was working on and his strained relationship with Lauren.

Ryan woke from one of his dreams and saw a red dot of light flashing on his bedroom wall. He instinctively recognized the red pinprick of light. Immediately throwing himself off the bed, he crouched next to it.

At the same instant his bedroom window imploded, the glass shattering, the shards raining down on him. The incoming volley of high-caliber rounds slammed into the wall, tearing chunks out of the wallboard in a crazy-quilt pattern.

His heart racing, Ryan grabbed his gun from the nightstand and was about to return fire, but the rifle shots got closer to him, whizzing only inches above his head. He sensed the red light dot on his forehead and dived to the floor just as more rounds slammed into the wall behind him and into the bed's mattress. He flattened himself on the hardwood floor as additional rounds poured into the room.

Chapter 36

Atlanta, Georgia

Scorpion had refused to meet the news executive at his WMN office, and instead chose Centennial Park, which was a few blocks away.

The billionaire strode into the park now, looking for the newsman. It was a chilly, rainy day, and the park, which was usually a bustling place, was mostly empty, the foul weather keeping people away.

Scorpion was wearing a bullet-proof overcoat over his $10,000 Armani suit. Walking alongside him was the ever-present Drax, his Doberman, while two bodyguards, one in front and one behind him, shadowed his every move, their heads on swivels as they scanned the park for potential threats.

The billionaire spotted Dan Marshall sitting at one of the stone benches beneath a canopy of trees. Walking up to him, he said, "Mr. Marshall, thank you for meeting with me on such short notice."

Marshall, a thin, balding man, stood and frowned. "You must be Scorpion." It was clear the news executive didn't want to be here and had only agreed because the billionaire owned a large share of WMN stock.

Scorpion gave him a cold smile. "That I am."

Marshall pulled up the collar of his raincoat. "My office would have been more comfortable for this meeting."

The billionaire wiped raindrops from his forehead. "Meeting there is not a good option for me."

"Why not?"

"If you'll bear with me, Mr. Marshall, everything will become clear. My men will have to search you to make sure you're not wearing a wire. And they'll take your cell phone. But don't worry, you'll get it back."

The news executive's face flushed, his anger growing. "Is this really necessary?"

"Do I have to remind you how many shares of WMN I own?"

Marshall sighed. "No. After you called to set up this meeting, I had your company checked out – you're a large shareholder." He frowned. "But your firm appears to be some type of shell organization – my people couldn't tell me where it was located."

Scorpion smiled once more, and again there was no humor in it. Then he motioned to his men, who approached Marshall, patted him down, and took his cell phone.

"Shall we sit down?" the billionaire said, perching on the stone bench. His Doberman stood stiffly next to him.

Marshall sat across from them, staring warily at the large, fierce-looking dog.

"Don't worry about Drax," the wealthy man said. "He's harmless unless provoked."

"So, what's this all about, Scorpion?"

"We're both busy men, so I'll cut to the chase. I want to buy controlling interest in World Media Network."

The news executive glared. "That's not possible. I own a substantial number of shares in the company and I don't want to sell them."

Scorpion wiped more raindrops from his forehead. "I thought you would say that."

"I'm assuming then that this meeting is over?" the news man said curtly.

"I'm afraid not."

Marshall frowned. "It looks to me like we have nothing else to discuss."

Scorpion flashed that cold smile again. "This meeting is far from over. You will sell me your shares. You have no choice."

The news executive rose abruptly. "I've tried being polite, but I gave you my answer. And it's no."

The billionaire nodded and his large dog barked and growled menacingly at the man. "Sit down, Marshall."

With alarm on his face, the man sat back down.

The billionaire ran a hand over his perfectly coiffed mane of silver hair, brushing off the moisture from the drizzle. "As I said, you will sell me your shares. You have no choice. Do you remember what happened to your star reporter, Mark Parker? I'm sure that you do. He jumped off a building in an apparent suicide. That was no suicide. My people eliminated him."

The news executive's eyes went wide with fear.

"And there's more, Marshall. Do you recall the car explosion last week? The one that killed your WMN producer? I'm sure the police told you that was no accident." Scorpion leaned closer to the other man. "My people did that also."

Marshall's face blanched white. "But ... but ... but why?"

"It was a warning – a warning to you. You will cooperate. As I said, you have no choice."

"You can't do this! I'll call the police."

Scorpion grinned coldly. "They can't help you. Nobody can. I'll have you killed minutes after you've left this park. And your trophy wife and your three adorable children who live in that beautiful home in Dunwoody? And your parents who live in Kansas City? I'll have all of them killed also."

Scorpion continued talking, stating detailed information about his family, including addresses, phone numbers, social security numbers, birth dates, schools, even pets names. "Like I said, I'll have them all killed." He snapped his fingers. "Just like that."

Marshall's face was a mask of fear. "Please ... please ... no...."

The billionaire leaned back on the stone bench and took an envelope out of his overcoat. "Some people call me ruthless. And maybe I am. But I'm also a very generous man when I get what I want. I'll pay top dollar for all of your shares of World Media Network." He handed the other man the envelope. "In there is an added bonus for you, something that sweetens my offer."

Marshall took the envelope. "What is it?"

"A bearer bond worth thirty million U.S. dollars."

"Why? Why do you want to own WMN?"

"It's obvious, isn't it? World Media is the largest news company on earth."

"I assume you'll fire me once the deal is completed."

"Oh, no, Marshall. You'll stay on. You'll still be the face of the network. Nobody will know who I am."

"What do you intend to do once you control the company?"

Scorpion leaned forward. "That's not your concern. Do you accept my offer?"

The other man's shoulders sagged, a look of resignation on his face. "Yes. You give me no choice."

Chapter 37

Atlanta, Georgia

J.T. Ryan sat in his living room and watched as APD cops and CSI techs bustled in and out of his apartment. The room, much like his bedroom, was a chaotic mess, the high-caliber rounds shattering furniture and penetrating the thin, now pock-marked walls.

Erin Welch came out of the bedroom holding a camera in her hands.

"Never figured you for a photographer, Erin."

She shrugged. "Since I'm 'not' on this case anymore, I can't bring my own crime scene techs. I want to have a record of what happened."

He grinned. "You're a jack-of-all-trades. And pretty, too."

"Wipe that smile off your face, Ryan. You almost got killed tonight."

The PI used humor to dispel tension and tonight was no exception. But he knew the woman was right. "Yeah. No doubt about it."

She waved a hand in the air. "Any idea who could have done it?"

"I don't know." He chuckled. "I know it's hard to believe, but some people don't like me."

"It's not *that* hard to believe."

"Now who's the wise-guy, Erin."

She set the camera down on the damaged coffee table. The table was gouged from the gunfire and covered with a mist of plaster board. "I went across the street," she said, "and checked out the high-rise apartment building there. The shooter probably fired down from the roof into your apartment."

Ryan nodded. "I agree. The cops find any spent shell casings on the roof?"

"No. The shooter was a pro. Policed his brass before he took off."

The PI rubbed the painful bruise on his forehead that came when he threw himself on the floor as the attack began.

"You should have that checked out," Erin said.

"I'm fine. I have a hard head."

"You do have a thick skull."

"Ouch," he said with a grin. "That's two zingers in one day. You should do stand-up."

Erin shook her head slowly and frowned. "You're rubbing off on me. And that's a bad thing."

Just then Ryan's girlfriend Lauren pushed past a cop at the doorway and rushed into the apartment. She had a terrified look on her face.

Lauren ran toward the PI and sat next to him on the couch. "I heard what happened. Got here as fast as I could. Are you okay?"

"I'm all right," Ryan said.

"Why didn't you call me, J.T.?"

"I didn't want to worry you, hon. Plus, we've been having issues, you and me."

Erin picked up her camera and said, "I'll leave you two alone. I've got work to do." Then she went toward the bedroom.

Lauren gently touched the angry bruise on Ryan's forehead. "Poor baby. Are you sure you're all right?"

He looked into her pretty hazel eyes, saw the deep concern there. "You know me. I'm invincible."

Lauren folded her arms across her chest. "You think you are, that's for sure." She gazed around the smashed-up furniture and the walls covered with holes, as if taking it all in for the first time. "Oh, my God. Your apartment ... it's a mess ...."

"But there's at least one consolation."

"What's that?"

He grinned. "It's all cheap furniture."

She punched him on the shoulder. "Quit joking around, J.T. This is serious. Someone tried to kill you."

"Yeah, you're right."

She gazed around the room once more. "What are you going to do now? You can't stay here tonight. This place is a wreck."

"I was going to get a hotel room."

"Oh, no you don't. You can stay at my place tonight, J.T. Plus I need to make sure you're okay. That bruise looks bad."

He stared into her eyes. "Are you sure that's a good idea? After what happened on Stone Mountain?"

She covered one of his hands with hers. "Just because we're not getting married ... and because we're not together anymore ... doesn't mean I don't care about you." She looked very sad and very lonely right then.

Never at a loss for words, Ryan this time didn't know what to say.

After a long moment he caressed her cheek. "Thanks. I appreciate the offer. I'll stay at your house."

*　*　*

An hour later Ryan and Lauren were at her house in the northern suburbs. They were sitting on the large sofa in the living room, as she applied a bandage to the bruise on his forehead.

That done, she rose and said, "You should be fine. But if it starts hurting, let me know. I'll drive you to the emergency room."

He gave her a mock salute. "Yes, nurse."

"I'm going to shower and get ready for bed, J.T. I'll bring you a pillow and some blankets when I'm done." She turned and left the room.

Ryan propped his feet on the coffee table as he leaned back and rested his head on the sofa. He had a throbbing headache, but otherwise felt okay. He'd been extremely lucky, he knew. *I could be dead right now.*

He heard the sound of running water from the second floor of Lauren's house and he closed his eyes as he visualized her lathering up her body. The pleasant thought excited him. But a moment later, totally exhausted from the shooting, he fell asleep fully clothed.

Suddenly he heard a noise, pulled his revolver from his holster, and bolted off the sofa.

But it was Lauren who had come into the room, her arms laden with a pillow, sheets, and a blanket. "Take it easy, J.T. It's just me." She placed the stack of linen on the sofa.

He re-holstered his gun.

She stood there with her arms across her chest, her long auburn hair, still damp from the shower, falling limply to her shoulders. She was wearing one of her 'granny nightgowns', the kind that cover you from head-to-toe, loose-fitting and with no cleavage. This one was pink and had tiny flowers printed on it. Although the garment was shapeless, he could still make out her petite, curvy figure. Even dressed as she was, Lauren looked magnificent and sexy as hell.

He stepped closer to her, breathed in her clean soap scent. "You look good, hon."

She ran a hand through her damp hair. "I wore this frumpy nightgown on purpose. I don't want you getting any ideas."

He grinned. "It didn't work. I already know what you look like under that thing. And I want to see it again."

Her hazel eyes sparkled and she blushed, the redness accentuating the freckles on her pretty face. He could tell she wanted him as much as he wanted her.

Ryan took another step forward and put his muscular arms around her slender shoulders. He pressed her to him and gazed into her eyes.

"Don't make this harder than it has to be, J.T."

Ryan laughed. "It's already hard."

She giggled. "I can tell."

He leaned his head down and kissed her softly on the lips, and she kissed back hungrily, her tongue exploring his mouth.

They stayed that way for a long moment, then she abruptly stepped away from him and crossed her arms in front of her.

"What's wrong?" he said.

"Nothing's wrong. I love you. But ...."

"But what?"

"I'm confused, J.T."

"Confused about what?"

She began pacing the room. "About you and me. About us."

"I love you, Lauren."

She stopped pacing and faced him. "And I love you too. More than anything. I never stopped loving you ...." Tears brimmed in her eyes. "I've been so lonely ... so miserable since we broke up ...."

Ryan shook his head. "That day up on Stone Mountain. We never broke up. You said you wouldn't marry me and you ran away. Then you wouldn't answer my calls."

Tears were flowing freely on her face. "I know. I'm sorry I ran away ... I'm sorry I didn't take your calls. I was very confused that day ... and I'm still that way now ...."

"We can make this work, Lauren. We can make us work. You have to give it a chance. Please."

She wiped tears from her eyes, but the anguished, confused look didn't leave her face. "I love you more than life, J.T. But I see now that you staying with me is making it too difficult. For both of us. I think after tonight you should find a hotel. Good night."

She turned, went to the staircase, and quickly climbed up the steps to the second story.

Depressed, Ryan took off his jacket and shoes, propped the pillow at one end of the sofa and lay down.

He closed his eyes but didn't get any sleep that night.

Chapter 38

Washington, D.C.

The Cadillac limousine stopped in front of the residential brownstone building on the quiet, tree-lined street. The only thing that made this particular building unique was the multiple satellite dishes that completely covered its roof.

Victoria "Vicka" Stark exited the car and walked up the steps to the edifice. She inserted her card in the entry device by the door, had her retina scanned, and keyed in her password.

Stepping inside, she made her way to the main operations room and once again keyed in her password to unlock the heavy metal door. Entering, she found the operations manager at his usual spot, sitting at a computer console at the back of the massive, auditorium-sized room. Similar consoles, all staffed, filled the space.

Covering the far wall of the auditorium was a large array of flat-screen TVs, all tuned to different television stations. The vast room was a bustling place, full of technicians wearing headsets, watching the TV screens and the computer monitors in their consoles. The place always reminded Vicka of the operations center at NASA.

Seeing her, the operations manager took off his headset. "Ms. Stark, I wasn't expecting you today."

"You know I like to show up unannounced. Keeps you on your toes, doesn't it Harold?"

"Yes, Ms. Stark."

She remained standing and stared down at the man sitting at the console. Harold Meeks had a worried look, which was good, she mused. She hadn't gotten her nickname of 'Dragon Lady' by accident. Vicka studied the bald, obese man with the rotund belly and rolls on his flabby neck.

"I see you haven't lost any weight since I was here last, Harold."

"No, ma'am."

"Enough chit-chat. How's O.O.V. going?"

"Fine, Ms. Stark."

"You told me that last time, but it wasn't true, was it?"

Harold's thick fingers fidgeted with his headset.

"I'll ask you again," she said in sharp tone laced with menace, "how are things going today? How many items have your techs flagged? And don't lie to me." She picked up a pencil from the console and snapped it in two. "You know what happens when you lie to me."

"Yes, ma'am. But things are going smoothly today."

She pointed to the large array of TV screens mounted on the far wall. "Show me."

"Yes, ma'am. On the top row of screens we're replaying the daily evening news casts from all of the major networks and the cable news outlets."

"Have you flagged any items today?"

"Only three, and they were minor infractions."

"That's good, Harold."

"Thank you."

"How about yesterday? How many stories did you flag?"

"Two, ma'am."

"For the whole day?"

"Yes."

"And everyone else was following the narratives we supplied?"

"Yes, Ms. Stark."

"That's good, Harold. That's a big improvement from when I was here last." She paused a moment. "You've contacted the news agencies that committed the infractions?"

"Yes."

"You personally called them?"

"Yes, ma'am."

Vicka nodded, satisfied with the results. "I'm pleased, Harold. And I know my partner will be pleased. You're to be commended."

His nervousness of earlier dissipated and he showed a hint of a smile. "Thank you, Ms. Stark."

Then she leaned down further so that their faces were only an inch apart. "But don't let it go to your head, mister. You're only a cog in my machine. An important one, but a cog nevertheless. You can be replaced."

She pointed a menacing finger at him. "And I don't mean a demotion or losing your job. You know way to much, Harold. There's only one solution if I don't get the results I want."

Chapter 39

Atlanta, Georgia

Erin Welch drove to J.T. Ryan's office building in midtown, and after parking her car in the lot, made her way up to his floor and knocked on the door.

After hearing him say "Come in", she opened the door and found Ryan aiming a pistol at her.

"Sorry," he said, as he put the revolver away in a drawer. "I'm kind of jumpy after someone tried to kill me other day."

"Understandable," she replied, sitting on one of the chairs fronting his desk.

He pointed to the coffeemaker on top of the filing cabinets. "Want some coffee and doughnuts? I just brewed a fresh pot."

She remembered the swill that passed for coffee, from the last time she was here. "No thanks."

Ryan grinned. "Oh, yeah. I remember. You only drink Starbucks."

Ignoring his remark, she glanced around the sparsely furnished office with its inexpensive metal desk and cabinets, mostly bare walls, and industrial carpeting. Then she spotted something new, a small cot in the corner.

"What's with the bed, J.T.?"

A frown crossed his rugged, handsome face. "I'm sleeping in the office, until my apartment gets fixed up."

"They have something called hotels now. Ever heard of them?"

"They're expensive, Erin."

A thought occurred to her. "Actually, I'm surprised you're not staying at Lauren's house."

Ryan grimaced. "Lauren and I ... we're not together anymore."

"That surprises me even more. You two have been an item ever since I've known you."

"It wasn't my idea to break up. I love her. Women are just ... complicated ...."

"Well, if it's any consolation, J.T., I always thought you made a great couple."

Ryan nodded, the dejected expression still on his face. He took a bite from a chocolate doughnut and a sip from his foam cup of coffee. "What brings you here, Erin?"

"Need to fill you in on some developments on the case, J.T. First, I'll be out of town for a couple of days. My boss wants to meet with me at the Hoover building in D.C."

"What's that about?"

She let out a long breath. "I don't know, but it can't be good. I think I'm being called on the carpet for not playing nice with Homeland Security."

Ryan took another sip of coffee. "Don't worry, the FBI won't fire you. You graduated top-of-your class at Quantico, and you've got countless commendations."

Erin shrugged. "That's true. But unfortunately, after 2008, everything in Washington is a lot more political. And my boss, the director of the Bureau, has a pension to protect."

"I understand. What else is happening?"

She leaned forward in the uncomfortable metal folding chair. "Alex Miller from Central Intelligence called me. His CIA operative, Rachel West, is in Spain now working the leads you obtained."

"Good. Has she made any progress?"

"Not yet, but I'll keep in close contact with Miller."

"Okay, Erin. Anything new on finding the perps who tried to kill me? Or the people who blew up the WMN producer?"

She shook her head. "No. But it's clear they were professionals. The lab results came back. They left no fingerprints or DNA trace evidence."

Chapter 40

Barcelona, Spain

Rachel West was worried. She hadn't heard from Cortez, her CIA field officer, in days although she'd left numerous messages for the man.

It was dusk and she was having a glass of wine at an outdoor cafe in *Las Ramblas*, a colorful and festive avenue bordered by boutique shops, flower stalls, quaint restaurants, and newsstands. The avenue's tree-shaded central walkway was crowded with people out to see and hear the street musicians, mime artists, and tarot readers that performed nightly in the area.

Rachel took out her encrypted cell phone and punched in the number for Cortez. Once again got voice mail. She hung up and glanced at her watch. It was six p.m. local time, making it noon in Langley.

She made another call and this time it was picked up on the first ring.

"It's Rachel," she whispered into the phone.

"Is this call encrypted?" her boss, Alex Miller responded.

"Yes."

"Okay, Rachel. Any progress?"

"Not a lot," she continued, keeping her voice low. "Listen, I've been trying to get a hold of Cortez for days with no luck. What's going on?"

"I don't know. You met with him when you arrived?"

"Yes. We went over the case. He was going to work with his informants and see what he could find out about the guy we're looking for, Scorpion."

"Okay, Rachel. I'm putting you on hold a moment. I need to make a call."

She drank her wine and watched as street musicians and several mime artists performed to a crowd gathered nearby.

Miller came back a few minutes later. "I just off the phone with the Agency's station chief in Spain. It's not good. Cortez hasn't checked in for two days. That's highly irregular. He hasn't been to his office, hasn't returned calls, and no one, including his family, knows where he is."

"He's missing?"

"That's right."

The CIA operative pursed her lips as she thought through the implications of this. "Too coincidental."

"I agree. Be careful, Rachel. If Scorpion can take out one of our field officers this quickly, he's a very well-informed and dangerous man."

Chapter 41

Hoover Building, FBI Headquarters
Washington, D.C.

Lies and bullshit. That's what I'm going to get today, Erin Welch thought, as she waited in the conference room for her boss to arrive. She just hoped she wouldn't get fired.

Ten minutes later a heavyset man with jet black hair entered the room and Erin rose from her seat.

"Director Tucker," she said, extending her hand.

"ADIC Welch," he replied as they shook. "Have a seat."

They sat at the polished walnut conference table and he gave her a wary look. "You probably know why you're here, Welch."

"Yes, Director. I have a pretty good idea."

Tucker's eyes narrowed as he glared at her. "When we talked several weeks ago, I thought I was quite clear."

"Yes, sir."

His nostrils flared and his face flushed. "Then why in hell am I getting calls from the director of Homeland Security *and* the Attorney General?"

"Let me explain, sir."

Tucker slammed his fist on the table. "I don't want an explanation. I gave you a direct order. I want it followed!"

"But –"

"No, Welch. I took you off this case. The Bureau has turned it over to DHS. It's *their* job to work it."

"Who gave you the order to turn over the case?" she asked calmly, trying to keep cool and diffuse the situation.

Tucker's face turned a bright shade of crimson. "What the hell does that matter?"

"With all due respect, Director, I think it's pertinent. Who was it?"

His jaw clenched and for a moment he seemed at a loss for words. "It came from someone very high up."

"Who was it, sir?"

"I can't say."

"Look, Director, I understand how politics works in D.C., specially at the top levels of government. I'm not trying to make your life difficult. I'm just trying to solve a multiple murder case which now spans the U.S. *and* Europe. I think we owe it to the American people to find out why their news reporters are being killed."

Tucker waved a hand in the air. "It's in the hands of DHS now. It's no longer our responsibility."

"Sir, you've read my reports. You're an intelligent man. This is clearly a conspiracy."

"I repeat, it's in their court now."

Erin took a long breath to calm down. "I believe the Department of Homeland Security has gotten their marching orders as well. I think DHS has been told to slow-walk this investigation."

A tired, haggard look spread on the director's face. "Even if what you say is true, we no longer have control over this matter."

"But, sir —"

He held up both palms. "Enough. I've let you speak. Now hear this. And hear it clearly. Do not pursue this. Let it go. Am I clear, Welch?"

"Crystal."

"Good." He rose from his chair. "Listen, Erin, you're a good Assistant Director. One of the best I have. You do a hell of a job running the Atlanta Field Office. If I remember correctly, you graduated first in your class at Quantico. You've solved a lot of big cases. Ten years from now, you might have a shot at becoming director of the Bureau." He paused a moment and his voice took on a menacing tone. "But if you persist with this witch hunt of yours, you'll be lucky to get a trainee-level job at the FBI Field Office in Alaska."

Then he turned and left the room.

Chapter 42

Atlanta, Georgia

J.T. Ryan had just climbed into his Tahoe and was about to pull out of the underground parking lot when he hard the loud squealing of tires.

A large, black SUV raced towards him, slammed on its brakes and came to a screeching halt in front of his vehicle, blocking his path. A second SUV pulled up behind the first.

Fearing a car-jacking, Ryan immediately drew his pistol.

Eight heavily-armed men wearing SWAT gear piled out of the SUVs, pointing their weapons in his direction.

"Put the gun down, Ryan!" one of the men yelled as he held up a badge. "Federal officers! Put the gun down and get out of your vehicle with your hands up! Do it now!"

Ryan, his heart pounding, couldn't tell if the badge was real, but their weapons looked lethal enough. And the odds, eight to one, were not in his favor.

The PI placed his revolver on the dash, slowly climbed out of his Tahoe and held his hands in the air. Pointing their guns, the eight men swarmed towards him.

"Hands against the car, Ryan!" one of the them ordered.

"Who the hell are you guys? What do you want?"

One of the men in SWAT gear stepped closer to him. "Hands on the hood. Do it now!"

Ryan turned and slowly placed his palms on the hood of his SUV. Someone came up behind him, roughly patted him down, pulled his arms back, and clicked on handcuffs. Then Ryan was spun around to face the armed men.

One of them held up his badge. "We're DHS."

"What the hell does Homeland Security want with me? I haven't broken any laws."

The man put away his badge. He was a thin, Hispanic-looking man with a mustache. "You're interfering with an ongoing investigation, Ryan."

"That's BS and you know it. I'm assisting the FBI."

The man gave him an ominous look. "The Bureau is no longer involved. DHS has taken over."

"What's your name?"

"Agent Castillo, DHS."

"Oh, yeah," Ryan replied. "I've heard a lot about you. And none of it is good."

Castillo glared. "I'm here to warn you. Stay the hell out of this investigation."

"Looks like overkill," the PI said with a chuckle, "sending a whole SWAT team to give me a warning."

"Take this seriously, Ryan. I can pull your PI license. I can lock you up. And even your FBI friend Welch won't be able to get you out."

Ryan was itching to punch the agent's lights out. And if he hadn't been handcuffed, he probably would have already done it. But he didn't doubt a word of what the man had just said. Homeland Security had a lot of clout.

The PI shrugged. "Okay. I heard your warning. Now can you un-cuff me?"

Castillo motioned to one of his men who unlocked the cuffs.

Then the DHS agent stuck his index finger on Ryan's chest. "You have been warned. If we have to come back a second time, we won't treat you so nicely."

Chapter 43

Washington, D.C.

Vicka Stark was giddy with excitement.

Soon she would be with her partner, her lover, a man she hadn't seen in over a month. *Too long*, she thought, *but unavoidable*. Between his schedule and hers, it was always complicated to arrange. And now that their operation was in full swing, it was even more difficult. Her lover's penchant for secrecy and her high-profile job made their trysts harder to schedule and keep covert. As it was, they had to meet at out-of-the-way places under assumed names. She had booked the current hotel suite with an alias.

Vicka sat at the small table and stared at her reflection in the hotel room's mirror. She didn't like what she saw. Even though she'd spent an hour applying makeup and styling her hair, something she rarely did, the results were lackluster at best. If nothing else, she was honest with herself. She was a dour and unattractive fifty-five year old woman. *No amount of makeup and primping can change that*, she thought sourly.

But that was the wonderful thing about the man she loved. He loved her dearly, despite her looks. *In his eyes*, she mused, her mood soaring, *I'm a beautiful and desirable woman. That's all that counts.*

Vicka brushed her hair one last time and stood up, and once again gazed at her reflection in the mirror. She had spent hours picking out the dress, a stylish black outfit that attempted, she hoped, to give her plain, flat-chested figure some semblance of femininity. She smoothed down the dress then sighed.

Just then there was a knock at her door, and her excitement soared, the prospect of seeing him again making her giddy. She giggled like a schoolgirl, then chided herself for being so silly. *I can't help it, the man brings out the best of me!*

Vicka went to the door and after glancing through the peephole, opened it.

Two bulky men with crew-cuts wearing ear-pieces and ill-fitting suits stood at the doorway. She nodded and let them in – she was used to the drill.

The men quickly went through the large, luxury suite, using hand-held scanners to sweep the place for video cameras and listening devices. Satisfied the rooms were clear of bugs, they made sure the glass slider leading to the balcony was locked and drew the blinds. Then they went back out to the corridor, taking positions flanking the door.

A moment later Scorpion walked in and closed the door behind him. His large Doberman Pinscher was at his side.

Her debonair and handsome lover was wearing a gray Armani suit that fit him like a second skin. His thick mane of silver hair glistened, and he looked and acted like a prince. The only feature that marred his good looks was a thin scar that ran down the whole length of his left cheek. But she had known him so long she barely noticed it. In her eyes, he was royalty.

Vicka felt like her chest was going to explode, she was so excited. She desperately wanted to rush up to him, hug him and kiss him, but knew that wasn't possible, not yet. Before she could approach him, the man always had to instruct his insufferable dog, Drax. The large canine had no compunction about biting her or anyone else who approached Scorpion.

Scorpion signaled to the dog and it instantly sat, although its eyes warily tracked her every move.

The man gave her a radiant smile, his perfectly-white capped teeth gleaming in the light. Then he spread his arms wide.

"Vicka, you look absolutely beautiful, as always!"

She smiled shyly and blushed, then ran into his arms, hugging him tightly. "It's been so long!"

The man hugged her back and looked down at her, his 1000-watt smile beaming. "I agree, Vicka. It has been too long. I wish we could meet more often." He caressed her face gently with a palm and she blushed again from the excitement of his touch.

"When the operation is complete," he continued, "we'll be together much more often."

"I hope so, Hans," she replied breathlessly. "I can't wait."

He pressed a finger to her lips, anger flaring on is face. "Don't call me that. Never use my real name. Never."

"I know, dear. It's just Scorpion sounds so – impersonal."

"I'm sorry, Vicka. But we're too close now to completion. We can't be linked in any way. My real name must remain secret."

She sighed. "Your men swept the room. It's not bugged."

"True." He pointed toward the sliding glass doors leading to the balcony. "But there are always birds up there, satellites picking up everything. You never know who's listening."

Vicka smiled. "I have a lot of pull in this town. I can suppress information."

"Even the NSA?"

Her smile grew wider. "Even them."

Scorpion nodded, but she could tell he remained unconvinced.

"Let's play it safe," he said. "Don't use my real name."

"As you wish. Let's sit down, okay? We have a lot to talk about." She grinned, and this time it was a lewd smile, the little girl giddiness of earlier gone. "And I want you to make love to me. I can't wait for that."

"Me neither. It's all I could think about on the flight over."

She caressed his arm. "Even with all of the beautiful women you have at your disposal? You still want me?"

Scorpion gazed deep into her eyes. "They are nothing to me, Vicka, those other women. You are the treasure in my life."

Deep down, she didn't know if he was being totally honest with her. But she didn't care. What mattered was that he was with her now, with her. "You always say the sweetest things, dear."

He gave her another radiant smile. "I love you."

"And I love you."

He sat down on the plush sofa and pointed to the wingback chair nearby. "Please, sit. We have much business to discuss before we can move on to more pleasant matters."

She sat on the chair, rapt at attention. "Of course, dear."

"I have excellent news to share with you, Vicka. I've concluded the pending deal in Atlanta. The news company there has agreed to my terms."

"So World Media Network is on board?"

"Yes."

"That's fantastic, Scorpion!"

"Yes, it is. WMN is the crowning jewel in the news business. With them in our pocket, it'll be easier to flip the rest."

She nodded, knowing what he said was true. "Was it difficult to convince Marshall to agree?"

Scorpion grinned and this time it was a cold smile. "No, once I made it clear he had no choice. The death of his producer in the car explosion was a brilliant idea. Thank you for suggesting it."

"We make a good team."

"Yes, we do, my beautiful Vicka."

Unable to suppress her desire for the man any longer, she got up from the armchair and sat next to him on the plush sofa. She placed a hand on his leg. Being so close to him, touching him, even fully clothed, filled her with sexual excitement. She stared into his eyes. "Make love to me."

"Vicka, dear, we haven't finished our business discussion. We have much more to talk about."

"Please, Hans – I mean Scorpion. I need you. I have to have you now. It's been too long, dear. We can talk later."

His lips pressed into a thin line and he glared. Then he took in a deep breath and exhaled slowly. Clearly he was angry but it was also evident to her that he was trying to suppress his irritation. After a moment he nodded. "All right, Vicka. We can talk later."

She giggled girlishly. "I love you!"

"I care for you very much, too."

She glanced at the large canine; the Doberman sat unmoving near the sofa, its black eyes tracking her every move. "Does your dog have to watch while we do it?"

"Of course. It's my policy. You know that. Where I go, Drax goes. You know how much I value my personal security."

"I think it's creepy," she said, giving the canine a nervous glance. *I hate that damn dog,* she thought for the thousandth time.

Scorpion caressed her cheek with a hand. "Don't worry about Drax. He's extremely well trained."

Vicka sighed. She knew it was an argument she wouldn't win. Scorpion was obsessed with personal security. In addition to the guard dog and the two armed men posted outside the hotel room's door, she knew there were two more of his bodyguards in the lobby.

She smiled salaciously and rubbed his leg with her hand. "Let's go to the bedroom. I bought a new negligee – I want to change into it." She caressed his leg again. "I think you'll really like it."

He gave her the 1000 watt smile. "I'm sure I will. But aren't you forgetting something?"

Acting surprised, she said, "What?" She knew what his next request would be, but had hoped to avoid it.

Scorpion pointed toward the floor in front of him. "You know what I like first."

Vicka grit her teeth, her enthusiasm waning. She detested this part. "Can't we skip it this time?"

He flashed the broad smile again. "Now, now, Vicka. You know what I like."

Her anger flared in spite of her attempt to suppress it. "Aren't you satisfied having all of your whores do that? You know I find it ... disgusting ...."

"It's always sweeter when you do it."

"Well, I hate it, Hans!"

"I know you're not fond of it. But we all have to make sacrifices from time to time."

She shook her head.

"Come now, Vicka, after you do this, we can have regular sex, just the way you like it."

"Please. Not this time."

He gripped her head forcefully with both hands. He was still smiling, but now it was a cold hard grin. "You know what you have to do."

With a feeling of resignation, she nodded.

Scorpion let go of her head, leaned back on the sofa, and unzipped his pants.

Vicka rose from the couch and knelt in front of him.

Chapter 44

Dallas, Texas

The truck driver tapped on the brakes, slowing the 18-wheeler rig a bit, as he kept an eye on the Infinity sedan three car lengths ahead of him. They were on a remote part of Interstate 35 heading away from the city. It was ten p.m. and traffic was light.

The truck driver would have preferred using a different method for completing his assignment, but his target, the man driving the Infinity, was well protected. The business executive lived in a gated estate and his office building had extensive security.

The truck driver sped up, keeping pace with the car ahead as he gauged the best time to make his move. He was familiar with this stretch of the Interstate and was calculating the optimum timing.

A minute later he spotted what he was waiting for, a bridge a quarter of a mile ahead. He quickly downshifted the manual gearshift, flicked the wheel left and smashed the accelerator pedal. The large diesel engine growled, the twin smokestacks of the 18-wheeler belched dark smoke, and the large truck surged forward, picking up speed. He came alongside the Infinity just as the two vehicles began crossing the bridge.

The truck driver flicked the wheel right, edging closer to the luxury car.

The Infinity's horn blared and the car began to speed up, but it was too late, the 18-wheeler's right flank crashed into the car, pushing it toward the bridge's railing.

Using both hands, the truck driver held on to the bucking steering wheel as the lumbering monster crushed the left side of the Infinity. Sparks flew and the sound of grinding metal, breaking glass, and the victim's screams filled the air.

Suddenly the bridge railing gave way and the partially crushed sedan flew off the bridge toward the river below. It splashed into the murky water and sank a moment later.

The driver, his heart pounding, drove the 18-wheeler past the bridge, slowed, and stopped on the shoulder. Climbing out, he glanced briefly at the damaged side of the truck. Its right flank was dented and scraped and half of its tires were blown out. But that wasn't his concern; he'd stolen the rig earlier for just this purpose. Taking a pint bottle of whiskey out of his jacket pocket, he splashed the contents on the truck's seat, then threw the bottle against the metal dash, where it splintered into a dozen jagged pieces.

Then, after taking off his gloves and stuffing them in a pocket, he began jogging toward his car, which he'd hidden earlier in the day under a stand of trees a half mile north.

Chapter 45

Atlanta, Georgia

"Interesting place to meet," J.T. Ryan said as he took a seat across from Erin Welch.

She was sitting at one of the back booths in the food court of the Georgia Aquarium in downtown. Closing the lid on the laptop in front of her, she said, "Not much choice, these days. Not like we can get together at my office or yours."

"That's a fact. I take it your meeting at the Hoover building in D.C. didn't go well."

Erin grimaced. "The director was not a happy camper. He made it crystal clear. I stay off the case or, if I'm lucky, I get a job cleaning toilets at the FBI Field Office in Anchorage."

Ryan let out a low whistle. "He's not kidding around."

She shook her head. "Not at all. If I disobey him again, I'm done."

"You explained that this is a conspiracy? That there's a cover-up going on?"

"He didn't want to hear it, J.T. He's got his marching orders."

"Who's pushing his buttons?"

"The director wouldn't say."

Ryan nodded. "Okay. By the way, I had an unpleasant meeting of my own. An old friend of yours paid me a visit."

Her eyebrows arched. "Who?"

"Agent Castillo from DHS."

"That bastard."

"One and the same, Erin. And to emphasize his point, he brought along a whole SWAT team with him. They cuffed me and read me the riot act."

"What did he want?"

"He gave me a warning. Stay off this case or he locks me up."

"He can do it too, J.T. And the worst part is, I'm not sure I could get you out."

Ryan rubbed his jaw. "I agree. So what's next? Do we give up? I've never been run off a case before and I don't want to start now."

"Me neither." She leaned back in her seat. "There's been another development, something I think is connected."

"What is it?"

"It was on the news yesterday, J.T. A man was killed in an apparent car accident in Dallas. His car was run off the road in a hit-and-run. They found an abandoned 18-wheeler nearby, the driver long gone. They also found evidence the truck driver had been drinking, but that could have been staged."

"And?" he asked.

"I checked on the victim. He was a well-known businessman in Texas. Part owner of a large chain of newspapers."

"You're right, Erin. Too coincidental." His anger flared. "So I ask again, do we walk away from this?"

"Hell, no. We can't. This damn thing is too big."

Ryan leaned forward. "That's what I wanted to hear."

They sat there silently for a long moment, both of them brooding over the BS that was blocking them at every turn.

Finally she said, "There may be a way for us to stay involved. But it'll mean you traveling overseas."

"Not a problem, Erin. Just tell me where and when."

"Okay. I got a call the other day from Alex Miller at the Agency. As you know the CIA operative he assigned to the case, Rachel West, is in Spain. Well, her field officer in Barcelona went missing. The Agency has been trying to track him down, but he's disappeared without a trace. How'd you like to go over there? It's not like you can do much good around here, with Homeland Security tracking your every move."

"That's a fact, Erin."

"You'll go?"

He nodded, took out his cell phone and began doing an Internet search.

"What are doing, J.T?"

"Checking airline schedules. There's a nine p.m. flight to Barcelona. I'll leave tonight."

Chapter 46

Barcelona, Spain

J.T. Ryan knocked on the hotel room's door and waited. He heard footsteps from inside and sensed being watched through the peephole.

The doorway opened and Rachel West stood there, holding a Glock at her side. "Come in, Ryan."

He stepped inside and she closed the door behind her and re-holstered the pistol.

"I never got a chance to thank you properly," he said, "for saving my life in Cartagena awhile back."

"Just doing my job," she replied in a cool tone, her piercing blue eyes inspecting him thoroughly, obviously trying to spot if he was armed. Even though both of them were on the same side, it was clear the woman was a professional and didn't take chances.

"You carrying, Ryan?"

"No. I couldn't take my weapon with me on the flight over. The Spaniards have strict gun laws."

"Tell me about it." She pointed toward the balcony at the far end of the hotel room. "I was having coffee out there – let's talk there and I can bring you up to speed. Want a cup?"

"Sure. I take it black."

She nodded. "Me too."

Ryan stepped out on the small balcony, which overlooked the bustling *Las Ramblas* area. The wide, tree-lined avenue stretched out below, and in the distance the busy harbor was visible. It was a cool, sunny day and he breathed in the crisp, sea breeze.

Rachel came out, handed him a ceramic mug, and then sat across from him at the ornate, wrought-iron table.

Taking a sip of the strong coffee, he studied the tall, slender, and attractive woman with long blonde hair. Her sculpted good looks hadn't changed a bit, he thought, since he'd seen her last in Colombia. And in fact, she was wearing similar clothes – tan work boots, faded jeans, and a long-sleeve blue denim shirt. But the casual clothes did little to disguise her curves and natural beauty.

"Any progress on the case?" he asked.

She shook her head. "Not much. You heard my field officer went missing?"

"Yeah, Welch told me."

"The Spanish cops just found his body."

Ryan raised a brow. "Murdered?"

"Clearly," she said, taking a sip of coffee. "A double-tap to the back of the head. Small caliber weapon. Probably a 22."

"A pro did it."

"No doubt about it. No fingerprints, no shell casings, no trace evidence."

"Is his murder connected to our case, Rachel?"

A gust of wind swirled onto the terrace and she tucked loose strands of her long hair behind her ears. "I think so. I met with him as soon as I arrived, asked for his help and he began talking with his informants. A week later they find his body in an alley with two bullets in his head."

"How many Agency people you got backing you up on this assignment?"

She flashed a thin smile. "Including myself, one person."

Perplexed, he said, "You're it?"

"That's right. You probably heard about the recent terrorist attacks in Japan and Sweden?"

"Yeah."

"Well," she replied, "all CIA assets are focusing on that. It's a good thing you're here to help. This case of the killed reporters is probably too big for one operative to handle alone. By the way, what happened back in Atlanta? Miller wasn't specific. Just told me you had to leave the U.S. for awhile."

Ryan grit his teeth. "Damn turf wars. DHS took over the case from the Bureau and threatened to pull my PI license and lock me up if I didn't stop investigating. Erin Welch, who's great at pushing back, is on thin ice herself. Coming here to Spain to help you was my best option to solve the case."

She leaned back in her chair, sipped coffee and gave him a long, hard stare as if sizing him up again. "Okay. Your skills will come in handy."

"Your boss, Miller, fill you in on my background?"

"I know all about you, Ryan." She set the cup down on the wrought-iron table. "Age 38. Former U.S. military. Rank of Captain in the Army. Airborne, Ranger, Green Beret. Then you went into the elite Delta Force, Tier 1. The best of the best in Special Forces." She gave him a thin smile. "Although the U.S. Navy SEALS would argue that point."

He grinned. "Do you know what SEALS aspire to be when they grow up?"

"What?"

"Be in the Army's Delta Force."

She chuckled. "Maybe. But you got to give the SEALS credit. They get all the press."

Ryan nodded, knowing what she said was true. Ever since Team SEAL 6 killed Osama Bin Laden, they received more accolades than any other Special Forces group.

Rachel continued talking, obviously recalling details she had learned about the PI. "After you got out of the Army, Ryan, you helped the FBI solve some big cases – the international drug case, the money counterfeiting conspiracy, and a few more." She paused a moment. "Although you're only 38, you're old-school in some ways. Your weapon of choice is a revolver, a Smith & Wesson .357 Magnum and you use jacketed hollow point rounds."

Surprised, he said, "How the hell do you know all this?"

"I'm CIA," she replied, amusement in her voice. "I know everything."

"Bullshit."

"I also know, Ryan, that you were in a long-term relationship with a woman named Lauren Chase and that you two broke up."

Ryan stared at her, startled by this. "How do you know –"

"I'm CIA, remember? I know the brand of beer you prefer, Coors, and that you're addicted to chocolate doughnuts. I even know about your rules. Ryan's Rules. Rule number 1: Only kill the bad guys. Rule number 6: Treat all women with respect. Rule number 13 –"

He held up a hand. "All right. Enough. You've made your point. But it doesn't seem fair. I know next to nothing about you."

The blonde nodded. "The Agency is tight-lipped about their operatives."

"Okay, Rachel. It doesn't matter that I don't know your background. You and your Agency team saved my life in Cartagena. I know I can trust you and that you're good at your job. That's all that counts."

She leaned forward. "Good. Glad we got that out of the way. You said you hadn't been able to bring a weapon over. I'll work on that. Get you a handgun." She pulled out a matte black pen from her shirt pocket and handed it to him. "You can have this in the meantime. I've got a spare."

He held the thick, metal pen in his hand and inspected it closely.

"It's a Tactical pen," she said. "It's standard issue for all Agency operatives. It's made of lightweight, aircraft-grade aluminum – the sharp metal point at one end is strong enough to break a windshield or poke out an eye. The serrated cap on top can be used to scratch skin and serve as a DNA catcher. I've used that pen to get me out of some tough situations when I didn't have a gun. The best part is, it acts like a regular pen and you can carry it through TSA checkpoints at airports."

"Thanks, Rachel. And you'll get me a gun? I feel naked without one."

"Yes. But it won't be old-school like a revolver. It'll be an automatic."

"Not a problem."

"Why'd you switch, Ryan? Not too many people in law enforcement carry one of those six-shot relics."

He shrugged. "I carried a semi-automatic most of my professional career. But I had one jam on me – almost got me killed."

"I understand."

There was a loud blast from a horn on the busy avenue below and both of them looked down. Then they sat there for several minutes, quietly sipping the strong coffee, lost in their own thoughts.

Eventually she checked her watch.

"Got a meeting coming up, Rachel?"

"No." She gazed at him, an amused look on her face. "I have to give you credit. You've been here an hour and you have yet to hit on me."

He returned her gaze and stared into her piercing blue eyes, once again struck by her beauty and understated charm, things she suppressed with a practiced cool professionalism. "Is that what you're used to?"

She smiled, nodded, and took another sip of coffee.

"Well, I can see why. You're an attractive woman."

"That has its pluses and minuses."

"I imagine so. Are there many females in the CIA?"

"Not many, Ryan. And the ones we do have are technical or research types at Langley. I'm one of the few Agency NOCs, and I'm the only one in Special Operations Division."

"What's a NOC?"

"CIA field agents with Non-Official Cover," Rachel replied, "hence the term NOC. Covert operatives. We do what's called HUMINT, or human intelligence gathering work; what you would refer to as espionage agents doing undercover work. Special Operations Division NOCs like myself kill the bad guys who need to be killed. We do all the dirty work nobody wants to know about, or talk about. NOC's like me aren't involved in satellite or communications surveillance gathering, which, in my opinion, the Agency is relying on way too much."

Rachel took another sip of coffee. "But don't get me started on that topic. I think the CIA, like many other government agencies, has become too concerned with MC/PC bullshit."

Ryan nodded. "I can't argue with you there. That's a big reason I never wanted to be an agent in the FBI. So. What's our next step?"

Rachel looked up from her cup, a determined expression on her face. "Now we go find the perps. Capture them if we can. Or, better yet, kill them."

Chapter 47

Atlanta, Georgia

As Erin Welch came out of her Buckhead townhouse and walked to her car parked on the driveway, she noticed a black SUV pull to the curb.

It was nighttime, and not expecting visitors, her hand instinctively went to the butt of her pistol. A man climbed out of the SUV and strode up to her.

She recognized him immediately. "Agent Castillo. What the hell do you want now?"

"We need to talk, Welch."

Erin shook her head slowly. "You're like a bad penny, Castillo. I can't seem to ever get rid of you."

The Homeland Security agent held up his palms. "It's not what you think. I'm not here to give you a hard time."

She rolled her eyes. "That'll be a first, you asshole."

"Let me explain," he said, and for the first time since she'd known the DHS man, his usual imperious and berating attitude was absent. Still, she was fuming from her meeting with the director of the FBI.

"Why should I, Castillo? You almost got me fired."

"I know. And I'm sorry about that."

"Sorry doesn't cut it, buddy. Now get out of my face and out of my driveway. I'm headed out to dinner and I'm hungry. And the last person I want to talk to is you."

"Please, Welch. Give me five minutes."

"I don't like you coming to my home. If you want to talk, make an appointment and come to my office."

"That's not going to work. We can't meet there."

It had been a long, frustrating day, she was tired and hungry, and she was still irate at the man in front of her.

"Please," he pleaded. "Just five minutes."

She sighed, then shrugged. "All right. But only five minutes. Then I never want to see you again. Got it?"

"Yes. Thank you."

Erin pointed back to her townhouse. "Let's go inside."

Castillo shook his head. "Not there. It may not be safe."

"What the hell do you mean?"

"I can explain." The man motioned to her Jaguar in the driveway. "We can talk in the car. That should be okay."

Confused but also intrigued by his mysterious comments and his abrupt change in attitude, she nodded. Taking the car's fob out, she unlocked the Jag and slid into the driver's seat, while he climbed into the passenger side.

"What's with all the cloak-and-dagger crap, Castillo? Why can't we talk in my house or office?"

His gaze swiveled furtively in all directions, scanning the area of her house and the street. No one was about and there was no car traffic in the quiet, upscale neighborhood.

"Expecting someone?" she asked sarcastically.

"No. I just want to make sure I wasn't followed."

She glanced at her watch. "You've got five minutes. Start talking."

Castillo turned his gaze back to her. "I think you were right."

"Right about what?"

"About this case."

She tapped her watch. "Explain. And fast. I'm hungry."

The DHS agent let out a long breath. "You remember the day we met, the day I took over the case and you turned over your files?"

Erin grit her teeth and felt bile surge up her throat. "I'll never forget it, you son-of-a-bitch."

"Look, I understand your anger. I really do."

"You have three minutes left, Castillo. Get to the point."

"You were right all along about this case."

"Explain."

"Remember the WMN producer?" he asked. "The guy who was murdered by the car bomb? And more recently, the business executive who was killed in a hit-and-run in Dallas?"

"Yes, of course."

"I've been investigating those cases. Considering your opinion of me, you may not believe it, but I'm actually a pretty good agent."

"You're right, Castillo. It is hard to believe you're a good agent. You always struck me as one of those imperious, know-it-all jerks we have in federal law enforcement."

He held up his palms. "I know, I deserve that."

"You *do* deserve it. You deserve a kick in the balls, too."

"Please, Welch. Give me a chance here. I'm trying to apologize for my behavior."

Startled by his total change in attitude from their earlier meetings, she said, "All right. I accept your apology. Now explain what's going on."

"Okay. Like I said before, I've been looking into the car bombing in Atlanta and the hit-and-run in Dallas."

"What did you find out?"

"That's the problem, Welch. I haven't been able to find out very much."

"And this proves you're a good detective? I'm not following you."

His head swiveled nervously again, scanning the area outside the car. Then he focused on her. "I've been *trying* to solve the case. But they won't let me."

"Who won't let you, Castillo?"

"My boss."

"Your boss at DHS?"

"That's right, Welch. But I think it's coming from someone much higher up in Homeland Security than my boss."

She jabbed her index finger on his chest. "I *told* you it was a cover-up. From day one I told you that."

"I know you did. I didn't believe you then."

"But you do now?"

"Yes, Welch. I think we're definitely dealing with a conspiracy."

Erin let out a long breath, her hunger and her frustration from the long day forgotten. This was the first glimmer of hope she'd had about the case in weeks. "I'm glad you finally realize the deception going on inside our agencies. Now tell me why we have to talk in my car."

"I think my phone lines are tapped."

"Tapped by who?"

"I don't know, Welch." He pointed toward her townhouse. "Your place may be bugged, too."

Erin thought about this a moment. "All right. That's a possibility, considering everything that's going on. So, are we finally on the same side?"

Castillo nodded. "Yes. We can work together, but we have to keep it secret. If DHS finds out, I'm toast."

She leaned back in the leather seat and stared at the man. "You said earlier the order to slow-walk this investigation was coming from high up. Who do you think it is?"

"I don't know, Welch. But whoever it is, they're high up the food chain. They've thrown a wet blanket on this and nobody, and I mean nobody, wants to talk about it. I've been a DHS agent a long time, and I've never seen anything like it."

Chapter 48

Atlanta, Georgia

Dan Marshall had a sick feeling in the pit of his stomach.

Although he'd agreed to the WMN buyout deal from Scorpion and had already deposited the $30,000,000 bearer bond into his Swiss numbered bank account, Marshall felt like a dead man walking.

He stared out the floor-to-ceiling windows of his office at World Media Network. It was a clear night and the city's brightly-lit skyline stared back at him. He quickly thought through his options. All of them were bad. He could remain Scorpion's puppet at WMN, under the man's thumb doing his bidding. Or, he could call the cops and hope they could keep him and his family safe from the reach of the maniacal billionaire. Lastly, he could make a run for it, leaving his family behind to face certain death.

After weighing his options for a long time, the newsman made a decision.

Swiveling his executive chair away from the windows, he faced his desk. Picking up the telephone's handset, he made a call.

Chapter 49

The Situation Room
The White House
Washington, D.C.

Vicka Stark listened as the Secretary of Defense droned on about the U.S. military's contingency plans, in light of the recent terrorist bombings in Tokyo. The man, a former Marine four-star, was a capable strategist but had a habit of over-complicating his briefings. He relied on extensive map, chart, and graph-heavy PowerPoint presentations. The slides of the briefing were now visible on the multiple video screens which lined the walls of the Situation Room. Vicka had a razor-sharp mind and had already figured out what the man's final recommendation would be fifteen minutes ago.

Vicka, who was sitting at one end of the long conference table, glanced at the meeting's other participants. As usual for National Security briefings, the country's top leaders were present. Among them were the Cabinet members and all the senior White House advisors. Also there were the heads of Homeland Security, the FBI, CIA, DIA, and NSA. But she gave them scant attention. Her focus was entirely on the man sitting at the head of the table, the president.

President Ackerman was a heavyset man in his early sixties, with sandy hair, an affable, charming personality and a disarming smile. Never a strategic thinker or a brilliant tactician, Ackerman however was a shrewd politician. He relied on pitting his opponents, be they Democrat or Republican, against each other until he was the last man standing. He had been elected to his first term by using this technique, and had won re-election four years later by dividing the U.S., pitting one social group against another. It was a brilliant strategy, a strategy Vicka herself had devised. Ackerman, who was more interested in the trappings of power than the actual running of the country, had adopted her strategy wholeheartedly.

Vicka had served the president for many years, first as his chief aide during his terms in the Senate, and since then as the White House CoS, the Chief of Staff. As Ackerman was fond of telling her in private, he would rather be on the golf course, or hob-knobbing with his Hollywood pals, than dealing with Congress or his Cabinet. "That's your job, Vicka," he would often say with a wink and a smile. Content to give speeches around the country to gin up his base, it was up to her to do the hard work of getting things done. This made for a lot of 80 hour weeks on her part, but she always felt it was worth it.

As the president's main gatekeeper, Vicka decided who spoke with him, what reports he read, and what meetings he attended. And she did her job with relish, ruling with an iron fist.

Feared and hated by inside-the-beltway Washington powerbrokers, Congressional leaders, and Cabinet members alike, they at the same time respected her total access to power. Behind her back they referred to her as the 'Dragon Lady'. She relished the nickname. *Better to be feared than liked*, she mused.

The Secretary of Defense finally concluded his long-winded briefing and President Ackerman turned to his Chief of Staff.

"Who's next, Vicka?" Ackerman asked.

"Mr. President," she replied, "the Director of Homeland Security wants to bring us up to date on steps he's taken to prevent a terrorist bombing like we saw in Japan."

"Of course," the president said, turning to the man. "Go ahead."

The DHS director launched into his presentation and when he was done, Vicka signaled to the Secretary of State to brief the room. Then the secretary commenced his remarks.

Vicka kept a close eye on Ackerman and when she spotted the president's eyes glaze over from the information overload, she said, "Thank you, Mr. Secretary."

"But I'm not done yet, Ms. Stark."

Vicka pointed to the thick binder resting on the conference table in front of her. Known as the PDB, the Presidents Daily Briefing, it contained the daily assessment on a whole range of national security issues facing the U.S. It was compiled from data supplied by the country's law enforcement and defense analysts, including the NSA, FBI, DIA, DHS, and DoD. "I'm sure your remarks are in here. Isn't that right, Mr. Secretary?"

"Yes, Ms. Stark," the Secretary of State replied.

Vicka turned toward Ackerman. "Very well, then. In that case, Mr. President, our briefing is concluded."

President Ackerman rose. "Good. I'm giving an award in the Rose Garden this morning and I've got to get ready." He glanced around the Situation Room. "Thank you, ladies and gentlemen. That will be all."

As the participants filed out of the room, Ackerman said, "Vicka, please stay a moment."

"Of course, Mr. President."

When Ackerman and his CoS were alone, the president strode to the door, closed it and locked it. Then he went to the media projector on the table and turned it off; the images on the screens disappeared. Finally, he sat down across from her at the table and slid his copy of the PDB towards her. "I don't have time to read it. If there's anything important in there, let me know, Vicka."

"Of course, Mr. President." She was used to this. In fact, she expected it. Ackerman rarely glanced through the PDB; he much preferred watching ESPN or the Golf Channel.

Vicka picked up the thick binder and stacked it on top of her own copy of the PDB. After this meeting was over, she would devour the document word for word, and follow up with the appropriate departments on items that needed to be addressed.

The president tented his hands on the table in front of him. "What are your thoughts on the terrorist situation?"

"It's contained, Mr. President. The bombings took place in Japan and Sweden, but I don't believe we have to worry about it happening in the U.S."

"That's good to hear. You know how I hate having to deal with those types of issues."

"Yes, sir. That's why you have me."

Ackerman nodded. "That's a fact." He waved a hand in the air. "If it weren't for you, I'd never be here."

"You're too kind, Mr. President."

"You underestimate yourself, Vicka. I'd be lost without you."

She smiled, very pleased at his remarks. His appreciation for her dedication to his legacy, his vision of change for the country, was what made all of her 80 hour weeks bearable, enjoyable even. Still, she never wanted to take credit for his success, knowing it was always better to stroke Ackerman's considerable ego.

"Nobody knows who I am outside the beltway," she said humbly. "You're the leader of the free world, Mr. President. The man America looks up to, to lead them during these troubled times."

Ackerman's chest puffed up, she noticed, and he nodded thoughtfully. "You're right, Vicka. Americans do love me. At least many of them do. But I do have one concern, and that's why I wanted to talk to you in private."

"Yes, sir?"

"I'm deeply concerned that recently my poll numbers have dropped. My popularity is slipping. Now that I'm in my second term, I'm looking toward my legacy, my accomplishments. When the history books are written, I want to be remembered not only as the best president the country has ever had, but also the most popular."

"It's what I strive for every day, Mr. President."

"I know you do and I appreciate it." He glanced around the empty room, as if to remind himself that their conversation could not be overheard. The Situation Room was designated a SCIF, or Sensitive Compartmented Information Facility. The room was outfitted with the most sophisticated anti-surveillance equipment, and it was the most secure area in the White House.

"One of the ways to insure my popularity, Vicka, is by making sure my policies, our policies, are presented to the American people in the very best light."

"Of course, Mr. President."

Ackerman placed his hands flat on the table in front of him. "How is the operation going?"

"Very well, sir."

"Our narratives are being followed?"

"Yes, sir. I visited O.O.V. a few days ago and everything is on track."

"That's good. Very good." He leaned forward in the high-backed executive chair. "I want you to redouble your efforts. I want to see as many positive stories about my administration as possible. Every day, multiple times a day. On all of the networks."

"Yes, sir."

"I know I can count on you."

"Of course, Mr. President."

Ackerman raised a brow. "Do you foresee any complications with O.O.V.? Any loose ends?"

"Only a few, and I'm taking care of them, sir."

"Excellent." Then a look of concern crossed his face. "You know, nothing of this can ever be connected back to me. My hands must remain spotlessly clean."

"Of course, sir. You always have plausible deniability."

"That's what I wanted to hear." The president settled back in the chair and he went quiet for a long moment. Then he said, "We speak with one voice."

"Yes, sir," Vicka replied. "We speak with one voice."

Chapter 50

Atlanta, Georgia

The power company repairman had been looking for the right house for most of the day. The process was more difficult because the remote area was sparsely populated, with the homes far apart, at times separated by miles of rolling countryside. That, and the fact he had no house number, only the rural road where it was located. That meant having to stop at each home and talking to the occupants before moving on to the next.

It was eight p.m. when he drove his Ford van into the driveway of a dilapidated farmhouse with a sagging roof. Lights were on inside, signaling someone was home. Grabbing his toolkit and clipboard from the passenger seat, the repairman climbed out of the van and knocked on the front door. He was wearing the well-known electric company's uniform of a blue shirt, tan pants and a tan ball cap. The shirt and cap were embroidered with the firm's colorful logo. Pinned on his lapel was a badge with his name. He'd stolen the uniform, along with the van, the previous day.

He heard muffled footsteps, the porch lights came on, and the door opened partway. An attractive Asian woman stood at the doorway.

"I'm Bob with Attria Electric," the repairman said with a smile. "There's been a power outage in the area and I'm checking to make sure your electricity is back up."

"Everything's fine," the woman said. "I haven't had an outage. In fact, I never called your company."

The repairman smiled again. "These thing are spotty. You know how it is. By the way, you're Mei Lin, the occupant of this house, correct?"

He had seen pictures of the Asian woman and was already sure it was her. But he was thorough and wanted confirmation.

"Yes, that's right."

"Good. I'll leave you my card," the repairman said. "If you have any problems, give us a call." He reached into his toolkit, removed the suppressed Ruger pistol stored there and quickly fired off four rounds.

The woman's forehead exploded in a bloody, pulpy mess as the high-powered bullets pierced her skull. Mei Lin collapsed and was dead before her body hit the floor.

Chapter 51

Barcelona, Spain

Waking up early, J.T. Ryan had taken a shower, shaved, dressed, and was about to leave his hotel room when he heard a knock at the door.

Opening it, he saw Rachel West at the doorway with a large, military-size rucksack slung over her shoulder. She was wearing dark blue jeans, a black polo shirt and a black leather jacket. The CIA operative came inside and he closed the door behind her.

"Just got a call from my boss at Langley," she said, setting the bag on the floor. "He received a lead about the informant my field officer was working with when he got killed."

"Good," Ryan replied. "That's what we needed. Where's this CI located?"

"Seville."

Ryan visualized a map of Spain, remembered the city was in Andalusia, in the southern part of the country. "We're flying there?"

"No." Rachel pointed to her rucksack. "Can't. We couldn't get what's in there through airport security. We'll go by train. They have high-speed rail here."

"Okay. When do we leave?"

"Now. I've already checked us out of the hotel."

"Did you get me what I asked for, Rachel?"

She opened the bag and took out a suppressed SIG Sauer 9mm pistol and two extra clips and handed them to him.

After checking the load, Ryan slipped the handgun under his belt at his lower back. "Thanks."

"You ready to go?" she asked.

Ryan went to the room's closet, took out a large duffel and slung it over his shoulder. "I'm always ready," he said with a grin.

***

Ryan had used Spain's high-speed rail before and knew it was an efficient system. And considering all of the usual delays at airports, it was a faster method of moving around the country. In fact, the AVE train they boarded in Barcelona would take only three hours to get to Seville.

Not having eaten since the previous day, Ryan was starved. He suggested going to the train's dining car and Rachel agreed. After stowing their gear in the overhead compartments, they grabbed a window table, ordered a meal, and watched the blur of countryside as they sped south.

The PI's head was on a swivel as he checked out the other diners on the train, trying to spot if he was being followed or watched. It was his usual protocol, and he noticed Rachel had been on the lookout as well, from the moment they had left the hotel.

"Situational awareness," Ryan said, referring to the term security specialists used for being aware of their surroundings.

"Roger that," she replied, taking a drink from her bottle of mineral water. "That's the first thing they taught us at the Farm, the CIA's training center."

Ryan nodded, and after taking one last look around, settled into his seat, satisfied they weren't being followed.

Their meal came, and she must have been as hungry as he was because she plowed into her food with gusto. And in fact, thought Ryan, the hearty *arroz-con-pollo* dish they were both having was mouth-watering.

"Got a plan?" he asked, between bites.

"Yes."

"Wanna share?"

"Sure, Ryan. We find the CI and question him."

"Simple as that? Do you want to elaborate?"

She took a sip from her bottled water but said nothing.

"You're a woman of few words, Rachel West."

She shrugged. "In my line of work, it's safer that way."

"We're on the same side here," he said with a smile.

Rachel stared at him. "You're right. I've just got a lot on my mind."

"About the case?"

"No. Personal stuff. Problems back home."

Ryan's thoughts drifted to his own problems with Lauren. As he watched the blur of countryside through the rail car's window, his thoughts turned somber.

Trying to shake off his gloomy mood and hers, he turned back to Rachel, who by now had cleaned her plate of food.

"You know what's worse than biting into an apple and finding a worm?" he said with a grin.

She looked puzzled, then realized he was telling a joke. "What?"

"Biting into an apple and finding half a worm."

Rachel shook her head slowly, her facial expression still stony. "I remember reading that about you. You're a wiseass."

"Helps pass the time." He glanced at his watch. "We got two hours to kill before we get to Seville. I've got another joke for you."

"All right," she replied, but he could tell she didn't really want to hear it.

"What's the worst part of office Christmas parties, Rachel?"

"What?"

"Looking for a job the next day."

This time she gave him a half-smile.

That's progress, he thought to himself. "Okay. Here's another: How does a man demonstrate he knows how to plan for the future? He buys two cases of beer instead of one."

Rachel chuckled.

"After a long business trip," Ryan said, "a man returned home and asked his wife, 'Did you miss me?' She replied under her breath, 'So far, with every bullet.'"

Rachel laughed out loud for a long moment and he could tell the woman was enjoying the banter.

"I've got a lot more," he said with a grin. "What do you get if you cross a snowman with a vampire?"

She smiled. "Okay. I give."

"Frostbite."

Rachel laughed again.

After drinking more water, she turned serious again. "Thanks for getting me out of my funk. But you do realize what we do is life and death, don't you? This isn't a joke. I kill people for a living."

"I know, Rachel. There are times I kill people too. The humor, the jokes, is a technique I grew into when I was in combat. Watching some of my buddies die, or lose their limbs ... it's horrible. It makes for some very dark nightmares. The jokes helped me, and a lot of guys in my unit, get through it."

The Agency operative nodded slowly. "Gallows humor. I have CIA friends who're the same way."

They were quiet after that for the rest of the trip, each lost in their own thoughts. He gazed out the windows and wondered what today would bring, and tomorrow. He recalled what he always repeated to himself when starting a new assignment. *Find the bad guys and bring them to justice. And stay alive during the process.* He'd been able to do that during his professional career. He hoped it would be true again.

Chapter 52

Atlanta, Georgia

Erin Welch knew something was wrong the moment she drove her Jaguar up the driveway to the old farmhouse. It was nighttime and lights were on inside the house and on the porch. And the front door was wide open.

Turning off the car, Erin immediately pulled her pistol and glanced around the property. No one was about and there were no vehicles visible. Climbing out, she heard muted sounds coming from the house, as if music was playing inside. Sweeping the gun in front of her, she cautiously approached the porch, went up the steps and peered inside through the open doorway.

Erin smelled it before she could see it – the distinctive stench of death. An experienced agent, she'd been to many crime scenes. The odor was unmistakable. In a crouch and with her weapon leading the way, she stepped inside.

Sprawled on the living room floor was a woman's body laying atop a pool of coagulated blood. Flies swirled around the room and on the corpse. Blood covered the vic's head and torso, and although the face was disfigured by multiple head wounds, the identity of the dead woman was obvious.

Ignoring the sick feeling in her stomach for a moment, Erin quickly scanned the room, then searched the rest of the house and grounds. Finally she returned to Mei Lin's inert body. Careful not to disturb the crime scene, she crouched beside it.

After saying a silent prayer for the Asian woman, she touched Mei Lin's neck. The skin was hard and cold. By the amount of rigor mortis, she estimated the reporter had been murdered at least 24 hours before, since it takes about 12 hours for a corpse to stiffen, and about 48 hours for rigor mortis to fade. Erin studied the victim's wounds. The face was covered with blood, brain matter, and bone fragments. It appeared the cause of death was a GSW, with four rounds penetrating her forehead. By the size of the entry wounds, it looked like a large caliber weapon had been used, probably a .357 Magnum or a 9mm.

Despite her experience in dealing with death, Erin felt a surge of nausea as she gazed at the bloody corpse. Mei Lin had been an innocent. A person who had only been trying to get to the truth. And for that the reporter had paid the ultimate sacrifice.

Turning away from Mei Lin's body, Erin pulled out her cell phone to call it in.

Chapter 53

Flying at 36,000 feet over the Atlantic Ocean

Scorpion settled back on the wide, deeply-upholstered leather seat and drank from his tumbler of bourbon. He was in the cabin of his Gulfstream G650 jet, and as usual he was the only passenger in a plane that could easily accommodate eighteen people. He was glad to be going home.

It was a productive trip, he thought. *Very productive.* World Media Network was now under his control. The plans were moving ahead with no major complications.

He reached down and idly patted his dog's head; the canine had been laying quietly at his feet the whole trip. Drax became instantly alert, its eyes scanning the cabin. Sensing no danger, the dog settled back down.

Yes, thought Scorpion, *it's good to be going home.* The home he was going to now was his favorite, although he owned many, in many different countries. Scorpion even owned a place in the U.S., although he spent little time there. He preferred Europe, the richness of its pageantry and history.

Just then the satellite phone resting on the table in front of him buzzed. Picking it up, he read the screen ID and recognized the caller instantly.

"Vicka," he said into the phone. "It's good to hear from you. I'm on my way home now."

"I figured as much," Vicka replied, her voice syrupy sweet. "I *had* to call you. I had such a *delightful* time during your visit." She laughed girlishly. "Seeing you, holding you, loving you again ... it was *truly* magical."

Scorpion chuckled inwardly at the unattractive woman's silliness. But he had to play along – she was an integral part of accomplishing his objectives. "As did I," he lied. "As I've told you many times, Vicka, you are the woman of my dreams. A true treasure."

"Ohhh," she cooed. "You say the sweetest things...."

He could visualize the woman blushing right about now and smiled. "Every word of it is true, Vicka."

"I love you so much, Hans –"

"Please, Vicka. Don't use my name."

"I'm sorry, dear."

Scorpion took a sip of his bourbon, felt the liquor's mellow burn as it went down his throat.

"I have some excellent news!" she said excitedly. "Something I know you'll love hearing."

He was tired of the woman's nauseatingly syrupy, sentimental mush and hoped her news was related to their operation. "Business related?"

"That's right, Scorpion."

"Is your line encrypted? Mine is here."

"Of course, dear."

"Good. Let's hear it, Vicka."

"Do you remember that pesky reporter the FBI woman was keeping under wraps?"

"Yes, I do. What was her name again?"

"Mei Lin," she continued, her excitement palpable. "Well, the people I hired finally found her. Lin was hiding in a farmhouse outside Atlanta."

"And?"

"Let's just say that the journalist won't be a problem anymore."

"She was eliminated?"

Vicka laughed. "Yes, dear."

"That is great news! You've done well. Very well."

"I knew you'd be happy."

"Very happy, Vicka. Mei Lin was a loose end and you know how I hate loose ends." Scorpion took another sip of the liquor. "I wish I was with you right now," he lied. "Making love to you."

She giggled. "Ohhh, I'd love that."

"Soon. I promise."

"I can't wait!"

"Okay, Vicka. I've got to go now. I have an important business meeting to attend."

"I understand, dear."

They said their goodbyes and he disconnected the call. He rested the phone on the table. Then he pressed a button on the console and he heard a click as the door opened from the plane's back compartment.

His stewardess walked up to him.

"Another drink, sir?" asked the pretty, Nordic blonde in the tasteful blue uniform.

"No. I've had enough." He gave her a cold, hard grin. "Go get comfortable in the bedroom back there. I'll join you in a moment."

"Yes, sir."

Chapter 54

Seville, Spain

The confidential informant lived in the *El Erenal* district of Seville, close to the Guadalquivir River. After having checked into a small inn, J.T. Ryan and Rachel West had driven their SEAT sedan rental there, and were now on the *Paseo de Cristobal Colon*, an avenue that bordered the river.

As they passed the *Plaza de Toros*, the historic bullring with the baroque facade, Rachel said, "It's the next street up ahead. Take a left."

"Got it," Ryan said. Slowing the car, he turned at the light, and spotting a place to park on the street, pulled to the curb and turned off the car.

"How do you want to play this?" he asked.

She stared up at the four-story apartment building, one of many on this street. "It's Saturday. This guy should be home today. We don't want to question him with his family around, so we'll take him back to the inn and do it there."

"And if he doesn't want to go?"

"You're a big, strong guy," she said. "I'm sure you'll be persuasive. And if he balks, I've got my Glock."

"Okay."

They exited the car, went into the building, and after climbing several flights of stairs, knocked on the apartment door.

"Estamos buscando al Senor Garcia," Rachel said to the matronly woman who answered the door. *We're looking for Mr. Garcia.*

"No esta aqui," the woman replied. *He's not here.*

By the woman's nervous attitude, Ryan suspected she was lying. He pushed past the matronly woman and went into the apartment. Hearing the creaking of a window being opened from one of the rooms in the back, the PI pulled his SIG Sauer and sprinted toward it.

A tall, wiry man was climbing out the bedroom window onto the fire escape. Racing over, Ryan grabbed the man by his collar and pulled him inside.

"You're not going anywhere, Garcia," Ryan said in Spanish, pointing the pistol at the man's face.

Garcia raised his palms. "All right! Don't shoot."

Rachel came into the room, her weapon drawn. She took out her Agency cred pack and held it up for Garcia to see. "I'm with the CIA. We're the good guys."

The man scrutinized the open wallet carefully and nodded.

"Why'd you run?" Rachel asked.

"I'm not safe," the man replied. "Not any more."

"What do you mean?"

Garcia shook his head.

Ryan heard Garcia's wife and children crying in the other room. "We can't question him here."

Rachel motioned with her Glock. "Let's go, Garcia. We're taking you back to our hotel."

***

Ryan stared down at the confidential informant, who was sitting on the narrow bed. They were in the PI's room at the inn. Rachel had been trying to get information from the Spaniard for half an hour with no success.

The CIA operative placed her hands on her hips. "C'mon Garcia, you've got to give us something."

"Like I said before, *senorita*. It's not safe."

"You've been a CIA asset for over a year. Cooperate with us now, and the Agency will assign you to another case officer. You'll continue making good money as an informant. I'll guarantee you that."

Garcia looked up at her, fear in his eyes. "Can you keep me safe? Can you keep my family safe?"

"We'll set you up in another city in Spain," Rachel said. "We'll protect you."

The man shook his head forcefully. "You couldn't protect one of your own. If they can kill Cortez, they can kill me too."

"This isn't getting us anywhere," Ryan said, his patience running out.

Rachel reached into her tote bag and pulled out an envelope. Opening it, she took out a thick wad of crisp 100 Euro bills. She riffled the wad of cash in front of the man's face. "This is yours," she said. "And I can have Langley wire me more. You'll be set for a long time, if you talk."

Garcia stared greedily at the money, then after a long moment shook his head again. "No. They'll kill me and my family."

"Is that your final answer?" she said.

"*Sí.*"

A look of resignation crossed her face. "I was hoping it wouldn't come to this." She turned to Ryan. "Looks like we have no choice. We'll have to waterboard him."

Ryan thought about this. Having interrogated people in the past, he knew the technique of waterboarding was effective, but at times it created a situation where the person, so afraid of drowning, would shout out whatever he thought his captors wanted to hear, regardless of its accuracy. The PI remembered something they had learned about Garcia and said, "No. I've got a better idea."

"Okay, Ryan. What?"

"You brought the duct tape?"

She reached into her bag and removed the roll.

Garcia, clearly frightened, jumped off the bed and ran toward the door but Ryan grabbed him from behind in a bear hug and held him tightly. "Duct tape his mouth, Rachel."

She tore off a piece of tape and slapped it across the man's lips. Then she wrapped more tape around his ankles. Ryan pushed the Spaniard to the floor and Rachel bound his hands behind him.

Garcia stared up at them, his eyes wide.

"You want to talk now?" Ryan shouted.

Garcia shook his head.

"Wrong answer."

Rachel turned to the PI. "Now what?"

"You'll see." Ryan grabbed the bedspread off the bed, spread it out on the floor of the hotel room, then dragged Garcia to one end of the quilt. He began rolling the man inside the bedspread like a roll of carpet. He felt the man struggling inside the rolled quilt and he used more duct tape to secure the cloth. Confident Garcia couldn't get loose, Ryan dragged the bundle toward the room's tiny closet and stuffed it inside and closed the door. He could hear Garcia's muffled screams through the closet door.

"Okay. Now what?" Rachel asked.

Ryan glanced at his watch. "Now we wait."

"Sure this will work?"

"You found out Garcia was claustrophobic. I've used this technique before. It should work."

"And if it doesn't, Ryan?"

"Then we do it your way and waterboard him."

The PI kept his eye on the time as he listened to the muffled screams. Eventually the screams turned into hysterical sobs and after another twenty minutes there was silence.

"That should do it," Ryan said. "Help me get him out of there."

They pulled the bundle out of the tiny closet, laid it on the floor and began unrolling the bedspread off of the man. When they were done, Garcia lay on the floor, staring up at them with panic in his eyes.

"Stand back," Ryan said to the CIA operative. "This won't be pretty."

He reached down and tore the tape off the man's mouth. As Ryan expected, Garcia vomited, expelling whatever he'd eaten that day. Then he began coughing uncontrollably.

Ryan waited a few minutes for the man to catch his breath, then said, "You'll talk now?"

"*Si! Si!* I'll talk!"

"That's better, Garcia."

He reached down, pulled the Spaniard off the floor and propped him into a sitting position on the bed. Then Ryan went to the bathroom, filled a cup of water, came back and held the cup to the man's lips.

When the cup was empty, Ryan said, "Tell us what you know about the billionaire we're looking for."

"He goes ... by the name of Scorpion," Garcia said hoarsely. "But that's not ... his real name."

"You're wasting my time, Garcia. We know that already."

"He lives in Spain," the man croaked. "But he's not a Spaniard. He has an odd accent."

Ryan thought about this. It confirmed what Sable, the Atlanta madam had told him. "What kind of accent? Russian?"

"It's possible. I don't know."

"What else? There's got to be more."

Garcia shook his head. "No! That is all I know. I swear!"

"Bullshit." Ryan turned toward the CIA operative. "Help me get this guy back in the closet. This time we'll leave him in there overnight."

"No!" Garcia shouted hoarsely. "Not that!"

Ryan reached over, grabbed the roll of tape and tore off a piece. He was about to slap it across the man's mouth when Garcia yelled, "All right! I know one other thing about Scorpion ..."

"What?"

"He lives in Madrid," Garcia spat out. "Scorpion lives in Madrid."

Chapter 55

Madrid, Spain

Scorpion was in the large study of his palatial estate, sitting on a leather wingchair, sipping 20-year-old bourbon. As he drank, he hummed along to Bach's Brandenburg Concertos, which were playing on the audio system. As usual he was wearing an impeccably tailored charcoal gray suit and matching tie.

His dog was laying next to the chair and he idly rubbed the canine's back as he waited for the woman to arrive.

A moment later the door to the study opened and a very attractive brunette wearing a silk robe stepped inside and closed the door behind her.

"Mariska," Scorpion said, "I'm glad you're here."

The young woman was one of his favorites and he always looked forward to her visits. She was expensive, but always worth it. A man who could afford anything, Scorpion always paid top dollar, and as a result always got the best money could buy.

As Mariska approached him, the Doberman sprang to its feet, growling and baring it's large, sharp teeth. "It's okay, Drax," Scorpion said soothingly to the dog. "No cause for alarm. Sit down and be still." The canine instantly sat back down on its haunches, but the woman still gave the dog a nervous glance.

"Relax, Mariska," the billionaire said. "Drax is harmless." He pointed to her robe.

Mariska pulled the sash and she shrugged off the silk bathrobe, revealing her shapely nude body. She stepped forward, a sly smile on her lips. "Did you miss me?"

The billionaire traced his hand over the woman's breasts. "You're one of my favorites, Mariska." Then he slid his hand to her hip and tugged her down to her knees in front of him.

Mariska tucked her long hair behind her ears, reached over and unbuckled his pants and unzipped him.

"Be careful with the suit," he said, "I don't want it getting soiled."

She nodded, then leaned forward and, opening her mouth, took him in.

Scorpion let out a low moan as her lips and tongue caressed him sensuously. He leaned back on the armchair and took a sip of bourbon. As he listened to the Bach concerto on the sound system, he watched excitedly as the woman increased her tempo. *There's nothing like having a woman who really enjoys her work*, he thought.

After another minute of this, he realized he was getting close. "Slow down," he said with a groan, placing a hand on her bobbing head. "I'm in no hurry."

Mariska's dark, sultry eyes met his and she slowed her rhythmic movements.

"That's better, Mariska."

Just then there was a knock at the door.

"Damn it!" Scorpion groused loudly. "What is it?"

He heard a muffled voice from outside the room. "It's Dietrich. I need to speak with you."

"Not now!"

"Yes, sir."

Mariska, her mouth full and still hard at work, glanced up at Scorpion questioningly. He caressed her cheek. "Go ahead. Take your time. Like I said, I'm in no hurry."

The young woman continued and Scorpion eased back on the armchair once again, enjoying the sensation of pleasure and pain as it increased to a crescendo.

Finally, when he couldn't postpone it any longer, he reached out with both hands, gripped her head forcefully and pulled it forward as far as it would go. Then he exploded in one long delicious rush.

A moment later Mariska leaned back, and careful not to stain his suit, zipped his pants and buckled them. With a satisfied smile she got up from the kneeling position and put on her silk robe.

"You like?" she said.

"Very much."

"Same time next week?"

"Of course, Mariska."

"You have something for me?"

Scorpion reached over to the table next to him and removed a thick envelope from a drawer. Handing her the package full of cash, he said, "I put something extra in there for you this week. I told you before. You're one of my favorites."

She kissed the envelope and was about to leave the room when he told her, "Send in Dietrich."

Scorpion finished his glass of bourbon and refilled it from the bottle of on the table. Taking a sip, he replayed in his mind the pleasurable sexual interlude. He patted his dog's back as he continued to listen to the music. The canine had remained quiet but vigilant during Mariska's visit, never taking its eyes off of the woman.

A large, muscular man with very short, black hair came into the study and closed the door behind him. He was wearing a black turtleneck, black slacks, and black loafers; holstered on his hip was a Desert Eagle pistol.

Scorpion gave the man a hard stare. "You know I don't like to be interrupted when I have girls over."

"I'm sorry," Dietrich replied. "It couldn't be helped." He had been Scorpion's head of security for many years and was well aware of this. But he also knew his boss was even more obsessed about security than his constant flow of high-end prostitutes.

"So what's so important, damn it?"

"Sir, I just learned something disturbing. Something that concerns O.O.V."

Suddenly alarmed, Scorpion forgot all about the sex. "What is it?"

"Do you remember the CIA operative, a man by the name of Cortez who was asking questions about you?"

"Of course. But you eliminated that problem."

"Correct, sir. But there's more of them nosing around."

"What the hell?" Who?"

"From what my sources tell me, sir, it's a woman agent named Rachel West and that private investigator from Atlanta, Ryan."

Scorpion gulped down the rest of his drink. "Ryan! That bastard again. He got away from us before." He grit his teeth, seething with anger. "Find them. Kill them!"

Chapter 56

Atlanta, Georgia

Erin Welch was in her office at the FBI building when she noticed her assistant poke his head around the door.

"There's a woman in the lobby," he said with an amused look. "Needs to talk to you."

"I don't have any appointments set up."

"She doesn't have one, Erin. Her name's Sable."

"Sable what?"

Her assistant smiled. "Just Sable. Said she had met with Ryan a while back and has more info for him. She told me she can't track him down."

Erin nodded. "Yeah. He's out of the country. What's with the smile?"

"You'll see when you meet her, Erin."

"Okay. Her name sounds familiar and I remember Ryan telling me something about her. Bring her up, but make sure she goes through the security checkpoint first."

"Roger that."

Five minutes later a striking, light-skinned African-American woman in her mid-forties elegantly strode in her office. Tall and slender with close-cropped, salt-and-pepper hair, she wore a stylish silk dress, gloves, pricey six-inch heels, and carried a Coach purse. Her clothes and accessories all matched in a sophisticated dove gray color. Erin had been in law-enforcement for years and could spot certain professions by their demeanor. Her assistant had also recognized it. The classy way the woman moved her hips in the elegant dress, the heavy-musk perfume, and her jewelry, all said call-girl. But very high-end.

"Sable," the woman said in a sultry, silky voice, taking off one of her gloves and extending her hand.

They shook and Erin said, "Have a seat."

The woman languidly slid on the chair and crossed her legs. "Mind if I smoke?" she asked.

"Sorry, that's not allowed in this building."

Sable nodded.

"Your name sounds familiar, Sable. In fact I remember now – J.T. Ryan got a lead from you on one of the cases we're working."

The woman took off her other glove and placed them on her lap. "That's right, Ms. Welch. He was looking for a European man. A man that I've had contact with in my business."

Erin recalled the details. "You run a call-girl ring here in Atlanta."

"I do *not*," Sable said defensively. "I arrange dinner dates between two consenting adults."

Erin rolled her eyes. "I'm sure. Now, what is it you want?"

"I've been trying to get a hold of J.T., with no luck. I have additional information about the man he was looking for."

"Okay, let's hear it, Sable."

"Not so fast. There's something I need in return."

"Like what?"

"I'm in a bit of a jam," Sable said, "with APD. I need your help to make it go away. In return I'll tell you what I know about Scorpion."

Erin leaned forward in her chair. "What kind of trouble are you in with the Atlanta cops?"

The woman waved a dismissive hand in the air. "It's a bullshit charge. Solicitation. You know the drill. There's a new lieutenant on the Vice squad who's been riding my ass, wanting to make a name for himself by bringing me down."

"I'm sure you have a high-paid attorney on your payroll; it can't be that much of a bullshit charge or he would have already been able to take care of it."

Sable waved her hand again. "Whatever. Anyway, I figure you, as the Director of this office, can make this go away."

Erin thought about this a moment. The search for Scorpion was hampered because they knew so little about him. Any lead would be useful. "All right. I'll intercede on your behalf. But only if the lead is good."

"Trust me, honey, it's good."

"Okay. Let's hear it."

Sable lowered her voice. "When I met J.T., I didn't remember at the time one important detail about this wealthy European. Scorpion always had a dog with him. A large guard dog. And he always kept the animal at his side, even when he was having sex with my girls. They thought it was weird, but hey, I run into weird every day in my business."

"I bet," Erin said. "What else can you tell me?"

"The dog had a name. Scorpion called it Drax."

Chapter 57

The White House
Washington, D.C.

Vicka Stark disconnected the call and replaced the receiver, a sick feeling settling in the pit of her stomach. *After all of our hard work*, she thought, *all of the progress we've made, and now this fucking thing happens.*

Vicka took a few minutes to compose herself, then pushed her chair away from her desk and rose. *I'm not a fucking quitter*, she reminded herself. *Never have been and never will be.*

Going to the wall cabinet in her sparsely furnished office, she unlocked it and scanned the stacks of neatly stored three-ring binders. Picking one, she placed it under one arm and relocked the cabinet. Then she marched out of her office and made her way toward the Oval Office.

As usual, two Secret Service agents were posted there, flanking the door to the Oval Office. And as usual, the agents simply nodded when they saw her approach. They were used to the president's Chief of Staff coming and going as she pleased.

Not bothering to knock, Vicka stepped inside the large, oval shaped room and closed the door behind her.

Seated in front of Resolute, the president's historic wooden desk were the Secretary of State and the Secretary of Defense. The two men were in a somewhat heated conversation with the president, who was behind the desk, leaning back in his high-backed executive chair.

President Ackerman looked up at her. "Vicka, I didn't know we had a meeting planned."

"We didn't, Mr. President," she said. "Something important has come up." She turned to the other two men in the room. "You'll have to excuse us, gentlemen. I need to speak privately with the president."

"But we're dealing with the crisis in Saudi Arabia," the Secretary of State said. "Our embassy there has been attacked and ransacked."

Vicka shook her head. "That'll have to wait. As I said, I have to speak in private with President Ackerman."

With aggravated looks on their faces, the secretaries gathered their papers and exited the room.

"You look worried," Ackerman said as he leaned forward in his chair. "What's wrong?"

Vicka glanced out the tall windows of the well-known office. It was a stormy day in Washington with dark, ominous clouds hanging low over the city. The foul weather matched her mood. She quickly thought through the best way to begin the conversation. Then realized there was no way to sugar coat it.

"Mr. President, I just got off the phone with my operations manager at O.O.V."

"And?"

"We've had a setback, sir."

"What kind of a setback?"

"A major one, Mr. President."

A stern expression crossed his face. "But you've told me things were going so well."

"They were, sir. But as you noted yourself, your poll numbers have been declining. That appears to have emboldened several news organizations. A few of the networks have refused to follow our narratives. They're broadcasting news stories that show the true poll numbers, and they have even dared to question some of your policies."

Ackerman's mouth dropped as a shocked expression settled on his features. "They went off script?"

"Yes, Mr. President."

"But that hasn't happened in quite some time, except at a few of the cable news outlets."

"Yes, sir, that's true."

He pointed to one of the wingback chairs that fronted his desk. "Please sit. You're making me nervous standing there."

"I prefer to stand," she replied, looking down at the man. She was too wired to sit.

Ackerman shrugged. "Okay, stand if you must. Now tell me how the hell are we going to deal with this? O.O.V. was working well. I wanted to roll out more of my signature policies during my second term. Policies that will cement my legacy and continue to transform the country into my vision for America."

"Of course, Mr. President. That's always been my goal as well. Your vision is my vision."

"So how do we fix this?" he said, his voice pleading, his eyes clouded with concern. "If other news outlets begin to reject our narratives, then my vision, my policies, could crumble."

"I won't let that happen, sir." She placed the thick three-ring binder she had brought with her on his desk. "I hoped it wouldn't come to this. But we have no choice. We must take action to keep O.O.V. on track."

Vicka pointed to the binder. "As you know, I'm a planner. Always have been. During your administration, I've prepared contingency plans on many issues. In there is the plan that will solve our current problem."

Ackerman picked up the document and quickly read through the first few pages. Then he looked up at her. "This is kind of drastic, don't you think?"

"I'm afraid, sir, that we have no choice. Drastic times call for drastic measures."

He rubbed his jaw slowly, deep in thought. After a moment, he nodded. "When would I give this speech?"

"I need to work out the details. I'll let you know, Mr. President."

"And the speech itself?"

"I've already written it, sir. It's in the back of that document."

"All right. And the setting?"

"It'll be a national address to the country. All of the TV networks will cover it during prime time. You'll give it here, in the Oval Office. That will show the country the importance of the speech."

Ackerman nodded again and he appeared calmer, more self-assured. "I knew I could count on you, Vicka."

"Thank you, sir."

"We speak with one voice."

"Yes, Mr. President, we speak with one voice."

Chapter 58

Toledo, Spain

After gassing up the rental car, J.T. Ryan and Rachel West got back in the sedan, this time with Rachel behind the wheel. They were headed north on the A4 highway toward Madrid. It had been a long, monotonous drive so far, past rural landscape of rolling hills and olive groves. Traffic had been light the whole way. Ryan was grateful for that, making it easier to spot someone following them.

"While you were pumping gas," Rachel said, "I called Alex at Langley. Gave him the new lead we got about Scorpion. Knowing the man has a dog named Drax might help us locate him. The Agency has sophisticated surveillance techniques. With two names to correlate, it'll be easier to track him down."

Ryan rubbed his jaw. "I hope so. We don't have much else, except that the man lives in Madrid."

"True. Hard to believe this guy is such a ghost. Specially these days where everything we do leaves a paper or digital trail."

"My guess is," Ryan said, "that Scorpion does everything through third parties: cut-outs and dummy corporations. If you're wealthy enough it can be done."

Rachel glanced at him, then back toward the road. "You're right. Money buys lots of things, including privacy."

They were quiet for the next half hour, each lost in their own thoughts.

Ryan, his eyes darting between his outside mirror, the rural landscape and the highway in front of them, spotted a dark vehicle behind them moving at high speed. "You've got a black SUV on your six. Closing fast."

Inclining her head, Rachel saw it on the rearview right away. "Got it. Looks like a Range Rover."

Ryan reached behind his back and pulled his SIG Sauer from his waistband.

"It may be nothing," he said, "but speed up if he tries to overtake us." Not taking any chances, he racked the slide on the pistol. His eyes were glued to the black SUV, which was now only three car lengths behind.

Rachel gripped the wheel tightly and buried the accelerator, but the Range Rover easily kept up and closed the distance, the rental car's anemic engine no match for the powerful SUV.

Turning around in his seat, Ryan faced backwards, aiming the pistol in that direction. His pulse quickened.

It all happened in a split second – the PI saw the muzzle flashes from the black SUV, heard the roar of the gunfire, and felt shards of glass pelt him as the back windshield imploded.

Ryan fired off three rounds at the Range Rover, but the bullets glanced off the vehicle. Clearly it was armored. Out of the corner of his eye he saw Rachel's head sag forward, her grip on the steering wheel slipping. He knew one of the attacker's bullets must have hit her, but he couldn't deal with that now. Instead he had to focus on the SUV.

Ryan squeezed the trigger again, this time blindly as the car began to swerve toward the concrete median separating the highway.

Grabbing the wheel with one hand from the unconscious CIA operative, he steered the car away from the median and toward the shoulder.

But Rachel's foot was jammed on the accelerator, and instead of slowing down, the sedan sped up toward the tree line that bordered the shoulder.

His heart racing, he realized he had no choice but to drop the gun.

Using both hands now, he grabbed the wheel, and using his leg dislodged her right foot off the gas pedal. He jammed on the brakes, then felt the rental car shudder, as the Range Rover struck it from behind, sending the much smaller vehicle spinning out of control.

With the steering wheel bucking wildly, he saw a blur of motion as the rental spun 360 degrees, swerved off the road, and crashed front first into a row of trees.

Dizzy and disoriented, Ryan picked up and pocketed the gun, yanked open his door, and using both hands grabbed Rachel's inert body out of the car.

Her forehead was bleeding and she was unconscious, but she had a pulse. Resting her body on the ground, he pulled his pistol, and using the car as a shield, peered through the cracked windows out to the road.

The black Range Rover had come to a stop nearby and its armed occupants exited with their guns drawn.

Aiming, the PI fired off three quick rounds. One of the men groaned and clutched his leg, as the others crouched behind the SUV and fired back, their rounds thudding into the rental's bodywork.

Ryan returned fire, this time emptying the magazine. But the furious volley from the other side continued, bullets shattering what was left of the sedan's windows, the glass shards raining down on him. Searching frantically in his pockets, he found the spare clip, and ejecting the spent magazine, slammed in the fresh one.

Feeling something touch him, he turned and saw Rachel staring up at him. Her eyes were glassy and her face pale. Blood trickled from her forehead.

"How many?" she whispered in a weak voice.

"Four men."

The CIA operative slowly reached for her gun and drew it, but her grip was weak and the pistol fell to the ground. Her hand reached for it again, but her eyes rolled white and her lids closed.

More gunfire erupted from behind him, the rounds crunching metal, glass, and plastic as they struck the sedan. With his heart pounding in his chest, he heard some of the bullets whiz overhead and also blow out the car's tires.

Peering around the front bumper, Ryan spotted one man sprinting toward the sedan and he squeezed the trigger in quick succession. The gunman flinched, cursed, and staggered to the ground.

Ryan couldn't see the others, but they were obviously closer to his position because the sound of their gunfire was louder. Reaching over the hood of the car with one hand, he fired off five more rounds. But the return fire continued and with his adrenaline pumping, he knew it was just a matter of time before their shots hit their mark.

Then in the distance he heard the faint wail of sirens.

With a sigh of relief, he peered over the hood of the car, aimed and fired the pistol. But the men were already climbing back into the Range Rover.

The SUV sped away as his rounds created star-shaped cracks on the back windshield; but the glass, obviously bullet-resistant, didn't implode.

Chapter 59

Atlanta, Georgia

Erin Welch felt the pounding of a migraine. It was past ten in the evening and she was still at her office in the FBI building, staring at her laptop screen.

It had been a long day, as she juggled a slew of new cases that had come into the field office during the last week. But she had set those aside hours ago, her focus now on the video clip she was watching.

Erin had not been able to shake off the image of the dead Mei Lin. The thought of her limp, lifeless body laying in a pool of blood haunted her and she was determined to find the killer.

Per FBI protocol, the safe house had CCTV surveillance cameras. The concealed one on the porch above the front door of the farmhouse had captured the image of the assassin as he exited the power company van, walked up the steps, and knocked on the door. Unfortunately the man was wearing a ball cap pulled low over his eyes, and it was difficult to make out his facial features.

Erin ran the security camera footage once again and then replayed it several times after that. She had viewed it dozens of times during the last few hours. The assassin was a non-descript man, of average build and height. Nothing about him stood out.

She rubbed her temple as she adjusted the clip to super-slow-mode during the one sequence when the killer briefly glanced up and his face was partially visible. But the porch lighting was inadequate so his facial features were still obscured.

With a sinking feeling Erin realized there was no way she would be able to identify him by watching the tape. She also knew there was another way to identify him, but that would take sophisticated facial recognition software.

The kind of software they had at the FBI's Operational Technology Division based in Quantico, Virginia. But since she wasn't even supposed to be working on this case, that avenue was closed.

Erin kept massaging her temples as her migraine grew.

Chapter 60

Madrid, Spain

Reclining in the hotel room's armchair, J.T. Ryan kept dozing off as he watched over Rachel West, who was asleep on the bed. On the table next to him was his SIG Sauer pistol, well within arm's reach. And Rachel's Glock was tucked under his waistband behind his lower back. As Ryan kept watch over the operative, he glanced alternately at the room's balcony and the door, half expecting another attack.

It had been a long day and then a long night after the shootout with the gunmen. He'd been questioned extensively by the Spanish police, who fortunately had made a well-timed arrival. Luckily the cops had been impressed with Rachel's credentials. After they called the CIA offices for confirmation, they arranged to have her taken to the nearest hospital for treatment of her injuries. After the clinic discharged her, Ryan had brought her here, a hotel that overlooked Madrid's *Parque del Retiro*.

Ryan picked up the SIG, got up and, walking to the glass slider, opened it and stepped out on the balcony. The sun was rising, casting an orange glow over the tree-covered park below. It was a cool, windy day and in the distance he saw the water rippling on the nature preserve's large lake. Early morning joggers traversed the park's numerous trails.

Satisfied there was no danger lurking, he want back inside. Resting the gun on the table, he moistened a small towel in the bathroom and, coming back in the room, sat next to her and applied the towel to her forehead.

She was pale and several bandages covered her face, but she had been lucky, he knew. One of the gunmen's rounds had grazed her forehead and given her a concussion, but according to the doctor at the clinic, she had suffered no permanent damage.

Rachel's eyelids fluttered open. She stared at him with a confused look.

"Hi Rachel. How're you feeling?"

She reached under the sheet covering her. "Where's my gun, Ryan?"

"Relax. It's right here," he said, pulling it from behind his back and placing it on the table.

At the sight of the weapon, Rachel seemed to relax. "Where are we?"

"Madrid."

"I remember driving," she said, "and the black SUV chasing us, and gunfire, the car spinning out of control, then nothing ...."

"You got lucky. One of their rounds grazed you, and you got bruised in the crash. But the doc said you're okay. All you need is rest."

She nodded. "And the gunmen?"

"I wounded two of them."

"Who were they?"

"Hard to tell, Rachel. But I'm sure they're connected to Scorpion."

With a hand she took the towel off her forehead, then felt the bandages on her face. "After I got knocked out, how'd you manage to get away from them."

"I'd love to say it was all skill," he replied with a grin, "but it was luck too. I held them off until the Spanish police arrived."

She pulled down the sheet covering her and stared quizzically at what she was wearing, a loose T-shirt and baggy sweatpants. "I wasn't dressed in this. Okay, Ryan, how'd I end up in this?"

"The doctor told me to make you comfortable. I changed you into that." He smiled. "If it's any consolation, I tried not to look."

"Yeah, I bet," she replied, her voice dripping with sarcasm.

"Scout's Honor," he said with a sheepish grin.

"Yeah, I remember. It's one of your 'Ryan's Rules'. Treat all women with respect." After a moment, she returned the smile. "I guess I should thank you."

"For what?"

"Saving my life."

"Seems like we're even now, Rachel. Since you saved mine in Colombia."

She touched the bandages on her face again. "I want payback for this." She sat up suddenly on the bed and picked up her Glock. "Let's go find those bastards."

"Not so fast, young lady. The doc said bed rest for a couple of days."

"Bullshit, Ryan. I'm ready now."

Then her face flinched in pain, her blue eyes clouded over, and she sagged back on the bed. She was asleep a minute later.

Chapter 61

The White House
Washington, D.C.

Vicka Stark stood off to one side and watched as the camera crew scurried around the Oval Office, making final adjustments on their equipment and adjusting the lighting. She scrutinized their every move, making sure all of the details for the prime time address were as she had planned.

Vicka glanced at her watch – ten minutes to go.

President Ackerman sat behind his impressive wooden desk, looking a bit nervous under the bright TV lights. Vicka had picked out the dark gray suit he was wearing, the starched light-blue shirt, the red print tie, and even the lapel pin of the American flag. The pin was something he detested wearing, but she had insisted and in the end he'd relied on her advice. A long row of American flags were positioned behind the president, something else the Chief of Staff had ordered for the occasion.

The speech tonight was being broadcast by all of the national TV networks and all of the cable news stations. Vicka had cajoled each of them into showing it during prime time, convincing them it was a major speech, a speech all of the American people needed to hear.

Vicka noticed beads of sweat forming on President Ackerman's forehead and she signaled to the makeup woman, who immediately approached him, wiped his brow and retouched the cosmetics.

She smiled at Ackerman to calm him down, trying to project a sense of confidence she herself didn't feel. Although he'd rehearsed the speech for days and she knew he was ready, she was still tense. It was an important address, one that would seal his legacy for the rest of his term as president and beyond. She wanted it to go without a hitch.

She glanced at her watch again – less than 30 seconds to go.

As the exact time approached, the TV news director counted down the seconds with his fingers. The camera signal lights changed from *Standby* to *On* and the TV lens zoomed from a wide angle of the Oval Office to a close-up of the president sitting behind his desk.

The nervous look on President Ackerman's face instantly disappeared as he stared directly and confidently at the camera.

Vicka breathed a sigh of relief – Ackerman, the polished politician, her politician, was back.

"Good evening," President Ackerman said in a somber voice. "I've asked to speak to you tonight because a new national threat is facing our country." He steepled his hands on the desk. "A grave threat, one that, left unchecked, could bring down this great democracy of ours."

"My fellow Americans," the president continued, his tone reassuring but also tinged with urgency, "I am deeply concerned that recently several news organizations have broadcast lies about my administration. Lies and distortions that are aiding and abetting our enemies abroad and endangering the security of the United States." His brows furrowed and his jaw clenched. "I will not let that stand," he stated forcefully. "As your commander in chief, I will not allow our great country to be torn down by the spreading of false rumors, innuendos, distortions, and outright lies."

Per Vicka's prior instructions, President Ackerman paused here a moment, then he continued in a grave, somber voice, "I have instructed the Attorney General to immediately launch investigations into these rogue news outlets that are spreading false rumors and blatant lies. As I said earlier, I will not allow our great nation, a nation that has endured for close to 250 years, to be destroyed by the falsehoods of a few news organizations. Organizations whose recent activities could be classified as criminal, and in fact, could be considered treasonous."

He paused again as Vicka had scripted, to give the audience a moment to let his words sink in.

Ackerman pointed a stern finger at the camera for emphasis. "I know some of you may think this is overstepping my reach, and that my actions somehow infringe on the First Amendment to the Constitution. But this could not be further from the truth. Despite what some misguided congressional leaders say about me, my only goal as president is to be a staunch defender of the Constitution."

He placed his hands flat on the desk in front of him. "I want what all Americans want – a strong country, a law-abiding country, a country built on equality and justice. I *will* ferret out these traitors, these enemies of the state. And I will do it in a fair way, a just way, and a legal way."

Ackerman leaned forward in his executive chair as Vicka had coached and delivered his closing remarks in a reassuring, confident voice. "My fellow Americans, as we proceed with this new chapter in the life of this great country of ours, I want you to know that your well being and your safety are my utmost concern. Good night, and God Bless America."

Chapter 62

Madrid, Spain

J.T. Ryan had just gotten up, shaved, showered, and threw on fresh clothes when he heard a knock at his hotel room door.

Picking up his pistol, he peered through the peephole. Ryan opened the door and Rachel West stepped inside. He closed the door behind her.

"You're looking a lot healthier," he said to the CIA operative, who was carrying a large duffel bag over one shoulder.

"Two days of sleep will do that, Ryan."

He studied her appearance. Despite the small bandage on her forehead, she looked as fit and attractive as ever. Her long blonde hair was pulled back in a ponytail and the cloudiness was gone from her blue eyes. Rachel was wearing dark gray jeans, a blue long-sleeve denim shirt, and a black leather jacket.

"Alex called me from Langley," she said. "They're still working on pinning down Scorpion's location. We should have an answer soon."

Ryan pointed to the bag she was carrying. "What's in there?"

"Some items that will come in handy. My CIA contact in Madrid dropped them off at my hotel room this morning." She opened the duffel and pulled out a suppressed MP-5, short-barrel machine pistol and handed it to him. "I already have one of these. This one's for you."

Ryan was very used to this type of sub-machinegun – it was the weapon of choice for special operators like the SEALs and Delta.

Then she took out a carton filled with grenades – the explosive type, the incendiary kind, and flash-bangs. Also in the duffel were two light-weight Kevlar vests, night-vision goggles, and a pair of binoculars.

"Very nice," he said, admiring the armaments.

Lastly she removed a small, spider-shaped device. It was constructed of black metal and about the size of a cell phone. A tiny camera was attached to the device.

Ryan nodded approvingly. "An aerial drone. I like it. Should come in handy for surveillance. You CIA types are well prepared."

Rachel grinned. "Might as well put American tax dollars to work."

Her cell phone rang and she pulled it out from a pocket. She listened to the caller for a long moment and her smile faded. With a grimace she disconnected the call and put the phone away. "That was Alex. They've hit a technical snag on tracking Scorpion's whereabouts. Looks like it'll take Langley another day or so to come up with it."

"Damn," Ryan replied. "I want to get started now."

"This really sucks," she groused. "I want to find that bastard and get payback."

"Let's get going anyway. We'll start nosing around Madrid, see what we can come up with."

Rachel shook head forcefully. "No way. My guess is Scorpion has a lot of contacts here. If we tip our hand too soon, he'll find out. It'll spook him and he'll vanish in the wind. Remember, he located us pretty quickly after we interrogated Garcia in Seville."

Ryan mulled this over a minute and realized the Agency woman was right. "Okay. I agree. So what do we do for the next day?"

She took off her jacket, slung it over a chair and began pacing the hotel room. She was silent as she strode back and forth like a caged tiger. Then she stopped pacing and faced him. "I've been cooped up, sleeping on-and-off for two days. Now my brain's wired. There's only one thing that's going to calm my nerves."

"What's that, Rachel?"

She reached into the duffel again and removed a bottle of Absolut vodka and held it up. "Ever do vodka shooters?"

He glanced at his watch. It was nine a.m. "Kind of early for a drink, isn't it?"

"You're such a Boy Scout, Ryan."

She walked toward the small kitchenette in the room, took out two glasses from a cabinet and set them on the table. After filling the glasses, she picked one up and slugged it back. She refilled it, sat at one of the chairs by the table, and motioned him over. "Come on. Have a drink. It won't kill you."

Ryan strode over, sat across from her, picked up the other glass and took a sip of the vodka.

She pointed to the bottle of Absolut. "Ever do vodka shooters?"

"I'm more of a beer man, myself."

"Yeah, I know," she replied with a smile. "Coors, right?"

"That's right." He took another sip, the strong liquor pleasantly burning down his throat.

"I was working a case a couple of years ago in Europe," she said. "In Sweden and Finland. I had some down time and I started enjoying shooters to kill the time."

"You're away from home a lot. Ever get lonely?"

She drained her glass, refilled it and drank again. "All the fucking time."

"Got anybody back home?"

She shook her head and slugged back the drink. "Used to. He was a good guy. A great guy, in fact. I thought he was the one. Mr. Right. I loved him and he loved me."

"What happened?"

Rachel's brows furrowed as she refilled the glass and gulped down more vodka. "It was great for a long time, then I realized he wanted a stay-at-home wife. Someone to have babies with. Someone to raise them, and shuttle them around to and from soccer practice."

"Living in a perfect, two-story colonial with the white picket fence?"

Rachel grimaced. "The whole nine yards. Can you see me driving a minivan?"

"No. You don't strike me as the type. Was this guy in the business?"

She drained her glass, refilled it and took a long pull. Then she laughed.

"The covert ops business?" she replied, slurring her words. "Hell, no. Far from it. He was in finance. High-powered job. Made tons of money."

She stared off in the distance. "Looking back on it, he probably imagined me as his trophy wife, throwing parties for his rich banker friends in our exclusive estate in a super-safe gated community."

Rachel drank more vodka, poured another glassful and took a long swallow.

"Take it easy," he said, motioning to the bottle of liquor.

Rachel's eyes were red-rimmed now and she grinned. "You really *are* a Boy Scout. You know that?"

Still smiling, she reached over and covered his hand with hers. "I like you, Ryan. I like you a lot."

"Is that the vodka talking?"

Rachel's blue eyes sparkled. "Maybe. A little. But that's not all of it, that's for damn sure. Like I said, I like you. A lot." She traced her fingers over the back of his hand. "I want you, Ryan."

Her touch felt warm and sensuous, and the sexual tension between them was palpable. She was a very beautiful woman, one of the most attractive he'd ever met. His adrenaline quickened and he was having trouble maintaining his cool. "Don't start something you'll regret later."

Lust glittered in her blue eyes. "Oh, believe me, I'm not going to regret it." Her fingers traced his arm. "Anyway, you did save my life the other day."

"You saved mine in Colombia. Remember?"

She smiled suggestively. "I remember. But this is different."

"How so?"

"Because I say it is, Ryan. Because I want it to be."

He took a sip of vodka and chuckled. "Women are hard to figure out, you know that?"

"Men too. You, for instance. I've been coming on to you for the last five minutes, Ryan. Most guys by now would have already ripped off my clothes, thrown me on the bed and fucked my eyeballs out. But not you, Ryan. Is this another one of your rules? Treat women with respect? Sometimes women want to fuck just as much as men do."

His breathing was labored from his desire. "I don't want to take advantage of you while you're drinking."

Rachel downed the rest of her drink in one gulp. She rose, unclipped her ponytail, and walked around the table and stood in front of him. "I'm not drunk. Far from it. I just know I want you."

Ryan looked up at her beautiful sculpted face, her piercing blue eyes, her mane of golden hair which cascaded past her shoulders. Her sensuous curves were accentuated by her form-fitting denim shirt.

"You really surprise me, Ryan. We've been working on this case together for over a week and you have yet to make a move on me."

"We're on a job. I thought you'd appreciate professionalism."

"Don't get me wrong. I do appreciate it," she replied. "It's a welcome change from the sleazy bastards I run into all the time. But you need to cut loose every once in a while."

She caressed his cheek with her palm. Her skin felt soft and warm and sensual. He knew she was going to be extremely difficult to resist, and deep down he didn't want to.

"I have someone at home, Rachel."

"Do you really? You said yourself you had broken up."

Ryan shrugged, his thoughts conflicted from his love for Lauren and their ugly breakup. He kept staring up at Rachel's vivid blue eyes, seeing the ardent yearning there. The air in the room was charged with sexual electricity.

"I like you, Ryan. And that's rare. Very rare. I've been with only a few men in my whole life. I like you a lot. You remind me of a young Tom Selleck, mixed with Ryan Reynolds and Rambo, all rolled into one. I even like your jokes, lame as they are. You make me laugh, something I rarely do."

Ryan watched as Rachel slowly began to unbutton her denim shirt. Her cleavage and her black bra were clearly visible by the time she had unfastened all of the buttons. His sexual excitement reached a fever pitch and he had trouble keeping his hands off of her.

"Don't start something you'll regret later, Rachel."

She smiled and licked her lips. "I'm not going to regret it." She reached down and placed her palm on his pants leg, then slowly slid her hand toward his groin.

Blinded with lust, he bolted up from the chair and engulfed her with his muscular arms. He kissed her hard on the mouth. She kissed back, hungrily, greedily, as they tumbled to the carpeted floor, eager to tear off each other's clothes.

Chapter 63

Langley, Virginia

Alex Miller stared at his computer, studying the satellite image displayed on the screen. It was an overhead photo of a very large estate sitting on a sprawling, wooded property not far from Madrid.

Miller was in his office at the Factory, the CIA's annex building. Using sophisticated telephone tracking software, his tech people had finally been able to intercept conversations which referenced two names: Scorpion and Drax. The conversations had taken place at the map coordinates of the estate. All it took from that point was to photograph the location using one of the Agency's satellites.

Miller nodded with satisfaction.

Picking up his encrypted cell phone, he placed a call.

Chapter 64

Hoover Building, FBI Headquarters
Washington, D.C.

"Guess you're wondering why I called you up here," FBI Director Tucker said as he came into the conference room and closed the door behind him.

Erin Welch, the only other person in the room, rose from her chair. "Yes, sir. Last time I was here, you almost fired me."

"Have a seat," the man said as they shook hands. He sat across from her and tented his fingers on the conference table.

Erin's eyes narrowed, expecting the worst. "As you requested, Director, I've stopped investigating the case of the murdered journalists." That statement was technically true. She personally was not working it, although she'd sent Ryan to Spain, something she hoped Tucker hadn't learned.

The FBI Director leaned forward. "I didn't bring you here to chew you out."

Erin breathed a sigh of relief. "That's good to know."

Tucker's forehead furrowed. "You saw President Ackerman's address to the nation a few days ago?"

"Of course, Director. I think most Americans did."

"What did you think of it?"

Erin weighed the question. She had been shocked by what the president was planning. But she also knew she was on thin ice – if she told the director what she really thought, her highly-paid position as ADIC could vanish and she might be filing for unemployment insurance. Still, it was imperative that she stuck to the truth and to her principles.

"May I be frank, Director?"

"Of course."

"Sir, what the president wants to do shreds the First Amendment of the Constitution. Trying to silence the press by threatening to prosecute news networks will have a chilling effect on freedom of speech."

Tucker said nothing for a long moment as he rubbed his jaw. "I agree with you, Welch."

"You do? Frankly, sir, after our last meeting, I would not have expected it."

The FBI Director nodded. "That's understandable. But what the president wants to do now crosses the line. This time the administration has gone too far."

"I'm very glad to hear that, Director. Does that mean I have your full support to reopen the investigation?"

Tucker's jaw clenched and his eyes looked guarded. "Yes and no."

"With all due respect, sir, what the hell does that mean?"

"It means I'm giving you the green light to investigate. But you have to keep it under the radar. I can't be involved, or have any knowledge of what you're doing. Is that clear, Welch?"

"Of course. Can I ask why?"

"Powerful people in Washington are trying to squash this investigation."

"Do you know who they are, sir?"

"I have my suspicions."

Erin mulled this over a moment. "When I reopen this case, I may find a link back to those powerful people. What then, Director?"

"Bring me the evidence, Welch. Then I'll have all the ammunition I need to nail those bastards."

That was exactly what Erin wanted to hear.

Chapter 65

FBI's Operational Technology Division
Quantico, Virginia

Instead of immediately flying back to Atlanta, Erin Welch rented a car and drove directly to the Bureau's technical and forensics center in Quantico. After clearing security, Erin was shown to the office of Henry Chang, one of the center's technical managers and a long-time acquaintance of hers.

The soft-spoken Asian man greeted her warmly. "Erin, it's great to see you. It's been a while."

They shook hands and she sat across from him as he took a seat behind his desk.

"Too long, Henry. Since I became ADIC of the Atlanta Field Office, I don't get to Quantico as much as I'd like."

Chang pushed his eyeglasses up the bridge of his nose. "So. You must be here on something important."

"Yes, it is."

Erin pulled a flash drive from a pocket and placed it on his desk. "There's a video clip in there from a CCTV security camera. I need you to run it through your facial recognition programs and tell me the identity of the man in the video."

Chang picked up the flash drive and smiled. "They have something called FedEx now. It would have saved you the trip."

Under normal circumstances, Erin would have chuckled at his joke. Instead she shook her head. "This case is too sensitive. As a personal favor, I'm asking you to keep this between you and me."

"I understand. Under what case number should I log it in?"

"No case number, Henry. No paper trail."

Chang nodded. "And when I get the results?"

"I don't want a written report," the FBI woman said. "Call me. And please make this a top priority. I need an answer ASAP."

Chapter 66

Madrid, Spain

Other than a few perfunctory words, J.T. Ryan and Rachel West had remained silent during the meal at the hotel's restaurant. Likewise, they didn't speak to each other as they loaded their gear into their rental SUV.

They climbed into the vehicle and before staring it, Ryan said, "This is awkward."

Rachel didn't turn to face him, simply stared straight ahead through the windshield. "Tell me about it."

"I'm sorry about what happened, Rachel. I should never have ...."

Her lips pressed into a thin line. "It was my fault. Entirely. I had way too much to drink yesterday."

"I know. Still, I should have stopped it."

The attractive blonde blushed and she covered her eyes with a hand. "I don't see how. I practically raped you to get you into bed."

The images of the torrid lovemaking flooded into Ryan's mind and he became instantly aroused. He pushed away the thoughts, focusing instead on the job. "It's still no excuse on my part. I should have had more self control."

She turned toward him and he could see the raw emotion there, just underneath the surface. "Just so you know, Ryan, it wasn't just the vodka. I wanted you. I would have wanted you without the booze."

He felt the same way and had enjoyed every minute of it. He wanted to hold her in his arms again.

Ryan let out a long breath, trying to regain his composure. "This isn't going to work. Not here. Not now. We're both professionals. We have a job to do."

She nodded slowly, sadness in her vivid blue eyes. "I know. We have to put yesterday behind us."

"Agreed," Ryan replied.

She extended her hand and they shook.

"Let's not talk about this anymore, okay?" she said in a cool, professional tone, the one she had used when the two had first met.

"Roger that, Agent West."

Rachel gave him a brief smile. "I think we can use first names, don't you?"

"Fine by me, Rachel."

He inserted the key in the ignition and fired up the SUV. Then he drove out of the parking lot and headed west. After passing the *Palacio Real*, Spain's royal palace in the Old Madrid district, they took the A601 highway north out of the city.

***

"You're sure this is the right place?" Ryan asked as he peered through the binoculars.

He and Rachel were on the crest of a ridgeline overlooking a miles-long wooded area. In a clearing at the center of the woods stood a massive home, bordered by at least three or four other buildings. He could make out a stable, a large garage, and an airplane hanger. There was also a long, asphalt runway in the area behind the house. He also noticed quite a bit of activity, with vehicles coming and going, utilizing the two roads that led to the home.

"Absolutely. This is the right place," she replied, keeping her voice low. "This is exactly where Alex said it would be."

Ryan refocused the binos. "Makes sense. That estate looks fit for a king."

"Scorpion's supposed to be a billionaire – he can afford it."

The PI put down the binoculars. "How do you want to play this?"

She glanced up at the sky, which was a deep azure blue. There were no clouds and it would be several hours before sunset. "We need to wait until nightfall, Ryan. Less chance of being spotted. Do you agree?"

"Yeah. But in the meantime, let's pull out that aerial drone. We can learn a lot flying it over the estate."

Rachel reached into her duffel bag and began unpacking the device.

***

Now outfitted with night-vision goggles, Kevlar vests, com headsets, and the MP-5 submachine guns, Ryan and the CIA operative slowly made their way down the ridge and into the forest that surrounded the large estate. After arguing about it earlier, Rachel had finally relented to have Ryan lead the way, but only after he reminded her of her recent concussion.

Ryan was on point now, his eyes scanning the tall stands of trees all around him. Everything had that hazy gray-green look of the night vision equipment.

He spotted a glint of reflection from the moonlight and froze. Going to one knee, he focused on the area directly ahead. The reflection of light was from a trip wire about a foot off the ground. Turning around, he saw Rachel about fifteen feet behind him, picking her way carefully through the dense vegetation. Like him, she was dressed in all-black clothing and wearing a black watch cap.

"Trip wire ahead," he whispered into his headset.

"Roger that," she replied through her own mike. She crouched, the MP-5 cradled in her arms.

Ryan pointed to himself and then forward, she nodded, and he advanced slowly until he was a foot in front of the metal wire. The wire was strung between two trees. No doubt, he thought, the whole forest was ringed with similar trip wires.

Careful not to touch it, he stepped over the wire, half-expecting an explosion or floodlights to bathe the area. When nothing happened, he continued forward deeper into the woods and kneeled again.

"Step over it," he said into his mike.

"Got it."

After the Agency operative cleared the wire, they picked their way forward, careful to remain as silent as possible.

It was relatively quiet in the forest. Only the sounds of crickets and small animals rustling across the ground could be heard. From the video the drone had taken, they had a pretty good feel for the layout of the property. They had decided to approach the mansion from the right hand side, well away from the two roads that led to the house.

An hour later they reached the clearing and Ryan crouched in a stand of trees that bordered it. Rachel was now to his left about ten feet from him. He focused the night-vision goggles, zooming in for a closer look of the home and the other buildings. Next to the runway stood a large airplane hanger. Painted on one side of that building was a sign that read *Scorpion Enterprises.*

"Check out the sign," he whispered into his headset. "This is definitely the right place."

"I see it," she replied. "We'll crawl forward the rest of the way, just like we planned it. But I'm on point this time."

"C'mon, Rachel. You vision may not be 100%."

"Bullshit, Ryan. I'm leading and that's final."

He let out a long breath. The woman was headstrong and he doubted he could change her mind. "All right, Rachel. But hold up a minute. I want to check something out."

"Roger that."

Something had been nagging at him for the last hour while they traversed the forest. They had cleared the initial trip wire and several more later, but he felt someone like Scorpion would have additional levels of security.

Adjusting his goggles, he turned on the infrared feature and spotted it immediately. Up ahead in the clearing was a crisscross of thin red beams of light. The latticework of red beams surrounded the mansion and the other buildings.

"Turn on your infrared," he whispered.

After a moment, she said, "Good catch, Ryan."

"You still want to take point?"

"Hell, yes."

He smiled inwardly. The woman had moxie. "All right. But don't screw it up. I'm sure Scorpion's got plenty of guards, ready to pull the trigger."

"Fuck you, Ryan," she whispered back in a humorous tone. Then in a serious voice said, "Going in."

Cradling the MP-5 on top of her arms, Rachel crawled forward on her hands and knees. When she reached the crisscrossing latticework of red beams, she got up into a crouch, slung the assault rifle over her shoulder, and moved closer to the lines of light.

Contorting her body, she climbed over and under the beams, which were at different heights. After she was through, she motioned him over with a hand then crouched to face the home, her MP-5 trained forward.

Ryan copied her moves, contorting his body while holding his breath, measuring his every step in order to prevent touching the red lines. One wrong move, he knew, and all hell would break loose. His heart thudding in his chest, he was finally on the other side. Crouching alongside Rachel, he held the submachine gun in front of him.

They were now facing the rear of the massive, three-story estate. No one seemed to be outside. An Olympic-size pool with a burbling waterfall feature was in the backyard. Spotlights illuminated the whole area, casting a harsh white light. He turned off his night-vision goggles.

Ryan glanced up at the large home and noted that none of the interior lights were on, which was understandable since it was well past midnight.

Just then a man with a rifle slung over his shoulder came around the side of the house. The PI and Rachel flattened themselves on the ground.

"Guard," Ryan whispered into his headset.

"You think there's more?" she replied.

"Let's wait and see."

The guard made a slow circuit of the back of the home, then moved toward the other side of the house and disappeared from view.

Five minutes later the same guard reappeared as he began making the rounds of the back yard.

"Looks like it's just one of them, Rachel."

"Yeah. I'll take him when he does his next loop."

"I got this, Rachel."

"No way," she whispered harshly over her headset. "This is what I do for a living."

Ryan shook his head and was about to object when he glanced over at her. She was pulling something out of a pocket.

Using the waterfall for cover, she sprinted forward and hid behind the large fountain. In her hands was a wire garrote stretched taut.

A few minutes later the guard reappeared and began his circuit. As soon as he turned his back, Rachel was on him. She came up behind him, looped the garrote around his neck and pulled tightly.

Even from where he was crouching ten feet away, Ryan could see the spray of blood from the guard's neck. The man collapsed to the ground immediately, his body twitching then going inert.

Rachel raced forward, pressing herself flat against the back wall of the home. The PI sprinted across the flagstone patio and likewise hugged the wall.

"Remind me never to piss you off," he whispered into the mike, and the CIA operative flashed a brief smile.

"We'll go in the way we planned," he said.

"Roger that."

Ryan cautiously approached the French doors at the back of the mansion. Peering through the windows, he saw no one inside; a night light near a wall cabinet gave off dim illumination. Figuring the French doors were wired with an alarm, he pulled a custom-made magnet from a pocket. Designed to override burglar alarms, the high-tech tool was something he always carried when on a job.

Placing the magnet at the foot of the door, he waited a full minute for it to work, then using his lock-pick set, jiggled the locks until it disabled the locking mechanism. Putting away his tools, he opened the door and stepped inside.

Rachel followed him in and they crouched silently in the dim room, which was a large kitchen with an adjoining dining area. They heard nothing except the ticking of a nearby clock.

He turned on his night-vision goggles and the room was clearly visible in a gray-green glow. Glancing at Rachel, he pointed to himself and then forward and she nodded.

Sweeping the room with his assault rifle, he advanced out of the kitchen and into the wide hallway, passing a den and several other uninhabited rooms. Eventually he reached a large, marble-step staircase at the front of the mansion, which led up to the upper floors. Curiously, there was also another staircase that led downward to a lower level. Across from the staircase was an elevator. Now that they were inside the home, he realized the place was even larger than it looked from the outside.

Squatting by the foot of the staircase, Ryan waited for Rachel to catch up. When she was next to him, he whispered, "I figure Scorpion is upstairs in one of the bedrooms there."

"I agree, Ryan."

"I'll take point."

Rachel rolled her eyes, then shrugged. "Men."

He began climbing the wide staircase, careful to be as silent as possible. The Agency woman followed behind. When they reached the second floor landing, he glanced both ways down the corridor. It was vacant and the numerous doors were all closed.

Ryan peered up the stairway leading to the third floor, and whispered, "You think he's up there?"

She nodded. "Most master bedrooms are on the top floor – that would be my guess."

The PI adjusted his night-vision goggles, turning on the infrared feature. To his relief he saw no latticework of red beams on the staircase leading up.

"It's clear," he murmured, and continued climbing upward as she followed behind.

Halfway up he heard a metallic click.

In a split-second the staircase and the corridors above them and below them were bathed in a harsh white light. An ear-splitting klaxon rang, the shrill sound bellowing throughout the house.

Both of them dropped to the ground, hugging the marble steps of the stairway. Moments later they heard the roar of gunfire as rounds whizzed over their heads and tore chunks of marble from the steps.

Shooting blindly, Ryan and Rachel returned fire, their rounds pock-marking the walls and ceiling of the third floor corridor. Racing down to the second floor, they crouched behind the wall for cover. His heart pounding in his chest, he kept his finger on the trigger, emptying his magazine as he fired upward.

Just then more shooting erupted, this time up from the first floor, the rounds ripping the wall above them as they kneeled by the landing on the second floor corridor.

"Fuck!" Rachel groused. "They have us pinned down!"

Ryan knew she was right – they were trapped on the second floor. Ejecting his spent magazine, he slammed a fresh clip into his submachine gun. "How many guards do you think?"

She glanced up. "From the volume of fire, at least two tangos upstairs and two downstairs."

He nodded, then heard a loud whirring noise. At first he couldn't place it, then realized it was the elevator moving down.

More rounds rained down on them, this time closer to their position.

He took out a fragmentation grenade from a pocket and got ready to pull the pin, when Rachel grabbed his arm. "You might kill Scorpion if you use those."

"We have no choice," he snapped. "We're dead if we don't."

Gunfire erupted, this time up from the first floor, the rounds chewing holes in the corridor ceiling above them, chunks of wood and plaster raining down on them.

Rachel unclipped a frag grenade from her jacket and pulled the pin. "I'll lob it down, you throw yours up, Ryan."

Simultaneously, they pitched the explosives toward the first and third floors, heard thuds as they clattered on the marble floors. An instant later an ear-splitting roar erupted and even from their position they felt the shock wave as the two grenades exploded.

Screams of pain filled the air and Ryan yelled, "Go! Go! Go!"

Sweeping the MP-5 in front of him, the PI raced up the steps and crouched by the landing to the third level. Rachel was close behind. Peering around the wall, he spotted one prone man laying in a pool of blood and debris. Another guard was on his knees, wounded, but he still managed to fire three more shots.

His heart pounding, Ryan pulled the trigger. One of his high-velocity rounds slammed into the guard's forehead, his head snapped back, and his body sagged to the floor.

Wasting no time, Ryan sprinted down the corridor, hurdling over the debris and the corpses, reaching the end of the hallway a moment later. A set of closed, double-doors was at this end and he assumed Scorpion was holed up inside. The PI took a position to the right of the door, and the CIA operative joined him a second later on the other side.

Ryan was about to reach over and turn the door knob when he heard a high-pitched whine. Alarmed, he stopped what he was doing. "What the hell's that?"

With a perplexed look, Rachel shook her head.

He listened another moment as the metallic whine grew louder into a roar. Instantly he recognized it. "Damn! That's a jet engine!"

Rachel grimaced. "Fuck. We saw the airplane hanger on the property. Scorpion got out of the house and reached the plane."

Knowing they only had minutes, maybe less to get to the man before the jet took off, the PI gripped his MP-5 and raced toward the staircase. Halfway there, out of the corner of his eye, he spotted a canister flying up from the stairwell. The object landed on the hallway floor.

Ryan froze in his tracks and his chest tightened with fear.

Immediately dropping to the ground, he hid behind one of the corpses as the grenade detonated. He felt the shock wave of the blast and its deafening roar at the same time.

The last thing he saw was a ceiling beam hurtling down toward him.

Then everything went black.

***

Ryan blinked his eyes as he regained consciousness. His vision was hazy but he knew he was on the floor, flat on his back.

"Ryan! Ryan!"

He heard a woman's voice as his vision cleared. Rachel was crouched next to him.

"Are you okay, Ryan?"

He had a hell of a headache and his whole body ached, but nothing felt broken. "Yeah," he replied groggily. "Scorpion?"

"Gone."

"You sure?"

Rachel nodded. "After you got knocked out, I searched the property. The airplane hanger was empty, the lights were still on and the door was wide open. The bastard got away."

"And the tangos?"

"I killed one guard. Wounded another – but he ran off into the woods somewhere."

Ryan tried getting up and felt lightheaded and queasy. Waiting a minute to let that pass, he sat up and leaned against the corridor's wall. "Find anyone else here?"

"One woman," Rachel replied. "I tied her up in one of the bedrooms."

"Anybody else?"

"No. They must have fled. The woman told me that aside from the guards, four other people live here – the butler, two maids, and a cook. They live in a separate house on the property – I searched all the structures but they were gone – I figure when the shooting started, they fled."

"Okay," Ryan said. "You question the woman about Scorpion?"

"Not yet. I wanted to make sure you were all right first."

Ryan tried grinning but his face hurt from the effort. "I'm too good-looking to kill," he joked. "And smart too."

She rolled her eyes. "Yeah. You are a *smart-ass*, all right."

After picking up his submachine gun from the floor, he held out his hand. "Help me up, will you? Let's go question that woman."

The CIA operative grabbed his arm and helped him to his feet. Then she led the way to one of the bedrooms at the other end of the hallway.

A woman in sleepwear was sitting on the bed, her hands tied behind her back. Her feet were bound as well, and a strip of duct tape covered her mouth. She was very attractive, with long, dark hair and a dark complexion. Ryan guessed she was probably Greek or maybe Turkish.

Rachel stood in front of her. "You want to do this, Ryan? I remember from your file you did a lot of interrogation work when you were in special ops."

He was about to say yes when a bolt of pain ran down his spine. Leaning against the bedroom wall for support, he said, "No. You go ahead."

Rachel reached over and tore the tape off the woman's mouth.

"Aow!" the woman yelped, her eyes wide with fear. *"Eso duele! "* she said in Spanish. *That hurts!*

The CIA operative closed a fist and held it in front of her. *"Esto te va doler mas!" This is going to hurt more!*

The woman's eyes grew wider and she cringed.

"No, por favor. No me golpes," she begged. *Please don't hit me.*

"Take it easy, Rachel," Ryan interjected. "She may give us more if you treat her with kindness."

The captive woman faced him. "I speak English too. And you are right, *senor.* I'll tell you whatever you want to know."

Rachel ignored all of this and slapped the woman hard across the mouth, breaking her lip. "Don't talk to him! Talk to me, lady! I'm the one asking the questions."

The hostage's face went white. *"Si! Si!"*

The PI was perplexed by Rachel's actions, then it dawned on him. She would be the bad cop and he would be the good cop in this interrogation. It was an effective technique, one he had used himself many times.

"Who are you?" the Agency woman asked, her tone harsh. "Scorpion's wife?"

The woman shook her head. "He's not married. I'm one of his women. He has many."

"What's your name?"

"Mariska," the woman answered.

"You're his girlfriend?" Rachel asked.

Mariska laughed, but there was no humor in it. "No. I'm one of his whores."

The CIA operative glanced at Ryan and said, "That tracks from what we know about Scorpion." She faced the captive again. "He fled in his jet. Where did he go?"

Mariska shrugged. "Who knows? This is his house. But he has others."

Rachel slapped her again, the blow leaving a bright red mark on the captive's face. "This isn't a fucking game, lady. You're going to have to do a lot better than that."

"I swear!" Mariska screeched. "I don't know where he is!"

The Agency woman crossed her arms across her chest. "You said he has other homes. Where?"

"In Europe. And America. Asia too. I heard he and his men talking about it."

"Where, specifically?"

Mariska shook her head slowly and her eyes showed panic as if she expected Rachel to strike her again. "I told you. I don't know. *Please* don't hurt me."

The CIA operative shook a fist in front of the woman's face. "I want the fucking truth!"

Mariska shrank back from her and closed her eyes tightly. "I swear," she replied, her voice trembling. "If I knew I would tell you."

Ryan noticed Mariska's body literally shaking. Then he noticed a damp spot on the woman's nightclothes in the area of her groin. She had obviously urinated from the fear.

Instead of punching the woman, Rachel opened her fist and began to gently caress the captive's long hair.

Mariska's eyes snapped open.

"Okay, honey," Rachel said sweetly, as she continued gently stroking the woman's hair. "You've told me what you don't know about Scorpion. Tell me what you do know about him."

Mariska nodded her head furiously. "Yes! I'll tell you. He liked sex. I was his favorite, or so he said. But I suspected he told that to all his women. And he paid me well. Very well. I made more money from him than from all my other customers combined."

"That's good, honey. What else can you tell me?"

"Scorpion liked oral sex best," Mariska replied. "But he liked other things, much kinkier things. Do you want to know about that?"

Rachel suppressed a smile "No. I don't care about that."

"All right," Mariska said. "Scorpion had a dog. The dog had evil eyes. I always hated that dog!"

"Drax, right?"

"That's right. The dog's name was Drax. And Scorpion always had that damn dog with him, watching us when we had sex. I think it gave Scorpion a thrill to have it watch, although he always said it was for security reasons."

"Give me a physical description of Scorpion," Rachel asked soothingly.

"He was tall. Well over six feet." Mariska pointed to Ryan. "Like him, but not as muscular. Scorpion had a thick mane of silver hair and he had the whitest teeth. He smiled often but it wasn't a warm smile."

"That's good, Mariska. What else?"

"Oh, I remember. He had a small tattoo of a scorpion on the inside of his wrist."

"Okay. Is there anything else about him you can remember?"

"He had a long, thin scar down his cheek, but it was faded, as if the cut happened a long time ago."

"I looked around the house," Rachel said, "and I didn't see any photos of him anywhere."

"That's right," replied Mariska. "He never wanted to be in any photographs. One time I was playing around with my cell phone and was going to take his picture. He grabbed the phone and smashed it against the wall. He told me he'd kill me if I tried that again."

"That tracks," Rachel said, turning to Ryan. "The guy is paranoid about his identity." She faced the captive again. "Can you remember anything else about him?"

"He wore very expensive three-piece suits. He was always telling me to be careful and not get them dirty."

"Besides the tattoo on his wrist," the CIA operative said, "did he have any other markings or unusual features on the rest of his body?"

"I don't know."

A perplexed look crossed Rachel's face. "You don't know? How's that possible? You had sex with him."

"Yes, I did. Many, many times. But he always wore his suits even then."

Rachel grimaced. "He was kinky."

"I told you."

"Okay," Rachel continued, "when I was searching this home and the other buildings, I didn't see any computers or file cabinets anywhere. Where did Scorpion keep his paperwork and his files?"

"I never saw any of that either," Mariska replied. "I suspected he kept that in his plane."

Rachel let out a long breath. "Fuck. This guy obviously planned ahead." She turned to Ryan. "You got any questions for her?"

"Just a couple," he replied, approaching the prostitute. "Mariska, did you ever hear him say the initials O.O.V.?"

"O.O.V.? No."

"Okay," he said. "We know Scorpion had a European accent. Was he a Spaniard?"

"That's true, he had a slight accent. But he wasn't from Spain."

"Was he Russian?"

Mariska shook her head. "I don't think so. I suspected he was German."

"German, huh? That could be a good lead," Ryan said. "He always went by the name of Scorpion. What was his real name?"

"That was a big secret. Nobody knew. But I remember one time he had a visitor. An American woman." Mariska scrunched her nose. "An ugly woman who wore drab clothes. Anyway, I overheard them talking and she called him Hans. Hans Krueger. I remember distinctly because he was furious at her calling him that."

Ryan nodded. "That's excellent. I'm glad you remembered that. Who was the American woman? What was her name?"

The captive shook her head. "I don't know. But from what I overheard, she was someone very important."

"So this American woman and Scorpion did business together?"

"Yes, they were discussing business. But she stayed for many days. And they spent nights together in his bedroom. I know because he didn't invite me or any of his other women to spend the night with him when she was around."

"They were lovers," Ryan stated.

Mariska scrunched her face in obvious disgust. "Yes. But I don't see why. Like I said, she was ugly."

Ryan considered this a moment. "You said she was important. Why do think that?"

"Because of the way Scorpion treated her. Like royalty. He treated her much better than he treated me. The butler told me after her visit that he'd overheard Scorpion say he loved this woman."

"Interesting. Describe what she looked like."

"Ugly."

"I got that part, Mariska. What else?"

She made a face. "She was flat-chested. And she had a hard face. A dour face."

"What color hair?" Ryan asked.

"I thought that part was odd. She was a brunette, with long curly hair. But her hair looked fake, like she was wearing a wig."

"Maybe she was trying to alter her appearance?" he said.

Mariska nodded. "Yes. I think so."

Chapter 67

Washington, D.C.

Vicka Stark was elated. The president's speech had worked wonders. Two of the networks which had been fighting the administration's narratives had now fallen into line and were broadcasting news stories favorable to the federal government.

The lone holdout, a cable news network that consistently reported the unvarnished facts, was still a problem. But Vicka had already contacted the Attorney General and that news company would be the first to be indicted for criminal prosecution.

All of this was going through Vicka's mind as she sat in the O.O.V. control room, observing the flat screen TVs mounted on the auditorium's far wall. The room's forty technicians were busy at their consoles, diligently monitoring their assigned news channels.

Vicka's operations manager hovered nervously by the workstation where she sat, no doubt trying to anticipate her next demands.

"Can I get you anything, Ms. Stark?" Harold Meeks asked.

She looked up at him. "That's the third time you've asked me that."

"Yes, Ms. Stark. It's just that you don't usually spend this much time in the control room. That's what you have me for."

"Harold," she replied in a low voice, so that none of the techs in the room could overhear. "We've had issues. Issues I've had to deal with." She tapped her pen on the workstation desk. "I'm making sure everything is going smoothly now."

"Yes, ma'am." He cleared his throat. "Are you satisfied all is well?"

Vicka picked up her briefcase, rose, and faced him. "Satisfied? For the moment. Now don't fuck it up, Harold."

Chapter 68

Madrid, Spain

"How soon do you head back?" Rachel West asked.

"Today," J.T. Ryan responded, after taking a drink of mineral water.

The two people were having lunch in an outdoor cafe overlooking the *Plaza Mayor*, the city's historic open square in the Old Madrid district. It was the first downtime they'd had since the shootout at Scorpion's estate.

Rachel tucked loose strands of her long blonde hair behind her ears. It was a cool, windy day, the breeze causing the large umbrellas covering the tables to sway. "Okay, Ryan. You talked to the Bureau?"

"Yeah. I filled Erin in on what happened. That Scorpion had literally flown into the wind."

"How'd she take it?"

"Obviously she was very disappointed," he replied. "But some things have changed back home. She's been given the green light to work on the case again. Erin said she's got leads for me to investigate."

"And that's why you're heading back today?" Rachel asked.

"That's right. How about you?"

A gust of wind blew and she smoothed her hair with a hand. "I talked to Langley. Alex wants me to stay here, continue to work the case."

"I'm glad, Rachel. You're a good operative. If anybody can track down Scorpion in Europe it would be you."

She drank water from her glass. "So. You looking forward to going back home?"

Ryan stared at the attractive blonde and fondly recalled their intimate moments. "Yes and no."

"What do you mean?" she replied in her cool, professional voice.

Feeling awkward about the intimacy they had shared, he faced a group of street musicians who were playing at the center of the plaza. He was quiet a moment as he tried to sort through his feelings for the CIA woman. There was no question he was attracted to her, but deep down he still hoped he and Lauren would eventually get back together.

Then Ryan faced the Agency operative. "I'm glad to be going home. I love Atlanta. But being with you has been ...." His voice trailed off.

Rachel held his gaze and although her cool, professional manner remained, under the surface, her glittering blue eyes told a different story.

She smiled. "I'm usually out in the field, on operations like this. In fact, Alex already told me that after I complete this assignment, he needs me to go to China. But I do get back home to Langley occasionally. That's not too far from Atlanta."

Chapter 69

Rome, Italy

Scorpion stared out the windows of his palatial villa in the outskirts of the city. It was a beautiful, sunny day, the kind of day he would have loved to be outside, soaking in the sunshine, breathing in the scent of his vineyard, strolling among the countless rows of vines, picking off and tasting the rich, flavorful red grapes.

But ever since the attack on his estate in Spain, he had remained inside, watching, listening, fearful of what might happen next. Luckily he had planned well and had devised a contingency for escape. Yet even now he didn't feel secure, didn't feel safe. It was a rare feeling for him. As a man who could afford the best protection and the best security, he had always felt invincible. Now he felt vulnerable.

Turning away from the windows, he went to his desk and picked up the handset of the encrypted phone. Dialing a number from memory, he waited for the other person to pick up.

"It's Scorpion," he said quickly. "I can't talk long. We have trouble, Vicka. Big trouble."

"What is it, dear?" the woman asked, her voice solicitous.

"My home in Spain. It was attacked. I suspect it was the American CIA people who were trying to track me down."

"How's that possible?" Vicka said, fear in her voice. "No one knows where you live or who you are."

His anger flared. "Obviously, *they* figured it out, damn it."

"Yes, dear. I'm *so* sorry. What can I do to help?"

"Nothing, Vicka. I have to sort this out. I'm calling to let you know so you can watch your back. Be extra careful."

"Of course, Hans. I love you. Where are you now?"

"It's better if you don't know."

"Yes, dear. I want to see you again. Are you coming to the States soon?"

"I don't know, Vicka. We'll see. I have to go."

He hung up abruptly.

Taking a long pull from his bourbon, he mulled over the situation, forcing his thoughts away from foreboding and toward action, toward resolving his current problem.

Formulating a new plan, he drew the window drapes closed and strode confidently out of the room.

Chapter 70

Atlanta, Georgia

Erin Welch stared at the whiteboard affixed to the wall of her FBI office. On the board she'd jotted the pertinent facts they had on the case of the murdered journalists. It was a jumble of information, a jigsaw puzzle she hadn't been able to solve.

Taking a sip from her cup of Starbucks, she scribbled an idea on the board and stood back, frustrated at her inability to connect the dots.

Just then there was a knock at her office door and she turned and noticed her assistant standing there.

"Ryan's here," the man said.

"Send him up."

A few minutes later J.T. Ryan came into her office. The rugged, good-looking man looked as fit as ever, but she noticed a slight limp in his stride.

"You okay, J.T.?" she asked as they shook hands.

He gave her a boyish grin. "Couldn't be better."

"What's with the limp?"

"I had a fight with a ceiling beam," he said with a chuckle. "The beam won."

Erin shook her head slowly. "Always the comedian."

Ryan pointed to the whiteboard. "What's this?"

"Everything we know about the case."

He nodded, pulled up a chair, and sat facing the board.

Still standing, Erin crossed her arms in front of her chest. "You catch any news since you got back from Spain?"

"Some. I saw what President Ackerman was planning on doing. I couldn't believe it."

"Me either, J.T. The president is a runaway train. If he pulls this off, we can kiss democracy goodbye in this country."

"I agree. You told me that the FBI Director has had a change of heart?"

"That's the only good result," she replied, "of Ackerman's speech. Director Tucker is in agreement with us and he's given me the green light to reopen the investigation. With conditions, however."

"What conditions, Erin?"

"I still have to play it close to the vest. Tucker suspects someone very high up in our government is involved in this conspiracy."

A frown crossed his face. "Obviously that's someone higher up than the FBI Director himself."

"That's right."

"That's not a large group of people, Erin."

"Correct."

Ryan let out a low whistle. "Okay. I see what we're up against." He pointed to the notes she'd written on the whiteboard. "Walk me through this."

Erin picked up one of the erasable markers and approached the board. She began checking off the items she'd jotted down earlier. "We have dead reporters," she said, "in the U.S. and Europe. We have a billionaire involved, Hans Krueger, AKA Scorpion. We have someone high up in the U.S. government involved. And the initials O.O.V. are connected to all this." She paused and underlined a name. "And now we have this man."

"Who is that?"

"His name is Zach Thomas," Erin said. "I reached out to my contact at the FBI's technical center in Quantico. I gave him the security camera video clip of the man who killed Mei Lin. My contact ran the video through facial recognition software and came up with this guy."

Ryan stretched his legs and rubbed his back in obvious discomfort. "Where's this Zach Thomas now?"

"We arrested him. He's being held on suspicion of murder."

"That's great, Erin. That's a big break."

The FBI woman shook her head. "Yes and no. Thomas has lawyered up and isn't talking."

"Damn," Ryan muttered.

Erin turned back to the whiteboard and underlined something else.

"I got a call today from Alex Miller at the CIA," she said. "After you left Spain, the Agency was able to track down Scorpion at a second location. The man owned another home, a villa in the outskirts of Rome. A CIA team headed by Rachel West raided the place but Scorpion was able to get away again."

"He's an elusive bastard," Ryan said.

Erin nodded. "Scorpion is that. Alex told me he's keeping Rachel West in Europe to continue working this case."

"Good. She's a good operative."

"I'm surprised to hear you say that, J.T. I know how much you like working solo. What's Rachel like, by the way?"

An enigmatic smile crossed his face. "She's a real firecracker."

"What do you mean by that?"

"Nothing," he replied, turning serious again. "She's a good operative."

"Okay."

He pointed to the board again. "Where's Zach Thomas now?"

"We're holding him in the detention center in this building. We can keep him locked up for some time, but eventually his attorney may be able to bond him out."

"Cut him loose now, Erin."

"Are you crazy?"

Ryan grinned. "Maybe. But that's not the point. Are you getting anything out of Thomas now?"

"No," she replied with a grimace. "I told you. He's lawyered up. He's not saying a word."

"So. He's useless to you sitting in jail."

"Pretty much."

"And I'm sure you won't let me question him while he's in here."

"That's a fact, J.T. I know all about your 'questioning' techniques. This is a federal office building, and in here, the laws apply. Water boarding, or whatever other interrogation methods you use are borderline illegal. Zach Thomas is a cold-blooded killer, but like everyone else, he has constitutional rights."

"Then slap an ankle bracelet on him and cut him loose," Ryan said. "I'll take care of the rest."

Erin thought about this for a long moment as she considered what the PI proposed. It was risky, since Thomas could flee and vanish in the wind like Scorpion.

Ryan grinned. "You hire me because I take care of the shit your *Special* Agents can't do. Isn't that right?"

Grudgingly, she nodded. "Yes."

"Okay, then. Cut him loose and I'll get answers."

Erin extended her hand. "All right. But on one condition. If Thomas flees, I cut your fee in half."

"You drive a hard bargain, lady," Ryan replied with a chuckle, as they shook hands.

Chapter 71

Atlanta, Georgia

Sitting in his Tahoe, J.T Ryan peered through the binoculars. He'd been watching the brick-front home for two hours, ever since Zach Thomas had gone inside. Ryan had followed the man from the moment he'd been released from the FBI building. The killer had taken a cab and come here, his home in the suburbs.

Parked half a block from Thomas's house, the PI was waiting to see if the man had any visitors. After two hours it looked unlikely. According to Erin he lived alone.

Propped on the dash of Ryan's SUV was a handheld device, its blinking green light indicating that the ankle bracelet on Thomas was operating and that he was inside the home. But Ryan had been a private investigator long enough to know that any tracking system, no matter how sophisticated, can be circumvented.

After checking the load on his Smith & Wesson .357 caliber revolver, the PI re-holstered the weapon and zipped up his jacket. Then he picked up the empty pizza delivery box on the passenger seat and exited the Tahoe. Still limping a bit from his injury, he strode to the home's entrance and rang the bell.

The door was opened partway by Zach Thomas, a non-descript man wearing slacks and a polo shirt.

Ryan held the pizza box in front of him. "Your pizza's here, sir," he said.

Thomas gave him a blank look. "I didn't order pizza."

"Are you sure? A large pepperoni with extra cheese. This is the right address."

"Listen, buddy. I didn't order it. Now get the fuck out of my face!"

"Well, sir, there's no reason to be rude. I'm just trying to make a buck."

"Get lost!" the man bellowed, beginning to shut the door.

Ryan dropped the pizza box, kicked the door forcefully and barged in. Closing the door behind him, he quickly pulled his revolver and pointed it at the man's face.

"What the hell is this?" Thomas barked. "Who the hell are you?"

"I'm your worse nightmare." Ryan motioned with the pistol. "On your knees. Now! And put your hands behind your back."

Thomas looked like he was going to make a run for it and the PI pressed the muzzle of the gun to the man's forehead. "I said *now.*"

The man complied and Ryan patted him down, flex-cuffed his hands and feet, and dragged him onto one of the living room's armchairs.

"If this is a robbery," Thomas said, "I have cash in the bedroom."

Ignoring this, the PI quickly searched the rest of the house, and finding no one else, returned to the living room. He noticed a stereo in a wall cabinet. He turned it on and put the volume on high.

"I have cash," Thomas repeated. "Lots of it."

"This isn't a robbery."

"What do you want, then? Who the hell are you?"

Ryan grinned. "I'm a pissed-off pizza delivery guy. You should have taken that pizza." His grin vanished. "Who hired you to kill Mei Lin?"

Thomas's jaw dropped. "What?"

"You heard me, Zach. I know all about you. I know you're a hit man. I want to know who hired you to assassinate the WMN reporter, Mei Lin."

"I don't know what you're talking about."

Ryan shook his head. "When you were in FBI custody, you could hide behind your lawyer. Unluckily for you, I don't have to play by those rules."

"You're with the FBI? I demand to see my attorney!"

"You *demand* it?" the PI said with a chuckle. "From my perspective, I don't think you're in a position to demand anything."

"Holding me at gunpoint is illegal, you moron."

His anger flaring, Ryan made a fist and punched the man hard across the jaw. Thomas's head snapped sideways and blood trickled from his cut lip.

"That was for killing Mei Lin," the PI snarled. "And for calling me a moron."

His eyes wide, Thomas said, "If I tell you anything, I'll incriminate myself. I'd go to prison for a long fucking time."

"Bullshit. You could deny you said anything. It would be my word against yours. Just tell me who hired you and I'll be on my way."

The man shook his head and said nothing. Blood continued to drip from his mouth, staining his green polo shirt.

"Okay, Thomas. I've been a nice guy so far. But you're testing my patience. Since you're not cooperating, I have to go to Plan B."

"What the hell's Plan B?"

"You're going to find out, my friend."

Ryan went to the kitchen, rummaged through the drawers, and finding the utensil he was looking for, returned to the living room. Holding the large kitchen knife close to the man's face, he said, "I used to do a lot of fishing years ago. In fact, I consider myself an expert in filleting fish. Fish can't talk, so I don't know if they felt any pain. But from my experience in interrogating people, filleting a person is another matter altogether."

Thomas's eyes went wide and he tried to squirm away.

Grabbing the man firmly by the neck, Ryan pressed the sharp blade to his cheek. The PI had used this technique before and had never had to cut someone, since the threat of pain and suffering was more terrifying than the act itself. Captives had always broken before the slicing began, and Ryan prayed it would be true again today.

The captive's face blanched and his eyes showed true terror. "I'll talk," the man whispered. "Please take the knife away."

"You're sure, Thomas?"

"Yes, I'll talk!"

Ryan pulled the blade away from the man's face. "Who hired you?"

"A man named Harold Meeks."

"Where do I find this guy?"

"I don't know for sure. But we met in D.C."

"Okay, Thomas. He paid you cash?"

"That's right. A hundred grand. Fifty at contract, fifty at completion."

Ryan nodded. "What's this guy do for a living?"

"I don't know. But after we met, I saw him get into a black sedan. It had government plates."

Chapter 72

Atlanta, Georgia

"I'm not going to ask how you got this information," Erin Welch said as she took a sip from her cup of Starbucks.

"That's good," J.T. Ryan replied with a grin. "Because you don't want to know."

They were sitting in Erin's Jaguar, which was parked in the underground lot of the FBI building. Erin drank more of the savory coffee. "Okay. Thomas told you the guy who hired him was a man by the name of Harold Meeks. Was he bullshitting you or telling the truth?"

"It's solid."

"And this guy Meeks probably lives in Washington," Erin continued, "and was driving a government car."

"That's right."

Erin stared out the windshield of the Jaguar, then faced the PI again. "That tracks with the other info we have about it being a government conceived conspiracy."

"Right," Ryan said. "I just thought of something. When Rachel and I questioned Scorpion's prostitute in Spain, she told us the billionaire had a visit from a woman. An American woman who, in Mariska's words, 'Scorpion treated like royalty.' This American woman was very important to him. They were lovers and business partners."

"Did you get her name?" Erin asked.

"No. No name, but I got a description of her. An unattractive, flat-chested woman with dark hair. Although Mariska thought the woman was wearing a wig."

"Okay," Erin said. "Maybe this woman is in the U.S. government?"

"It could be."

"All right, J.T. This is a great lead."

Ryan laughed. "I know. I should raise my fees."

Erin smiled but shook her head. "No. Not that great."

"What do you want me to do now?"

"Get some rest, J.T. I need to chase down these leads. I'll call you when I get something."

"Roger that," he said.

Then she watched as he got out of her car and walked to his white Tahoe, which was parked a few vehicles away.

Chapter 73

Washington, D.C.

"You should have let me handle this on my own," J.T. Ryan said, as he drove the rented Chevrolet Impala.

"Not this time," Erin Welch replied, who was in the passenger seat. "We've got government people involved."

Ryan glanced over at the FBI woman. "I get faster results."

"True. But this time I need hard evidence. Evidence I can take to Director Tucker. Since top federal employees are involved in this conspiracy, I can't have you running loose on your own in D.C., shooting up the place. Your Rambo methods get results, but this time you need adult supervision. The director green-lighted my investigation, but he also cautioned me to tread lightly."

"All right," he replied, realizing this was an argument he would not win.

Ten minutes later Erin said, "That's the building on the right. Find a place to park."

Ryan pulled to the curb a moment later and studied the brownstone, which was located on a quiet street lined with similar buildings. He pointed to the edifice's roof. "Check out the satellite dishes. The roof's covered with them."

"According to what I found out," Erin replied, "this place is a government call center. Harold Meeks is a Federal government high-level manager. He's employed by the State Department, but for the last three years he's been on 'special assignment' at this location."

Ryan turned off the Impala. "What kind of 'special assignment'?"

"The records don't say. That's what we're going to find out."

The PI unzipped his jacket, pulled out his pistol and checked the load.

"You're not going to need that, J.T."

Ryan re-holstered the weapon. "Probably true. But I like to be prepared."

They exited the car and walked to the building's entrance.

"Check out the retinal scanner," he said, noticing the device by the doorway. "Pretty sophisticated security for a call center."

Erin nodded as she pressed the buzzer. When the door was answered by a tall, athletic-looking man a moment later, she held up her Bureau creds. "I'm Erin Welch with the FBI. I need to speak with Harold Meeks."

The man inspected the credentials carefully, then stepped aside and let them in. He led them down a long, wide corridor to a vacant conference room.

"Please wait here," the man said. "I'll go get Mr. Meeks for you."

A few minutes later a very obese man in a tight suit stepped into the room.

Erin flashed her creds again. "I'm Assistant Director in Charge Erin Welch, Mr. Meeks. And this is J.T. Ryan."

Meeks stared nervously at her badge, then pointed to the conference room chairs. After they had all sat, Meeks said, "What's this about?"

"We're investigating a murder," Erin replied, "a murder that took place in Atlanta."

Meeks eyes darted furtively to Erin, and then at Ryan, and back to the FBI woman. "A murder? What does that have to do with me?"

"I'll get to that in a moment," Erin said as she waved a hand in the air. "What is this place?"

The obese man tugged at his shirt collar and loosened his tie a bit. "It's a call center."

"What kind of call center?"

The man seemed uncomfortable with the question. "We do research."

"What kind of research?" Erin said in a hard voice.

"Surveys. We survey American consumers on the effectiveness of federal government programs."

"I noticed you had a retinal scanner at the front door," Ryan interjected. "Why do you need that kind of sophisticated security if all you do is consumer research?"

Meeks unfastened the collar button of his white shirt. "D.C. has a high crime rate."

"You're a top-level manager," Erin said. "In fact, your position is the highest level a civilian employee can attain in the Federal government. It seems to me you're way overqualified to be supervising something as simple as conducting surveys."

"We do important work here," the obese man replied nervously.

Erin leaned forward. "Who do you work for?"

"Work for?"

"Yes. Who do you report to, Mr. Meeks?"

Beads of perspiration formed on Meeks's forehead. "I'm the Operations Manager here. I'm in charge."

"Yes," Erin replied. "But everyone has a boss. Who's your boss?"

The man pulled out a handkerchief and mopped his brow. "That's classified."

The FBI woman raised a brow. "Classified? That's odd, since all you do is conduct surveys."

Meeks's face flushed. "You said you were here about a murder," he said, obviously trying to change the subject.

Erin nodded. "That's right. Do you know a man by the name of Zach Thomas?"

The man's eyes bulged. He said nothing for a long moment, then stammered, "Zach Thomas? No, I never heard of him."

She removed a photograph from her jacket and placed it on the conference table. She pointed to it. "Do you recognize the woman in this photo?"

Meeks stared at the picture and his face turned white.

"That's Mei Lin," Erin stated harshly. "She was a reporter who was murdered recently."

"What's that have to do with me?" the man asked in a weak voice.

"You hired Zach Thomas to kill her, didn't you?"

Meeks shook his head furiously. "No! Of course not!"

"We have Thomas in custody," Erin said. "He says otherwise."

The obese man's eyes darted between Erin and Ryan, seeming unsure what to say next.

"If you cooperate with us," Erin said, "I can probably get you a deal with the District Attorney. Perhaps take the death penalty off the table."

"What do you ... want to know?" Meeks replied, his voice cracking.

Erin leaned forward. "Who do you work for?"

Meeks grimaced, then whispered, "Victoria Stark."

The FBI woman was shocked. "Victoria Stark? The Chief of Staff at the White House?"

"That's right."

"Now tell me what you really do in this building," Erin demanded.

"This is the operations center for O.O.V."

Erin and Ryan exchanged glances when they heard this. Then the FBI woman stood up abruptly.

"I need to search this building," she said.

Meeks stared up at her, his face a mask of fear. "Do you have a search warrant?"

"No. But I can get one."

The obese man shook his head. "I've said too much already. I want a lawyer."

Ryan unzipped his jacket and was about to pull out his weapon when Erin tugged his arm. "No, J.T. Now's not the time for that."

The PI scowled, then let out a long breath to calm down.

Giving Meeks a hard stare, Erin said, "We'll be back."

Chapter 74

The White House
Washington, D.C.

Vicka Stark's stomach twisted into knots as she listened to the caller describe what had happened. Sitting in her office, she gripped the receiver tightly and rubbed her forehead with her other hand. "And you told them you worked for me?"

"Yes, Ms. Stark," Harold Meeks replied. "I'm sorry. But they were insistent."

"Tell me again who these FBI people were."

"The woman was named Erin Welch, and the man with her was J.T. Ryan."

Vicka gritted her teeth. *Damn it*, she thought. *I should have had that bitch Welch killed also, along with Mei Lin.*

The Chief of Staff's mind raced as she tried to sort through her options. *Remain calm. You can handle this.* Trying to keep her emotions in check, she said, "But you prevented them from searching O.O.V.?"

"Yes, Ms. Stark."

"That's good, Harold."

"What do you want me to do now?"

"Go about your regular duties. I'll contact my attorney – he'll come see you at O.O.V. today. It'll take Welch a few days to get that search warrant. In the meantime, say nothing about this to anyone. All right?"

"Yes, Ms. Stark. I'm sorry about all this."

Vicka was furious at the man and wanted nothing more than to literally strangle him. Instead she calmly said, "Don't worry, Harold. We'll get through this. You'll see. I'll take care of everything."

She hung up the phone. Rising from her chair, she strode out of her office and made her way down the hallway. When she reached the Oval Office, she nodded curtly to the two Secret Service agents posted there, opened the door and stepped inside.

Fortunately President Ackerman was alone, writing at his desk.

"Vicka, did we have a meeting planned?" he said as he looked up.

"No, Mr. President. Something's come up. And its urgent."

Ackerman sensed her alarm and closed his folio. "Of course. Have a seat."

She perched on one of the wingback chairs fronting his desk. "Mr. President, we have a serious problem regarding O.O.V."

"What is it, Vicka? I thought things were proceeding smoothly ever since I gave my speech."

"Yes, sir. The press has been very cooperative since your address to the nation. This is something else entirely."

Ackerman raised a brow. "Tell me."

"The FBI visited the operation this morning. They questioned my operations manager and wanted to search the place."

"FBI? I thought you had that covered. Didn't you squelch their investigation?"

"Yes, Mr. President. The Attorney General has been on board. He's kept the Directors of the FBI and Homeland Security in check."

"So what the hell's happened?"

"I'm still trying to sort that out, sir. But it's clear one of the Bureau's agents is actively pursuing an investigation. I can give you all of the details if you'd like."

President Ackerman raised a hand. "No. I don't want to know."

"Yes, sir."

Ackerman's face clouded with worry. "If news about O.O.V. gets out to the public, it could bring down my whole administration. All I've worked for, all we've worked for, would go down the drain."

"I agree, Mr. President."

Ackerman swiveled his executive chair away from her and faced the tall windows behind him. It was a dark, overcast day, and a cold drizzle was falling on D.C.

She kept quiet, knowing the man had to come to the correct solution, the only solution, on his own. He was the president after all, and she had to preserve the illusion that he was in control. After a few minutes, he swiveled the chair and faced her again.

"As much as it pains me to say this, Vicka, I think we have to shut down the operation."

Vicka nodded, relieved she hadn't had to prod him. "I agree totally, Mr. President."

He raised a brow. "You'll take care of it?"

The Chief of Staff stood. "Of course, Mr. President."

Chapter 75

Washington, D.C.

J.T. Ryan was nursing a beer at the hotel bar, itching to get back to the call center building and kick ass. Just then Erin Welch walked into the upscale place and headed towards him.

He swiveled his barstool as she sat next to him. "Well?"

"It's in the works," Erin replied as she signaled the bartender. "We'll have the search warrant by tomorrow."

The bartender came over and took her drink order. After the man moved away, Ryan patted his jacket, which concealed his holstered pistol. "My way's faster."

Erin shook her head slowly, then gave him a brief smile. "In case you've forgotten, I'm a *law* enforcement officer. That means I have to do things *legally*."

Ryan shrugged. "By the way, do you think Meeks was telling the truth about the White House Chief of Staff being involved?"

Erin took a sip of her wine. "I do. Have you ever seen a photo of Victoria Stark, or seen her in a news clip?"

"No," Ryan replied. "I don't follow Washington politics as closely as you do."

"Well, Stark looks a lot like the woman Mariska described, except she has short, blonde hair."

Ryan rubbed his jaw. "That makes sense. Mariska said the woman was probably wearing a wig. The jigsaw puzzle is coming together. Scorpion and his lover, Victoria Stark, appear to be conspiring together to kill reporters. The question I have is, what's their ultimate goal?"

"Stark's motivation is clear to me," Erin said. "She obviously wants the news media to present a rosy picture of the administration's policies. If you can get television stations and newspapers in your pocket, it's much easier to get Americans to accept government policies. Even very bad policies. Including ones that are contrary to the U.S. Constitution. It's exactly what happens every day in Russia and China, countries where the government controls the press."

Ryan nodded, realizing Erin made sense. "What about Scorpion? What's his motive?"

"That's unclear. We don't know enough about him to understand how he fits into the picture."

Just then Erin's cell phone rang and she took the call. After telling the PI she'd be back in a few minutes, she walked out of the bar to talk to the caller.

While Ryan waited, he pulled out his own cell phone and checked his messages, hoping for a call back from Lauren. Ever since he'd returned from Spain, he'd left countless messages for his ex-girlfriend, but she had yet to return any of his calls. He still loved her and desperately hoped they could get back together. Punching in her number, he fully expected it to go to voicemail.

But this time the call was answered on the first ring.

"Lauren! I'm glad I caught you. I've been leaving messages for a week."

"I know, J.T.," she replied in a sad voice. "I got them."

Ryan gripped the phone tightly, excited to hear her voice again. "I'll be back in Atlanta soon. I want to get together and talk about us, about our future."

There was a long silence from the other end.

"J.T. ... there is no us," Lauren said haltingly, her voice cracking. "I've spent a lot of time ... thinking ... I just don't see ... how we can ... make it ... work ...."

"Please don't say that, Lauren. I love you."

"And ... I love you ... too. But we want different things ... out of life ... I realize that now ... I want a family ... kids, and a husband who's around ...."

"We can make it work, Lauren."

"You always said," she continued, her voice shaky, interrupted by sobs. "That you were a warrior ... warriors don't retire, J.T. ... they die with their boots on ... it doesn't matter that you don't wear an Army uniform anymore ... you're still a warrior at heart, chasing the bad guys ... kicking down doors and dodging bullets ... you'll always be chasing the next big case ...."

"Please, hon. Don't give up on us."

She said nothing, but he heard her jagged sobs. When the crying stopped, she whispered, "It's over, J.T."

Then she hung up.

His eyes welled and he brushed the tears from his face. He was devastated. More depressed than he had been in a very long time.

Chapter 76

Washington, D.C.

Vicka Stark stood at the far end of the O.O.V control room as she waited for all of the employees to file into the vast auditorium. She was holding a microphone because without it, her voice wouldn't carry in the cavernous room. The auditorium had a three-story-high ceiling to accommodate the TV flat-screens mounted on the wall.

The TVs were all turned off. Also turned off were the computer monitors in the workstations. She glanced over at Harold Meeks, who was standing in the first row of the assembled staff. The man appeared nervous as usual, and she smiled at him in an effort to calm him down.

Vicka counted heads again, and realizing all of the building's employees were in attendance, began her talk. "Thank you, everyone, for coming ... I know some of you were off shift, so I want you to know I appreciate you coming back in today."

She pointed to the dark TV screens mounted on the wall behind her. "You're probably wondering why the screens are not on and why the workstations have been turned off. Well, there's a reason for that, which I'll get to in a moment. But first, I want to congratulate each and every one of you for the fantastic job you've done over the last several years. I want to specifically congratulate Harold Meeks, my very capable operations manager, for the exemplary job he's done." She paused a moment, and turning toward the man, began clapping.

As the rest of the assembled employees in the amphitheatre joined in the clapping, Meeks beamed.

"I also want everyone to know," Vicka continued, "that President Ackerman is very aware of your excellent efforts. To emphasize how much the president and I appreciate your outstanding work, at the conclusion of my talk, I will be handing out bonus checks for $100,000 to each of you as a reward for your hard work and dedication."

Vicka paused, and as she had expected, a chorus of cheers broke out in the room.

When the cheering and clapping subsided, she said, "However, today I also bring some sad news. Because of recent budget cuts, our fine work at O.O.V. must come to an end."

There was a stunned silence in the auditorium as the meaning of her words sank in.

"I know this is unexpected," the Chief of Staff said. "However, I want all of you to know that although the operation here will cease to exist effective immediately, all of you will be transferred to other federal government jobs. These jobs will pay the same or more than you make now. And to make the transition easier for you and your families, in addition to the $100,000 bonus checks, you'll also receive and additional check for $75,000 to facilitate your transition to your new government job."

Harold Meeks began clapping and the whole room joined in.

"Earlier today," Vicka said, "I asked Harold to make this a special occasion and he has carried out my instructions. At the other end of the room, you'll find a buffet table and an open bar. While I go get your bonus checks and transition checks, I want you all to enjoy the free food and drinks. When I return in a few minutes, I'll be handing out your checks."

Vicka smiled broadly as the assembled group began to clap again.

She turned off the microphone and watched as the employees headed to the back of the auditorium for the free booze and food. Festive music came on over the loudspeakers, something else she had asked Meeks to arrange.

The operations manager came up to her and she extended her hand.

"Excellent job, Harold," she said with a smile.

He nodded and shook her hand, but a sad expression was on his face. "I'm sorry it all has to end."

"As am I, Harold. As am I. We've done good work together. Excellent work." She beamed at him. "But don't you worry, Harold. I'm going to make sure you land on your feet with a better job. A higher paying job."

"Really, Ms. Stark? What about the FBI investigation? The people who came to O.O.V.?"

"Don't worry. I'm handling that. You can rest easy."

"That's a big relief, ma'am. I was very concerned."

"I'll take care of everything, Harold. You've been my rock at O.O.V. There's no way this place could have functioned without you." She paused and smiled again. "In fact, I've got big plans for you. I'm working on getting you a senior position at the White House. How does that sound?"

Meeks's jaw dropped. "The White House? Me?"

She clapped his back. "That's right. I want you with me, at the center of power."

The man smiled broadly.

"Now go mingle with the employees, Harold, while I go get everyone's checks."

"Yes, Ms. Stark! Whatever you say!"

As Meeks went toward the back of the room, she strode out of the auditorium. She walked down a corridor to the building's security room and stepped inside. Going to the control workstation, she sat down and glanced at the surveillance monitors. One of the security cameras was showing the interior of the large auditorium. The O.O.V. employees were talking among themselves, as they feasted on the food at the buffet table and drank liquor. She could hear the festive music from the loudspeakers.

Then Vicka focused on the computer keyboard in front of her. She began to key in a long series of numbers and letters. It was a password only she knew. When she was done, she hit the enter key.

A moment later she heard a series of loud metallic clicks as the locks on the auditorium's four exit doors slid into place. Then an explosive surge of electrical current caused the building's transformer to blow, but not before setting off a series of electrical fires in the auditorium. Sparks erupted from the room's workstations and TV screens, igniting the carpet and draperies. In a moment, the whole space was engulfed in flames and smoke.

Vicka heard the employees screaming as panic set in. Their panic increased when they raced to the exits and realized they were locked in the cavernous room.

She raced out of the control room, down the corridor, and exited the O.O.V. building.

Her contingency plan had worked flawlessly.

Chapter 77

Flying at 34,000 feet over the European continent

Scorpion turned off the TV, disturbed by the news report he had just seen on CNN. Taking a pull from his bourbon, he leaned back on the wide leather seat. He was in the cabin of his Gulfstream jet. He was alone, except for the ever-present Drax, who was lying on the floor next to him. Picking up the satellite cell phone on the table in front of him, he punched in a number.

"It's Scorpion," he said when Vicka Stark answered.

"I was just about to call you," she replied.

"I saw the news, Vicka. They said a government call center in D.C. had burned down, killing over 80 people. I checked on the location and realized it was the O.O.V. building. What the hell happened?"

"I'm sorry, Hans. I had no choice. The FBI was getting too close. I couldn't let that happen."

Scorpion's gut wrenched into knots. O.O.V. was a critical part of his scheme. "Damn it, Vicka! This is totally unacceptable."

"I know, dear. But don't worry. We'll rebuild. You'll see."

He gritted his teeth. The woman made it sound so simple. But he knew it had taken them years to get this far. Scorpion was not a young man – starting O.O.V. from scratch would be a long, arduous process. And the threat of discovery was much higher now that the FBI was actually investigating.

"Where are you now, Hans?"

"In the air. I've had some setbacks of my own. The CIA found my home in Rome. I was lucky to get away."

"Where are you going now?" the woman asked.

"I'm not sure yet, Vicka. So much has happened." He clenched his fingers around the tumbler of bourbon. "And none of it good."

"Can you come to the U.S.? I want to see you again. To make love to you again."

Scorpion's thoughts churned, then an intriguing idea formed in his mind. "That may be possible. I've got one thing to take care of first. Then I will come to America again. I want to see you, Vicka."

"I can't wait!"

"I love you," Scorpion said and hung up the call.

Chapter 78

Washington, D,C.

J.T. Ryan slowed the Chevy Impala as soon as he spotted the fire trucks and police cruisers blocking the street ahead. Gawkers crowded the area outside the barricades that had been erected.

"Let's walk the rest of the way," Erin Welch said, from the passenger seat.

Ryan pulled the Impala to the curb and turned off the engine. As soon as he climbed out, the stench of heavy smoke filled his lungs.

Working their way through the throng of onlookers, Erin flashed her FBI creds and they were waved past the barricades by the uniform on duty. When they reached the burned-out brownstone a block later, they realized the scene was worse than they'd seen earlier on the news. Not only had the 'call center' burned down, but the adjacent buildings had also sustained severe fire damage. It appeared the flames had all been doused, but plumes of black smoke rose from the structures, blanketing the area.

Erin spotted a man in a fire chief's uniform close by, and she held up her badge. "Chief, I'm Erin Welch, FBI. Do you have an initial assessment of what happened?"

The chief, a brawny, middle-aged African-American man stared at her badge. Wiping some soot off his face, he said, "An electrical fire. It spread from the center of the building and engulfed it in a matter of minutes."

"You think this is accidental or intentional?"

The chief coughed from the smoke. "We don't have all the facts yet, and my investigative team is still in there, but I've been doing this kind of work for twenty years. It looks accidental. But my gut tells me different."

"Okay, Chief," Erin said. "Any survivors?"

"No. That's the strange part. We found all the bodies in a large auditorium; they were trapped inside. The fire was intense and almost everything was charred, but it appears that the auditorium's exit doors may have been locked."

"All right." Erin pulled out a business card and handed it to the man. "I'd appreciate it, Chief, if you could keep me wired in on this."

The man coughed again. "No problem, Welch." He moved away toward one of the fire trucks.

"You think Harold Meeks was one of the people who died in the fire?" Ryan asked.

"Maybe," Erin replied. "We'll know for sure when the ME identifies the bodies. In the meantime, I'm treating this as a possible crime scene."

Ryan stared through the hazy, smoky air at the burned-out building. "Makes sense. It's very suspicious that the place goes up in flames right before we get a chance to search it. What's next, Erin?"

The FBI woman shook her head slowly. "Harold Meeks and this so-called 'call center' was the best lead we had."

"We have one other lead," Ryan said. "The one Meeks gave us. According to him, he worked for Victoria Stark."

"I haven't forgotten, J.T."

"Okay, then. Let's get back in the car and go question her."

She brushed some ashes from her face. "You make it sound so simple. She's the Chief of Staff at the White House. We can't just barge in there and interrogate her."

"You're an FBI ADIC, for Christ sakes," Ryan said. He pointed to the brownstone. "And this is a crime scene. Over 80 people are dead."

"Possible crime scene," Erin corrected. "But you're right. Stark is our only lead right now and we need to talk to her." Erin pulled out her cell phone. "I'll call Director Tucker. Explain everything that's happened. I'll ask him to call the White House and arrange a meeting." She moved a few feet away to make her call.

Erin returned five minutes later. "Okay. It's in the works. I talked to Director Tucker and he'll call the White House and arrange for us to meet the Chief of Staff."

"When will we get to talk to Victoria Stark?" asked Ryan.

"Hard to say. Hopefully tomorrow, or possibly the day after that."

Chapter 79

Fairfax County, Virginia

The armor plated Cadillac Escalade made its way through the sparsely-populated rural area, eventually reaching the little-used nature park. The driver pulled to a stop under one the parking lot's dim lights and shut off the vehicle.

The bodyguard, who was sitting in the passenger seat, turned and faced Scorpion who was in the back seat. "Sir, we're here. This is the place."

"Good," Scorpion replied, settling into the plush and spacious rear seat area of the Escalade. He glanced through the windows at the deserted, heavily-wooded park. No cars were around, and since there was only a quarter moon on this night, the area was mostly dark.

Scorpion took a long pull from his tumbler of bourbon as he idly patted Drax. The large dog was laying at his feet.

Ten minutes later Scorpion noticed headlights in the distance and soon after a black Mercedes sedan parked next to the Escalade. Seeing Vicka climb out of the car's driver side, he reached over and opened the rear door of his SUV.

Vicka slid into the Escalade, a worried look on her face. "Why are we meeting here, Hans?" she asked, shutting the door behind her. "I was hoping we could meet at the hotel as usual."

Scorpion pressed a button on his armrest and an opaque privacy panel slid up, closing off the rear compartment from the front, providing complete privacy.

"It couldn't be helped, Vicka."

After giving the Doberman a wary look, she hugged Scorpion. "It's not important, Hans. The only thing that matters is that we're together again." She looked up into his eyes. "It's so good to hold you."

Scorpion gave her a radiant smile. "I've missed you."

"Have you really?" she replied in the silly, girlish voice she used sometimes when she was around him.

"Of course. Every day."

She smiled coquettishly. "Maybe tomorrow we can go to the hotel. So we can, you know ...."

He beamed at her. "Nothing would please me more, Vicka. But first we must discuss business."

The woman's smile faded. "Yes. Of course. Business. As I told you on the phone, things have not gone well recently."

"Is O.O.V. completely gone?"

"Yes, Hans. Like you saw on the news. The building burned to the ground."

"And the employees?"

"All dead," she said. "They died in the fire."

"What about your operations manager?"

"Harold Meeks is dead also," Vicka replied.

"Good. Is there anything left that could lead the FBI to you? Or to me?"

Vicka placed her hand on his chest and suggestively rubbed his white shirt and silk tie. "Nothing. We're safe, dear."

"That's excellent news!"

"Yes, it is. And you'll see, Hans. We can rebuild O.O.V."

Scorpion gave her a hard stare. "About that. After much thought, I believe we should cut our losses and move on."

"What do you mean? Operation One Voice has been our dream – mine, yours, and President Ackerman's. To create a society that shares our vision of equality and fairness. When we control the media, nothing can stop us."

Hans Krueger, AKA Scorpion, shook his head. "That was your dream, Vicka. And the dream of that puppet of yours, Ackerman. It was never mine."

A confused look settled on her face. "I don't understand, dear. You're not making any sense. We started Operation One Voice in order to create a more equal and fair society. A socialist society based on wealth redistribution."

"That's where you're wrong," he said, his tone harsh. "My goal was never about fairness or equality. It's always been about power and control. Once I controlled the media, the news, nothing could stop me. To do what I want. One Voice was never about an idyllic American voice, nor a European one. You never realized this, you *stupid* bitch. It was always about *my* voice. It was about *me* obtaining power and control."

Vicka's jaw dropped. "I can't believe you're saying this, dear. Is this some kind of sick joke? Well, it's not funny!"

"It's no joke, Vicka."

She grimaced. "This is crazy. Please, we've been planning this for years." She hugged him tightly but he didn't reciprocate. "I love you, Hans."

Scorpion pulled away from her. "I need to move on," he said in a harsh tone. "You fucked up Operation One Voice. It would take us years to rebuild. And with the FBI and CIA closing in, it's too dangerous now. I need to cut my losses."

Her eyes welled up with tears. "What are you saying, dear? Don't you love me anymore?"

Scorpion laughed cruelly. "Love you? I have many beautiful women at my disposal. Do you really think I could love someone who looks like you? You were a means to an end. And now your usefulness to me is gone."

Tears ran down her cheeks. "You're leaving me?"

He laughed harshly again. "Actually, it's you who'll be leaving me." He reached across and opened the rear door of the Escalade. "Now get out!"

"Please don't do this," she pleaded, the tears flowing freely. "I love you, Hans!"

"You're a liability to me now," Scorpion barked. "You know way too much about me. I'll give you a minute head start."

"What do you mean?"

"Get out of the vehicle, Vicka. I'll give you a minute head start before I let Drax loose."

The woman's eyes went wide as the ominous meaning of his words sank in.

Scorpion snapped his fingers and the large Doberman instantly came to its feet. Baring its razor-sharp teeth, it emitted a menacing growl.

"60 seconds," the billionaire began counting down, "59 seconds, 58 seconds, 57 seconds ...."

Vicka, her heart pounding in her chest, jumped out of the SUV and stumbled to the asphalt pavement, spraining her ankle. Quickly getting up, she hobbled as fast as she could toward her Mercedes, which was parked nearby.

Reaching the car, she tried unsuccessfully to fling open the driver's side door. Recalling she had locked it, she frantically searched her pockets for the keys. Locating the fob, she pressed the unlock button, while hearing the thudding of the dog's paws pounding on the pavement behind her.

Panicking, she turned around and saw the Doberman leap towards her, its jaws wide open, exposing its large, razor-sharp teeth.

Scorpion, still sitting in the back seat of the Escalade, heard her screams for the next five minutes.

Chapter 80

Hoover Building, FBI Headquarters
Washington, D.C.

"Thank you for seeing me on such short notice," Erin Welch said, as she and FBI Director Tucker shook hands and sat down in his office.

"I hope this is important, Welch. I have a very busy day today."

"Yes, sir, it is important. No doubt, Director, you've heard the news of Victoria Stark's death."

"Of course." He shook his head. "Strange situation. Being mauled by a wild animal in a remote part of Virginia."

"Director, I think it's more than strange. I think it was murder."

Tucker's eyebrows shot up. "What makes you say that?"

"It's too coincidental, sir. First, there's a fire killing over 80 people. And one of those who died was Harold Meeks, a suspect in my case. Meeks told me he worked for the Chief of Staff at the White House. Now she's dead a few days later."

The director tented his fingers on his desk. "I see your point. But Victoria Stark was the victim of an attack by a coyote or a wild dog. The Virginia State Police forensics people are trying to ascertain that now."

"I have no explanation for that," Erin replied. "But I believe that whatever happened to Stark, it was staged to look like an accident."

"Okay, Welch. I agree with you that the timing of all this is suspect. And you were right all along about this being a conspiracy. So I trust your instincts. What are you proposing we do now?"

Erin leaned forward in her chair. "I need to search the Chief of Staff's office and her home. Stark must have kept documents and files of her master plan."

"What you're asking is highly irregular, Welch. Since this is possibly a murder, I can get you a search warrant for her home with no problem. But her office at the White House is another matter. The Secret Service has jurisdiction there."

Erin's jaw clenched. "Sir, I'm not interested in inter-agency battles. I just want to solve the damn case."

Tucker considered this for a long moment. "All right. I'll set it up. On one condition. You'll be going to the West Wing of the White House. The seat of power for the United States. Conduct your search *strictly* by the book."

Chapter 81

The White House
Washington, D.C.

After going through the security checkpoint at the White House gate, Erin Welch drove the Chevy Impala to the parking area for the West Wing. Pulling into a spot and shutting off the car, she turned to J.T. Ryan who was in the passenger seat.

"Give me your weapon," Erin said.

Ryan un-holstered his pistol and handed it over.

After locking the gun in the glove compartment, she said, "Director Tucker was very specific in his instructions. We do this by the book. No cowboy tactics."

Ryan rubbed his jaw and smiled. "Cowboy tactics?"

Erin pressed her lips into a thin line. "This is a serious matter. Here are the ground rules: I'm in charge of this investigation, so I'll do all the talking in there. I'm bringing you along because you've been on this from the beginning and you may pick up something I miss. Any questions, J.T.?"

"No."

Smiling again, he took out his comb, and looking in the rearview mirror, passed it over his short, brown hair.

Erin frowned. "What are you doing? Your hair looks fine."

"I want to make sure I look presentable," he replied with a chuckle. "Next I'm going to buff up my shoes."

The FBI woman rolled her eyes. "That's another thing. No joking in there. The Secret Service has no sense of humor. Got it?"

He gave her a mock salute. "Yes, ma'am!"

Then he turned serious and they exited the car. After going through another security checkpoint at the door, they were led into the West Wing by a stern-faced Secret Service agent. They followed the agent down several corridors until they came to a closed door.

"This is Victoria Stark's office," the agent said to Erin, as he unlocked the door. "Will you need anything else, ADIC Welch?"

"No, thank you. I'll take it from here."

"Okay. I'll wait out here until you're done." The agent opened the door, Erin and Ryan stepped inside and he closed the door behind them.

Ryan surveyed the small, simply furnished office and noticed the inexpensive metal desk and cabinets. "Not very opulent for the Chief of Staff of the White House."

"I never met Stark in person," Erin replied, "but I saw her in news clips. She always wore cheap, off-the-rack business pantsuits, flat shoes, and no makeup. This office fits her personality."

Ryan gave Erin an appraising look, noting her designer dress, classy high heels, and expensive leather briefcase. "No Louboutins for her, huh?" he said with a grin.

The FBI woman shook her head slowly and sighed. "You can't help yourself, can you? Always joking around."

He raised his palms in front of him. "All right. I'll be good."

"Yeah, I'll bet," she murmured under her breath. Then, setting her briefcase on a side table, she clicked it open and took out two pairs of latex gloves. After handing one pair to Ryan, she pulled on the other pair.

"I'll take the lead on doing the search," she stated firmly. "I'll look at the documents first, then I want you to go through them."

"Okay."

She began going through Victoria Stark's desk, opening drawers and inspecting the contents. Afterward, the PI repeated the process. Finding nothing incriminating, they moved on to the row of metal filing cabinets. They spent the next hour scrutinizing the documents but found nothing out of the ordinary.

Lastly they tackled the tall metal wall cabinets. The first one was stocked with office supplies and books, but the second cabinet was locked.

"Interesting," Erin said. "This is the first locked cabinet or drawer we've found. Wonder where the key is?"

Ryan reached in his pocket and took out his lock-pick set. "I'm sure Stark had it with her when she died. But it's no problem. I got this."

The FBI woman averted her eyes. "Since I'm a law enforcement officer, I'm not going to ask what you're going to do."

"Good," he replied with a grin. He quickly unlocked the cabinet and opened the door. "Damn," he grumbled as he peered inside, noticing it was empty. He studied the interior of the cabinet closely, and noticing an odd alignment in the back panel, pried it open. Behind the false back was a smaller, closed metal cabinet with a high-tech lock dangling from the hasp.

"Take a look at this," Ryan said.

"That lock seems very sophisticated," Erin replied.

"It is. I'm familiar with this device. The company that manufactures it makes the most secure locks in the world."

"Okay, J.T. I'll go get the Secret Service agent. Maybe he knows where the key is."

"Let me try, first. I've never met a lock I couldn't pick." The PI began to work on it and a minute later the mechanism clicked open.

Erin grinned. "If your private investigative work ever dries up, you can always make it as a crook."

Ryan returned her smile and opened the door with a flourish.

Inside the cabinet was a stack of three-ring binders; there were over ten of them in total. Erin picked up the binder that was laying on top.

"Shit," she uttered, looking at its cover. Printed in large block letters were the initials, O.O.V.

She quickly went to the desk and rested the binder on top of it. Then she leafed through the contents, which outlined a very detailed plan of action, listing names, dates, and locations. When she closed the binder a few minutes later, a look of disgust was on her face. "Now I know what O.O.V. is."

"What is it, Erin?"

"Operation One Voice," she replied. "And it's much worse than we ever imagined."

Chapter 82

Hoover Building, FBI Headquarters
Washington, D.C.

Erin Welch and J.T. Ryan were in the conference room, waiting for FBI Director Tucker to arrive. Resting on the table was a large cardboard box.

Minutes later Director Tucker came into the room.

"Director," Erin said, "this is John Taylor Ryan. He's the contractor I've told you about who's been helping me."

Tucker shook hands with the PI, and after they all sat down, the director said, "What's in the box?"

Erin reached into it and took out the binder labeled O.O.V. She slid it in front of Tucker. "Sir, we found these documents when we searched the Chief of Staff's office. Ryan and I have read and made copies of all of them. The document you have in front of you is a blueprint for an operation named One Voice. It confirms our suspicion that the administration has been involved in a conspiracy to silence and control the news media, starting with TV networks and newspapers at the national level, and eventually at the local level. The plan also called for the censoring of Internet news."

"Who was involved in the conspiracy?" Tucker asked. "Vicka Stark?"

"Yes, sir," the FBI woman said. "But it was much bigger than Stark. President Ackerman was involved as well."

"You're sure?" the director demanded.

"Yes, Director."

"Anybody else involved?"

"A third person is mentioned," she said, "a man named Hans Krueger. He's a German billionaire who goes by the alias of Scorpion. We've been after Scorpion for some time, but he's eluded us so far. His relationship with Vicka Stark is murky, but from the documents it appears Krueger supplied the funding for this whole operation."

"And all of this information is contained in these documents, Welch?"

"Yes, sir. It's all here, in black and white. Dates, names, all the details." Erin reached into the box again and pulled out several more binders and slid them toward Tucker. "And there's more, sir. As soon as the president's administration had been able to fully control the press, they had other plans they intended to implement."

Tucker grimaced. "What kind of plans?"

"Ways to subvert the U.S. Constitution," Erin said, "and eliminate the Second Amendment, thereby outlawing the ownership of guns by private citizens. And there's more, Director. Much more. They planned to eventually dissolve the Congress and the Supreme Court. It's all there, sir."

The director began quickly leafing through the documents.

When he finished, he looked up at Erin and Ryan. The color had drained from Tucker's face. "A dictatorship, plain and simple."

Erin nodded. "That's correct, sir. That's what President Ackerman wants to do. He wants to remake America into his vision of utopia."

The director rose abruptly from the table and began pacing the conference room, deep in thought. After a minute he stopped and turned toward them, his face flush from anger.

"Leave these documents with me," he stated in a firm voice. "This is exactly the kind of ammunition I needed."

"What do you want us to do now, sir?" Erin asked.

The director extended his hand. "You both have done an excellent job." He shook Erin's hand, then Ryan's.

"Now, as FBI Director," Tucker added, "it's my turn."

Chapter 83

Near Baltimore, Maryland

Scorpion sat in the back seat of the armor-plated Cadillac Escalade as it sped on the Interstate highway. His mood was dark. Although he'd eliminated the Vicka Stark problem, he still had much to worry about.

The CIA had located three of his homes. The one in Spain, then Italy, and lastly in Berlin, Germany. He had been extremely fortunate to escape alive, but the three attacks had decimated his platoon of bodyguards. Worst of all, he was running out of options. It seemed everywhere he went, the Agency was able to find him.

He gulped more of his bourbon and listened to Bach's Brandenburg concertos over the sound system, trying to ease his tension.

After another hour of heavy drinking and tortured internal debate, he made a decision.

Scorpion pressed a button and the partition separating the rear and front compartments of the vehicle lowered. In the front seat was his driver and Dietrich, his head of security.

Dietrich turned back to face him. "Yes, sir?"

"Change in plans," Scorpion ordered. "Take me to the safe house."

"Yes, sir."

Chapter 84

The Oval Office
The White House
Washington, D.C.

FBI Director Tucker was admitted into the Oval Office by the Secret Service agents and he marched inside.

President Ackerman, who was sitting at his desk, glared at him. "I agreed to meet with you, Director, but I can only give you a couple of minutes. I'm extremely busy. Ever since the tragic death of my Chief of Staff, I've had to deal with many issues all on my own."

The FBI Director, not waiting for an invitation to sit, perched on one of the wingback chairs fronting the desk. He placed his briefcase on the floor next to him.

"I've given this a lot of thought, Ackerman," Tucker said, his voice hard. "And I've decided you only have one option regarding your future."

President Ackerman grimaced. "What's the meaning of this? What the hell are you talking about? And I *demand* you address me by my title as president. That's protocol."

"Fuck protocol," Tucker replied. "After you hear what I have to say, that title won't be yours much longer."

Ackerman's face turned beet red and his hands formed into fists. "I should have you thrown out of my office for using that kind of foul language in here."

"The last thing you'll need to worry about is profanity, Ackerman."

The FBI Director picked up his briefcase, clicked it open, and took out two three-ring binders. He placed them on the desk and slid them toward the president. "These are two of the documents your Chief of Staff, Victoria Stark, held in a secret compartment in her office. The first one is titled O.O.V., and it spells out, in great detail, the planning and execution of Operation One Voice. An operation that you and Stark carried out. The second document is your plan to dissolve Congress and the Supreme Court. Luckily for the country, we found these documents before you were able to implement them. In my possession I also have an additional eight documents which detail other parts of your conspiracy to completely nullify the Constitution and run the Unites States as a dictatorship using Executive Orders."

The president's face turned white as he heard this. He briefly leafed through the two documents on his desk. It was obvious he was aware of their contents because he quickly pushed them away as if they were on fire.

President Ackerman opened his mouth, but nothing came out. Speechless, his face drained of all color, he closed his jaw. Then his shoulders slumped and he hung his head.

"You have one option," the FBI Director stated harshly. "Resign, or face criminal prosecution for treason against the United States. Which is punishable by death."

He reached into his briefcase again and took out a thick envelope. He held the envelope in the air. "In here is a warrant for your arrest and an indictment for prosecution."

He slid the envelope toward Ackerman. "I've already met with the Attorney General, the Speaker of the House, the Majority Leader of the Senate, and the Chief Justice of the Supreme Court. I have shown them your plans. They were all in total agreement with me. The only way you can avoid prosecution is by resigning as president of the United States effective immediately."

A tortured, confused look settled on the president's face as Tucker's words sank in. Then Ackerman picked up the envelope and quickly read through the arrest warrant and the indictment. The tortured look on his face etched deeper. The president pointed to the binders on the desk. "What about those?"

Tucker reached over, picked them up, and stored them in his briefcase. "These will remain with me for safekeeping, Ackerman. But the leaders of Congress, the Chief Justice of the Supreme Court, and my staff at the Bureau have copies. In order to spare the nation the disgrace of finding out their president betrayed them, I, and the parties I mentioned, agree that if you resign quietly for 'health reasons', no one will know the details of your treachery."

President Ackerman's eyes sunk in their sockets and his shoulders sagged. He appeared to have aged ten years in the last ten minutes. "You said I would resign immediately?"

"That's correct." Tucker pulled out a folded sheet of paper from his suit jacket. "I've taken the liberty of typing out your resignation letter." He unfolded the letter, placed it on the desk, and handed the president a pen.

After giving the letter a brief glance, President Ackerman signed it, his hand trembling with every stroke.

Chapter 85

Atlanta, Georgia

J.T. Ryan was driving north on Interstate 85 when he felt his cell phone buzz. Slowing the Tahoe, he pulled out the phone and answered the call.

"It's Rachel," the woman said.

"Rachel West," he replied with a chuckle. "My favorite CIA operative. And the prettiest too."

The woman laughed. "Tell me, J.T. How many female CIA agents do you know?"

"Besides you?"

"Yes."

"None," he said.

"Then that's not much of a compliment, is it?"

He turned serious. "Not true. You're a very skilled field operative. Is this a social call or business?"

"Business, J.T. As you know we've been tracking Hans Krueger, AKA Scorpion, across Europe after you left Spain. We almost got him in Rome, and in Berlin, but he managed to get away. Now we've got a new lead on him."

"Great."

"Unfortunately," she continued, "we think he's now in the United States. I'm sure you're aware the CIA is expressly forbidden from operating in the U.S."

"Yes. What's the lead?"

Rachel West gave him the information and then said, "It's a good thing you can work on this, because after President Ackerman resigned a couple of weeks ago, our focus on the case changed. Alex is reassigning me. I'll be leaving for China in a day or so."

"All right, Rachel. Thanks for the info on Scorpion. I'll follow up. But I've got a similar situation with the Bureau. Since the president resigned, the FBI isn't treating this as a priority."

"Copy that."

"When will you get back to Langley, Rachel?"

"Hard to say. It depends how long my assignment in China lasts. But when I do get back, I'll give you a call." She paused. "It's not a long drive from Atlanta to Virginia." Then she disconnected the call.

As Ryan continued driving in the heavy, midday traffic, his thoughts turned to the lead Rachel had given him about Scorpion.

Chapter 86

Hoover Building, FBI Headquarters
Washington, D.C.

Erin Welch paced the empty conference room as she waited for the FBI Director to arrive. Although she felt she'd done a good job on the case of the murdered journalists, she also knew that D.C. politics was a murky labyrinth of lies and deceit. Many times the good guys got screwed, while the guilty went free. Hopefully this would not be the case today, but whenever she visited Washington, she always prepared for the worst.

Director Tucker walked in a moment later, a solemn expression on his face. After they shook hands, Erin said, "What am I being called on the carpet for today, sir?"

"What makes you say that?"

"Experience," she replied, trying to keep her tone neutral.

He smiled briefly. "I guess I deserve that." Then he shrugged. "If you had my job, you'd realize that dealing with the sewer of D.C. politics is no easy task."

"Actually, Director, I do realize it."

They sat down across from each other and Tucker said, "You did a good job on the case. If it hadn't been for your work and Ryan's, the U.S. would be in a very precarious position right now. After the President resigned, his cabinet did as well. And now that the Vice-President has replaced Ackerman, I believe the country is on the right track again."

Erin nodded, agreeing with what the director had just said. The new president, in her opinion and the opinion of many, was on the path to making America a true democracy again.

"So why am I here, Director?"

"I want to assign you to a new job in the Bureau."

Erin instantly recalled his acidic remarks from awhile back. "The Alaska Field Office?" she asked with a frown.

Tucker smiled. "Far from it, Welch." He placed his hands flat on the conference table. "Have you ever heard of the FBI's J.T.T.F.?"

"Of course, sir. The Joint Terrorism Task Force. It's the Bureau's premier group for fighting terror."

"That's right. I want to put you in charge of it."

"That would be a big step up for me, Director. I'm honored to be considered for that position. But I love Atlanta. And I'd hate having to move to D.C."

The FBI Director waved a hand in the air. "I knew you'd say that, Welch. And I have a solution. You can keep your position as Assistant Director in Charge of the Atlanta Field Office. You can promote one of your managers there to assist you with those duties. And I would assign you an office here at the Hoover Building. You can travel back and forth. And, along with the title of Director of J.T.T.F., you'd receive a very substantial increase in salary."

Erin mulled this over, tempted by the opportunity. The new position would be a fantastic stepping stone in her long-term goal of one day being appointed as FBI Director. Still, being in D.C. more frequently meant having to deal with the morass of Washington politics.

Tucker leaned forward in his chair. "I've already talked to the president and filled him in on your credentials. After what you accomplished on your last case, he agrees with me that you'd be a perfect fit for this job." The director extended his hand. "The country needs you, Welch."

"All right, sir," Erin said as they shook hands. "I'll take the job."

Chapter 87

Atlanta, Georgia

J.T. Ryan awoke early.

He showered, shaved, and dressed, his thoughts totally focused on his upcoming day. Yesterday he had met with Erin Welch, who had informed him of her new, expanded responsibilities at the FBI. Although he was happy for her promotion and knew she was imminently qualified, he was disappointed her focus had shifted away from solving the last piece of the puzzle, the capture of Scorpion.

Luckily she had agreed to let him keep working the case. And though he'd be on his own, she had granted him access to the FBI's armory in Atlanta, where he'd been able to borrow a host of high-tech weaponry. The weapons were locked in a closet in his apartment. Going to the closet now, he selected several items, including a rapid-fire Model 870 Remington tactical shotgun, an M-4 assault rifle with RPG grenade capability, and other gear, all of which he packed into a large duffel bag. After checking the load on his Smith & Wesson .357 Magnum, he re-holstered the revolver and hoisted the bag over his shoulder.

He made his way out of his apartment and into his Tahoe, which was parked in the building's underground lot. It was a cold, damp, overcast day, the dark clouds promising rain. As he drove north out of the city, he turned on the heater and considered the lead Rachel West had provided. CIA satellites and telephone intercepts had been able to pinpoint a location for Hans Krueger in the north Georgia mountains. Unfortunately, when Ryan had plotted the GPS coordinates on a topographical map, he realized there was nothing there. No towns, no villages, no structures of any kind in the rugged mountainous area for twenty miles.

The PI wondered if the CIA intel could be faulty. He remembered that it was Agency intelligence, along with British MI-6, who had incorrectly determined that Saddam Hussein had nuclear weapons in Iraq in the early 2000's.

Still, Ryan had no other leads.

Raindrops splattered on his windshield and he turned on the wipers. Soon the drizzle turned into a torrent of rain, and the foul weather remained for the balance of his trip north into the mountains of Georgia.

Two hours later he reached the small town of Blue Ridge, nestled high in the Blue Ridge Mountains. Checking into an inn where he had previously stayed, he had lunch at the hotel restaurant. Watching the heavy downpour from his window table, he realized he'd have to wait out the storm before trekking into the rugged wilderness.

After lunch he pulled out his cell phone and once again tried in vain to reach Lauren. The call went to voice mail; he'd lost track of how many messages he'd left her. Lauren had made her intentions crystal clear during their last conversation, which was underscored by his unreturned messages. He didn't want to give up on the woman he loved, but it was clear she had given up on him. Disheartened, he put away his phone and watched the torrential rain continue to fall in sheets.

***

The following day was overcast, but luckily the rain had stopped.

That morning he put on a warm flannel shirt, blue jeans, and hiking boots. After donning the body armor he'd borrowed from the FBI, he put on his black, weather-proof North Face jacket and a black ball cap. He exited the hotel room and stored his large duffel bag in the cargo compartment of his Tahoe.

Ryan then drove north out of the town of Blue Ridge. What little development there was receded the further he drove. The mostly wooded, hilly terrain was sparsely populated. Besides an occasional gas station, some of which were shuttered and obviously abandoned, he saw little human activity.

The higher the elevation he went up the mountains, the less vehicle traffic he spotted. Eventually he concluded that he was the only one in the area. The state road narrowed as it twisted and turned upward, until it became one long series of continuous switchbacks. By the side of the road, he did see a few weather-beaten and rusted-out trailers, but here again, they appeared to be abandoned. Soon the paved road turned into a gravel trail and after another few minutes the gravel gave way to a muddy path.

Rechecking the coordinates on his hand-held GPS device, he noticed he was still going in the right direction. Although his SUV had 4-wheel drive and could navigate the soggy mud path, he decided to continue on foot. If Scorpion and his men were in the area, the PI wanted to maintain the element of surprise and go in as quietly as possible.

Pulling off the trail, he drove the Tahoe into a copse of trees and heavy vegetation. Getting out of the SUV, he pulled out the M-4 assault rifle from the cargo compartment and hoisted the duffel over his shoulder. He began hiking up the muddy path. Because it was a dark, overcast day and the trail was bordered on both sides by a dense forest, the area was dimly lit.

As he continued deeper into the woods, he listened closely for unusual sounds but all he heard was the sucking noise of his boots as they sank and lifted over the mud trail.

The incline on the path increased dramatically over the next hour and he sensed the air getting thinner as he went up the mountain. Checking the GPS coordinates every ten minutes or so, he knew he was still headed in the right direction.

Ryan encountered no one during his trek. And except for the rustle of trees, the call of birds, and the whistling of the wind, he heard no other sounds. He saw no signs of human activity. He detected no tire tracks on the path – but since it had rained heavily the previous day, evidence of vehicle traffic could have washed away.

He continued trudging up the rugged, mountainous terrain for several more hours, his duffel bag feeling heavier the further he climbed through the dense forest.

Eventually the woods thinned out and he reached a clearing on a ridge. Just ahead, maybe a hundred yards in front of him, large boulders jutted out from the muddy ground. Consulting his GPS device, he realized this area was the exact location Rachel West had given him.

Resting the duffel on the ground, he un-slung the M-4 assault rifle and advanced forward cautiously. When he reached the boulders, he scanned the area thoroughly, turning 360 degrees, looking for any signs of life. He saw nothing except trees and rocks and mud. The CIA got it wrong, Ryan thought. *I guess this was a wasted trip.*

He spent the next hour exploring the area and found nothing out of the ordinary. Glancing at the darkening sky, he recognized it would be nighttime soon. Tired from the long trek, he decided not to retrace his steps down the mountain tonight, but rather set out for home in the morning.

Finding a sheltered area under some trees, he constructed a crude bivouac. Afterward he ate protein bars and lay down on the damp, cold ground to get some sleep.

Two hours later, after a restless nap, he awoke suddenly. Grabbing the M-4, he crouched by a tree and listened for sounds. All he heard was the howling of the wind and the rustle of branches. Still, he sensed something was different, although he couldn't identify it. It was totally dark now and he slipped on his night-vision goggles. The area around him became visible in a gray-green haze. Willing his muscles to freeze, he once again listened for human activity. There was nothing. Then he took in a breath and knew what it was immediately. A cooking smell; the faint scent of food being prepared.

Holding the assault rifle at the ready, he moved forward slowly, his head on a swivel as he scanned the area again. He saw it and froze. A wisp of smoke coming from one of the large boulders.

He approached it cautiously and peered up to the top of the boulder, and now noticed a tiny metal grate, obviously an exhaust vent, spewing out a thin trace of smoke.

Ryan began climbing over the smaller rocks up the jagged face of the boulder. The irregular, craggy rock was wet and slippery, and he had to sling his M-4 over his shoulder in order to free his hands. Using the crevices on the surface, he pulled himself up and soon after reached the top of the boulder. He studied the small exhaust vent. The cooking smell was much stronger here and smoke was definitely spewing from the grate. He also noticed that the feel of the rock surface up here was different. Ryan rubbed the rock face and realized it wasn't rock at all, but rather something synthetic. A very hard plastic, he thought, painted and shaped to look natural.

He slowly retraced his steps back down from the top of the boulder and crept cautiously to the rear of the massive rock, which was concealed by heavy vegetation.

There was a fairly flat area on the boulder about seven feet high and seven feet wide where it met the rocky ground.

He ran his hand over the irregular, flattish rock and recognized this part was also constructed of synthetic material engineered to look like natural stone. As he studied the area closely he determined that a vehicle could easily drive into the 7' by 7' rock-like panel when it was open.

Checking the GPS coordinates again he noticed that this was the exact spot the CIA believed Hans Krueger was located. Then Ryan remembered something else, something he'd read a while back about the Blue Ridge Mountains. A century ago there had been mining in this area. The ore had played out long ago, and the mines had been abandoned. But it was evident to Ryan now that Scorpion had located one of the abandoned mines and built a secret home here. What better place to hide than in the middle of this wilderness?

Ryan quickly thought through his options. The safest way was to call Erin and get backup. But she was already on her way to D.C. and by the time she dispatched an FBI team from Atlanta, it would be many hours before they reached this area. In the meantime Scorpion might detect Ryan's presence and flee. The billionaire had already eluded the CIA several times. *No, I can't take that chance*, he thought. *I can't let him get away.*

The PI raced back toward his duffel bag, took out the Remington tactical shotgun and RPG grenades for the M-4 assault rifle. Then he went back to the area with the synthetic door which resembled a rock wall. He paced a safe distance away and turned around to face the wall. After loading the rocket propelled grenade into the M-4's launch tube, he crouched on one knee. Aiming the weapon, he held his breath and squeezed the trigger.

Chapter 88

The Safe House
Blue Ridge Mountains, Georgia

Hans Krueger awoke instantly from the muffled roar of the explosion.

He bolted upright on the king-size bed. As usual, the man was fully dressed except for his shoes. A phobic about exposing his body to other people, he only slept in the nude when he was by himself. A beautiful, naked brunette lay next to him – his latest prostitute. Undisturbed by the explosion, the woman continued sleeping in a drug-induced slumber, while emitting a slight snore. He knew the coked-up whore could sleep through anything.

Krueger jumped off the bed and raced to the bedroom door. Opening it, he saw his chief of security running down the corridor.

"What the hell was that?" Krueger yelled.

"The outer door," the man replied as he drew his Desert Eagle semi-automatic. "Something blew it up. We're under attack, sir."

Krueger watched as several more of his bodyguards raced out of their rooms toward the first level of the underground house. While the home's furnishings were ultra-modern and the floors were lushly carpeted, the rough stone walls and curved, rocky ceiling betrayed the house's true origins as an abandoned mine.

Krueger's ever-present Doberman was by his side, it's eyes alert.

Damn, thought Krueger, *I can't believe they found me again!* He silently cursed Vicka Stark, the CIA, the FBI, and everyone else he could think of, anyone but himself, for putting him in his present predicament.

But all of that was forgotten when he heard the muffled roar of a second explosion. Not wasting another moment, Krueger raced toward the vault.

Chapter 89

The Safe House
Blue Ridge Mountains, Georgia

J.T. Ryan quickly reloaded the M-4 and fired a third RPG round at the synthetic door. The grenade exploded and this time the steel-reinforced door shattered, creating a large, jagged-shaped opening into the cave. Ryan peered through the smoky haze of the explosions. It revealed a well-lit interior. Taking off his night-vision goggles, he sprinted forward, knowing the element of surprise was gone. The grenade detonations would have awakened the dead.

Crouching by the jagged opening, he stared inside. It was a wide tunnel with rocky walls and ceiling leading to what appeared to be a garage. The large garage area was lit by overhead fluorescent tubes. He could make out several vehicles: two Jeep Grand Cherokees and a black Cadillac Escalade. The howl of a loud alarm filled the air.

Spotting no one, Ryan crept into the tunnel and then the garage, his assault rifle pointed forward. Reaching the Cadillac Escalade, he hid behind it and looked toward a closed metal door at the far end of the garage.

Suddenly the door swung open and two armed men sprung out. Ryan fired a long burst from his M-4, the spent brass clattering on the concrete floor. The high-velocity rounds struck one of the men and he staggered and fell. The second guard took cover behind a row of metal storage units and returned fire, his rounds denting but not penetrating the armor-plated Escalade.

Ryan squeezed the trigger on his assault rifle but nothing happened. His heart stopped as he realized the M-4 had jammed. Dropping the weapon, he un-slung the Remington shotgun, chambered a round, and fired in the direction of the guard. The shotgun shell tore a large hole in the storage unit the man was using for cover.

As the *boom* from the shotgun's report echoed in the low-ceilinged, cave-like room, Ryan watched as more armed men poured out the door and hid behind the Jeeps. They began firing toward him, their rounds ricocheting off the Escalade and the rocky walls and ceiling. Chunks of stone rained down on him and he felt the SUV shudder from the pounding of their incoming high-velocity rounds.

Pinned down by the blaze of gunfire, he knew he was badly outnumbered. Soon they'd outflank him and finish him off. His heart thudding in his chest, he frantically thought through his options, knowing he had to act now.

Peering around the SUV's bumper, he squeezed off another shell from the shotgun. Unzipping his jacket, he grabbed one of the grenades clipped to his Kevlar vest. Pulling the pin, he lobbed it over his head toward the Jeeps.

The explosion was deafening, drowning out the wail of the alarms. When the detonation's echoes abated, he heard the muffled screams of pain. Once again peering around the bumper, he saw two bloody corpses by the heavily damaged Jeeps. Another man was limping toward the door at the far end. Opening it, he went inside and slammed it shut behind him.

Sprinting up, Ryan raced toward the back of the garage, using the demolished Jeeps for cover. Among the debris of shattered glass, plastic, and metal, were the two mangled corpses.

317

He stared at the closed metal door. Not bothering to check if it was locked, he fired off another two shotgun shells, which blasted a jagged hole in the door's lock plate. With his ears still ringing from the explosions and gunfire, Ryan raced forward and flung open the door. Stepping inside, he crouched and scanned the well-lit interior. It was a large area, a living room filled with expensive leather couches, teak wood tables, and a wall unit filled with high-end electronics and a massive flat-screen TV. Lush gold tone carpeting covered the floor and the only rustic feature of the place was the rocky, cavern-like ceiling. He saw no one, but he spied a trail of blood, obviously from the guard he'd wounded earlier.

Holding the tactical shotgun at the ready, the PI advanced slowly, following the trail of gore. It led out of the room and into a corridor. He passed a vacant dining room, a kitchen, and another sitting room, all filled with sleek, opulent furnishings and appliances. At the far end of the hallway he found a wide staircase leading down. Descending the stairs cautiously, he reached a lower level. On this floor he found six bedrooms: five small ones and one much larger. Five of the rooms were unoccupied, but in the master bedroom he found a naked, comatose woman. He also found another dead guard in the hallway. Continuing to the end of the corridor, he noticed a narrow set of stairs, also leading down. He descended the stairs cautiously and came to a closed, vault-like metal door that resembled the entrance of a bank vault. The door was massively thick and obviously constructed of high-grade metal, probably titanium. It was clear to Ryan that this closed room was Scorpion's last line of defense.

Chapter 90

The Safe House
Blue Ridge Mountains, Georgia

"What's he doing now?" Hans Krueger demanded, as he stood looking over Dietrich's shoulder. His chief of security was sitting at a workstation staring at a TV monitor.

"He's right outside the vault door," Dietrich replied.

"What the hell do we do now?"

"We have one option, Mr. Krueger."

"What?"

Dietrich pointed to one of the buttons on the workstation's control panel. "This."

"Do it!" Krueger screamed. "Kill him!"

Chapter 91

The Safe House
Blue Ridge Mountains, Georgia

Ryan crouched by the vault-like door, trying to figure out a way to break in. He was certain his grenades weren't powerful enough to knock it down. It would take a massive explosion to blast through the door.

As his thoughts churned, he heard a slight hissing noise. Perplexed by the sound, he scanned the area. Looking up toward the rocky ceiling, he noticed an air vent spewing faint smoke. Instantly he recognized what it was. As the mist filled his lungs, he coughed and covered his nose with a handkerchief. Turning around, he raced back to the stairs. Sprinting up two rungs at a time, Ryan watched in horror as a metal panel began descending down from the ceiling at the top of the stairs. He knew that in seconds he would be trapped inside a poisonous gas chamber. Reaching the top step, he threw himself on the floor and rolled out of the chamber just as the panel *clanged* shut behind him.

Gripping the shotgun tightly, he hid behind a wall cabinet, his adrenaline pumping. Sniffing the air, he realized this part of the house was free of the poisonous gas.

Suddenly he heard a creak from behind him.

Whipping around, he saw an assault rifle pointed at his chest. Ryan fired, the shotgun shell literally blasting the guard's head off. Blood spurted everywhere as the man's body collapsed to the floor.

Comprehending that this guard must have come in from the garage area, the PI retraced his steps, and carefully searched the multiple underground levels and the garage, but found no one else in the house.

Then he returned to the corridor with the staircase that led down. The stairs were now sealed off by the metal panel. Ryan fired off three shotgun shells in quick succession, the powerful rounds shredding the panel. Then he retreated and waited ten minutes to allow the poisonous gas to dissipate.

Going back to the demolished metal panel, he went past it. He stood at the top of the staircase and gazed down at the massive vault-like door at the foot of the stairs. Doubting it would work, but not having any other options, the PI took out his last explosive-type grenade. Pulling the pin, he threw the grenade down the steps and then raced in the opposite direction.

Chapter 92

The Safe House
Blue Ridge Mountains, Georgia

Hans Krueger saw a bright flash on the workstation's TV monitor and heard a muffled blast. The TV screen went dark.

"What the hell happened?" Krueger barked.

"The man set off a grenade," Dietrich replied. "But don't worry, sir. That door is impenetrable. No grenade can blast it open."

Krueger pointed to the dark TV screen. "Did we lose the video feed?"

"Yes, sir. The explosion took out the security camera."

"What do we do now?" Krueger asked, a nauseous feeling in his gut. He wasn't used to being afraid, didn't like it one bit.

"We wait, sir. We have enough food and water to last us two weeks. The man outside the vault can't get to us. We're safe in here. I've already contacted the guard who was buying supplies in Atlanta. He'll hire more gunmen. They'll be here by tomorrow."

"You're sure the man outside can't get to us?" Krueger asked.

"Don't worry, sir. We're safe in here."

Chapter 93

The Safe House
Blue Ridge Mountains, Georgia

J.T. Ryan's thoughts churned as he crouched outside the vault door, its high-gloss metal finish only scratched and dented by the exploded grenade.

He took stock of the weaponry he had left. A handful of shotgun shells, one incendiary grenade, two smoke grenades, and his .357 Magnum revolver. *Not much*, he thought grimly. Shaking his head slowly, he recognized there was no way he could penetrate the massive door.

Then a new idea came to him.

It was a long-shot, but it was all he had. Turning around, he sprinted back up the stairs to the first floor of the house. He searched all of its rooms. Not finding what he was looking for, he made his way to the floor that contained the bedrooms. Searching it, he finally located what he was after: the heating/air-conditioning units, which were in a large utility room. This room also contained the water heater, an electrical generator, a water filtration system, and assorted other equipment to service the three-level underground home.

Ryan was certain the vault room downstairs had a separate back-up power generator, so cutting off the power from this main unit was futile. But he guessed that the air vents that supplied the whole house originated here in the utility room. He closely inspected the duct work leading out of the heating/AC unit. Eventually he found a duct that led down toward the lowest level. Disconnecting the duct, he peered into the tube's dark opening. *It's a long-shot*, he thought again. *But it's all I've got.*

Unclipping the last three grenades from his Kevlar vest, he pulled the pins on the smoke grenades and pushed the canisters down the duct. Then he pulled the pin on the incendiary grenade and repeated the process. He heard the rattle of the three metal canisters as they rolled down the tube. Then he quickly closed off the top of the duct.

Chapter 94

The Safe House
Blue Ridge Mountains, Georgia

Hans Krueger smelled the smoke. Then saw it coming out of the air vent.

He panicked when a flash of fire shot out of the vent. Flames spewed out of the opening, dropping onto the carpeted floor, igniting the carpet on fire.

Chapter 95

The Safe House
Blue Ridge Mountains, Georgia

J.T. Ryan, his shotgun at the ready, waited cautiously outside the vault door.

It had been five minutes since he'd activated the grenades. There was no way for him to know if his plan had worked.

After waiting another two minutes, he figured he had failed. Knowing there was nothing else he could do on his own, he pulled out his cell phone and punched in Erin's number. Luckily he reached her and he explained the situation. She told him she'd dispatch an FBI team to the area, but it would take several hours for them to arrive.

The PI put his phone away. Then he sat on the floor to wait, with his shotgun resting on his lap.

To his amazement, the massive vault door creaked open slowly and a cloud of black smoke began spewing out.

Instantly gripping the shotgun, he got up on one knee, expecting Scorpion's armed men to rush out.

When nothing happened, he peered inside the opening. Through the hazy smoke he spotted a powerfully-built man sprawled on the floor; next to him was a fire-extinguisher canister.

Ryan entered the small room, which resembled a bank vault. Approaching the inert man, he noticed the guy had suffered burns all over his body. Checking his pulse, he realized the man was dead.

Going to the back of the room, the PI found a second corpse laying next to a workstation. This man was older, and well dressed, wearing a starched white shirt, expensive slacks, and a custom-made suit jacket. Although burns were evident on his body, it appeared to Ryan that the man had died of smoke inhalation. Next to the man's body was a dead canine, a large Doberman.

Ryan coughed as the acrid smoke filled his lungs. Glancing around the rest of the space, he found no one else. Using his boots, the PI stomped out the remaining embers on the scorched carpeting.

It's clear what happened, Ryan thought. His grenades had ignited a fire; a fire the room's occupants had not been able to contain. In a desperate attempt to escape the flames and the intense smoke that filled the room, one of the men opened the vault door, but by then it was too late.

The PI went back to the well-dressed corpse. *Is this Scorpion?* he wondered. *Probably.* Kneeling next to the body, he tugged the cuffs on the man's long-sleeve shirt. Ryan saw it immediately on the man's wrist. A tattoo of a scorpion.

It's ironic, Ryan mused. *Scorpion's safe room had become his tomb.*

Chapter 96

Atlanta, Georgia

"Good job on finding Hans Krueger, AKA Scorpion," Erin Welch said as she slid an envelope across her desk.

J.T. Ryan, who was sitting opposite her in her office, picked up the envelope. "What's this?"

"A bonus."

Ryan opened it and glanced at the check inside. He let out a low whistle. "Nice. Thanks."

"Don't mention it. You earned it, J.T."

Ryan slipped the envelope in his jacket. "How are your new expanded responsibilities working out?"

The attractive brunette smiled. "It's keeping me very busy. But I like it."

"Good. So what's next, Erin?"

She opened a desk drawer, removed a file and handed it to him.

"What's in here?" he asked.

"The next case we'll be working on."

Ryan opened the file and read through it. By the time he reached the last page, his heart was thudding in his chest. "This is big," he said.

Erin nodded, a grim look on her face. "Yes, it is. Our biggest case yet. You don't have to work on it, if you don't want. But I could really use your help." She paused a moment. "Are you in or are you out, J.T?"

Ryan considered this for several minutes, knowing the case would be extremely challenging and could change the rest of his life.

"Hell, yes," he said. "I'm in."

END

***

About the author

Lee Gimenez is the award-winning author of 12 novels, including his highly-acclaimed J.T. Ryan series. Several of his books were Featured Novels of the International Thriller Writers Association, among them SKYFLASH, KILLING WEST, and THE WASHINGTON ULTIMATUM. Lee was nominated for the Georgia Author of the Year Award, and he was a Finalist in the prestigious Terry Kay Prize for Fiction.

Lee's books are available at Amazon and many other bookstores in the U.S. and Internationally.

For more information about him, please visit his website at: www.LeeGimenez.com. There you can sign up for his free newsletter. You can contact Lee at his email address: LG727@MSN.com. You can also join him on Twitter, Facebook, Google Plus, LinkedIn, and Goodreads. Lee lives with his wife in the Atlanta, Georgia area.

***

Other Novels by Lee Gimenez

Skyflash
Killing West
The Washington Ultimatum
Blacksnow Zero
The Sigma Conspiracy
The Nanotech Murders
Death on Zanath
Virtual Thoughtstream
Azul 7
Terralus 4
The Tomorrow Solution

SKYFLASH

is available at Amazon and many other bookstores in the
U.S. and Internationally.
In paperback, Kindle, and all other ebook versions.

KILLING WEST

is available at Amazon and many other bookstores in the
U.S. and Internationally.
In paperback, Kindle, and all other ebook versions.

The
Washington
Ultimatum
Lee Gimenez

THE WASHINGTON ULTIMATUM
is available at Amazon and many other bookstores in the
U.S. and Internationally. In paperback, Kindle, and all other
ebook versions.

Lee Gimenez's other novels, including
- Blacksnow Zero
- The Sigma Conspiracy
- The Nanotech Murders
- Death on Zanath
- Virtual Thoughtstream
- Azul 7
- Terralus 4
- The Tomorrow Solution

are all available at Amazon and many other bookstores in the U.S. and Internationally.
In paperback, Kindle, and all other ebook versions.

Made in the USA
Charleston, SC
30 January 2017